Never Haunt a Historian

by Edie Claire

Book Seven of the
Leigh Koslow Mystery Series

Cover art by pbj creative studios

This book is a work of fiction. The names, characters, places, and incidents are products of the writer's imagination or have been used fictitiously and are not to be construed as real. Any resemblance to persons, living or dead, actual events, locales or organizations is entirely coincidental.

Dedication

For every reader who has ever taken the time to send me an email or a Facebook message. Your encouragement means more than I can say. Thank you so much!

Chapter 1

"Aunt Leigh," the young voice said with as much authority as a barely thirteen-year-old boy could muster. "We have a problem."

Leigh tried hard not to startle. Yes, she had been sound asleep. But since her visor had been pulled down over her eyes as she rocked in her "brainstorming hammock," her cousin's son did not necessarily know that. She was supposed to be working. She *had* been working. Until she fell asleep.

She lifted the visor slowly, not at all surprised to see her "nephew" Mathias flanked solidly by his little sister and Leigh's own twins, all four of whom stood like soldiers, arms akimbo and faces serious.

The sight did not bode well.

Leigh cleared her throat and shook the cobwebs from her weary brain. "What's that?"

"It's Mr. Pratt," Mathias announced. "We think that something's happened to him."

Leigh swung her legs out of the hammock and sat up, noticing as she did so that Archie Pratt's wandering hound, Wiley, was once again in her backyard, cavorting with her own always-happy-to-dig-with-a friend corgi. The two dogs were behind her raspberry bushes, no doubt in pursuit of the resident ground hog.

"Because of his dog running loose?" she asked hopefully, knowing full well that the good-natured, slobbering black mutt could be found anywhere this side of Snow Creek Road at any time, whether his master was home or not. Archie didn't believe in leash laws. Or in neutering.

"It's not just that Wiley's been over here more than usual," Matthias continued. "He's been acting weird. Like he doesn't want to go home. We were over by the farmhouse after school yesterday, and he only went in his dog door once, and then he came right back out again."

Leigh's brow furrowed. She wasn't grasping the problem yet. But she knew it was coming.

"We thought Mr. Pratt was home because his truck was there," Leigh's son Ethan chimed in earnestly. "But when we went over just now and rang the doorbell, he didn't answer!"

Mathias silenced his cousin with a resentful look. Older than the others by two years and then some, he considered himself the Pack's official spokesperson. "The truck was parked in the exact same place as yesterday, Aunt Leigh," he continued. "But Mr. Pratt wasn't home. And we know he hasn't driven it because—"

His sister Lenna could not control herself. "There was this big spot of bird poop right on the driver's side of the windshield yesterday," the blond, blue-eyed beauty blurted excitedly, "and today it's still there!"

Her brother glared.

"There's more, Mom," Leigh's daughter Allison said quietly. Smaller than the other children by a head, the dark, diminutive Allison looked nothing like either of her parents but was the spitting image of Leigh's father Randall. Which was fitting, as the child had been determined since toddlerhood to follow in her grandfather's veterinary footsteps. "I don't think Wiley's been eating right. He threw up a bunch of cardboard and plastic earlier, and you know if Mr. Pratt was going out of town, he would have asked somebody to feed him."

Leigh stood up. "That is odd," she conceded. When her family had moved into their house five years ago, Archie Pratt had functioned like a one-man welcoming committee and neighborhood association. Never mind that they didn't actually live in a neighborhood. The handful of houses that fronted Snow Creek Road between her cousin Cara's farm and Archie Pratt's equally nonfunctional one were a motley and utilitarian bunch, all built a half century ago with the singular goal of staying above the flood plain. Nevertheless, Archie had greeted all the newcomers with a map of the area, the names and phone numbers of all their other neighbors, two bottles of Rolling Rock, and a plastic pen from a defunct insurance company. Archie liked everybody, and everybody liked Archie.

Leigh's relationship with the man might be casual, built on randomly occurring chats at neighbors' homes and by the creek that ran through all their backyards, but she was certain that he would never intentionally take off and leave his dog unattended. When he traveled out of town, which he often did, he took Wiley with him.

"All right," she agreed. "I'll go over and check on him. Maybe he was home but didn't hear the bell. Or maybe he's not feeling well."

She moved forward, and the Pack fell instantly into step behind her.

Or maybe…

A cold wave of foreboding stopped her in her tracks. "You guys stay here," she ordered. "Offer Wiley a little bit of Chewie's kibble; see how he takes it. But put Chewie in the house first. We don't want a war on our hands."

The Pack frowned in unison at the disinvite; but thankfully, didn't argue. Leigh watched them scamper off, then looked down the valley toward Archie's place. His farmhouse wasn't visible from her yard. Being on the other side of the creek, around a bend, and behind a patch of woods, it wasn't visible from any of the other houses, except maybe the O'Malleys', which was closest to it. She decided to take the road.

Archie was perfectly fine, she was sure.

Really. She was.

A cool nip wafted on the air, warring with the late September sunshine and promising colder weather to come. Leigh's shoulders shivered, but she kept moving. She strode past the house of her nearest neighbors, a young couple named Derrick and Nora Sullivan, and was relieved to hear no sound from within. Their baby had been colicky lately, screaming unmercifully every evening and well into the night. The sound went straight to Leigh's marrow, taking her back to those foggy, ill-remembered days when Allison had done the same.

Passing by the Browns' house next, she hastened her steps. Lester and Emma ran a personal care home, catering to two elderly women and a man they treated more like houseguests than patients. But the fact was, any of the five adults living there (and several of the temporary help) could carry on a two-hour conversation with a fire hydrant, and Leigh was on a mission.

The fourth house on the strip was the O'Malleys', home to Patty, Joe, and their decidedly unpleasant offspring, Scotty. If it was hypocritical for Leigh to lecture the Pack about tolerance and acceptance while she herself avoided the little twerp at all costs, so be it. Scotty wasn't actually the kind of kid who would pull the wings off of flies, but he was the kind of kid who liked to talk about it.

At the gravel turnoff to Archie Pratt's house, Leigh stopped short. The door of his metal mailbox stood open slightly, with several envelopes sticking out beyond the brim. As she stepped over and pulled down the door, a fresh twinge of concern assaulted her middle. The mailbox was stuffed to overflowing.

She paused a moment, looking uncertainly down the road in either direction. Archie was hardly the type of man to ignore his mail. How long had he been gone?

After another moment's indecision, Leigh pulled the mail out of the box and shut the door. At least if she moved this load to his porch, he could continue to get deliveries. She set off down the gravel drive and toward the small bridge spanning the creek, her steps growing increasingly hesitant.

She failed to notice the figure in the water until she was within a few feet of it.

"What are you doing here?" an impudent young voice demanded.

Leigh jumped a foot.

The source of her fright chuckled with laughter. Eleven-year-old Scotty O'Malley was standing knee deep in the creek in soaked cargo shorts and a tee shirt, holding a muddy fishing net in one hand and a bucket in the other.

"I could ask you the same question," Leigh retorted, although she did not particularly want to know the answer. According to the Pack, Scotty was an avid collector of anything that anyone else might consider "gross."

"You looking for Mr. Pratt?" the boy demanded, his expression suddenly intent.

"I thought I would take his mail to him," Leigh answered carefully.

Scotty's eyes widened. He scrambled up out of the water, dropped his tools, and moved to stand beside her on the bridge, shorts dripping, bare feet and legs coated liberally with green-brown mud. He leaned in toward her and dropped his voice to a stage whisper.

"I think he's dead."

Leigh took a quick step back. "Scotty O'Malley!" she

admonished, using her best "calm mother" tone, even as her blood ran cold. "Why on earth would you say that?"

The boy's voice remained sober. "Because I seen his ghost!"

Leigh released a breath. Of course. The ghost thing. She'd been hearing that old song for years. The original Frog Hill Farm, whose farmhouse and remaining outbuildings Archie now owned, had been settled by a Civil War veteran who had spent the remainder of his eighty-some-odd years there. Various neighbors, including Archie himself, found this fact to be so enthralling that they encouraged oral legends about the place, including dubious tales of the founder's heroism at Gettysburg and even more dubious tales of his ghost coming back to haunt the farm—in full Union regalia. Leigh was no expert on the supernatural, but given that she'd always heard that ghosts haunted the place where they died looking how they did *when* they died, the farm's being haunted by a Civil War soldier didn't make much sense. But it did make a better story than being haunted by a geriatric farmer in overalls.

"You mean the solider ghost?" she asked.

Scotty shook his head.

"Nuh-uh!" he answered. "That one's got a head!"

Leigh took in a long, slow breath. Why was she letting this kid's macabre nonsense get to her? Archie's ghost, indeed. The man was in his early fifties and healthy as a horse. "What are you talking about?"

"I seen him last night!" the boy insisted, moving close enough to drip creek water onto the tops of Leigh's shoes. "There are these dancing lights, you know, that come with the hauntings. Orbs, they call them. I can see them from my room! And a couple times, when I walked out here to the creek, I seen the ghost himself—the soldier one! But this one last night, it had a different kind of coat. More like a rain coat. It was tall, and all hunched over like, and *headless!*"

Leigh looked deep into the pale green eyes of the disturbingly genuine-sounding middle schooler, and a chill started up her spine.

She stifled it. "Mr. Pratt is not particularly tall, nor does he strike me as the type to wear a raincoat when it isn't raining. Whatever you think you saw, I don't believe it was a ghost, and I'm sure it wasn't Mr. Pratt." She gave a little shake to her handful of mail. "He's obviously been out of town."

Scotty's eager expression hardened into a frown. He turned and scrambled back down into the creek with a splash. "Wouldn't go over there if I was you," he said offhandedly. "I'm just saying."

Leigh felt a cold sensation and looked down. The toes of her sneakers were soaked through. "Thanks for the warning," she said wryly. "But I think I'll deliver his mail all the same."

She turned and started toward the farmhouse again.

"Won't do him no good," she heard the boy mutter as she walked away. "Can't read when you got no head."

He's making it all up, Leigh assured herself, sticking to her path. *Just to make trouble.* Were her own twins not constantly rolling their eyes at the boy's various schemes and delusions? And they were younger than he was.

Archie Pratt was perfectly fine. He had probably gone out of town with a friend, and whomever he had asked to feed his dog and collect his mail had dropped the ball for some reason. A miscommunication, perhaps. It happened all the time.

Leigh turned a bend in the gravel drive and Archie's unmistakable pickup truck came into view through the trees. As she drew closer to it her brow furrowed, as it always did when she tried to decipher the jumble of faded bumper stickers that were Archie's message to the world. *Save the Whales* and *Live Free or Die* were posted on the upper left tailgate, slightly overlapping. Towards the right were *You'll get my gun when you pry it from my cold, dead fingers* and *Peace, Love, and Harmony*. In the middle was a large, circular sticker with a picture of a bespectacled caterpillar, a violin, and a musket with the caption entirely (and maddeningly) worn off. The bumper itself proudly displayed, from left to right: *Give us Liberty, Not Debt; Support Public Education; Drill, Baby, Drill;* and *We are the 99%*.

Leigh shook her head and kept walking. She had heard Archie talk about a lot of things, but politics wasn't one of them. Which was probably a good thing.

She reached the front steps of the farmhouse. She steeled herself and started climbing.

Everything around her seemed perfectly, harmlessly normal. The farmhouse was old—as old as Cara's, having been built shortly after the turn of the twentieth century when the Harmony Railroad Line began shuttling people in and out of nearby Pittsburgh at the amazing speed of sixty miles per hour. Cara's house had been both lovingly and meticulously restored, but Archie's ministrations had addressed only half of that equation. He kept saying that he was "fixing up the place." But while Archie appeared to have a wide variety of vocations, including insurance salesman, high school teacher, Civil War reenactor, and sometime e-trader—a carpenter he was not.

Leigh gasped and jumped aside as a board under her foot made a cracking sound. She saw no damage, but she stepped carefully off the beaten path the rest of the way to the door. Falling through a rotting porch onto God only knew what lay beneath was not on her agenda this afternoon.

Neither was seeing a headless ghost. She was delivering a man's mail. That was it.

She leaned over and laid the stack of envelopes and fliers neatly on the wrought-iron bench that sat under the front window, weighting them down with the arrow from a broken weathervane whose various pieces (including the rooster) now decorated Archie's windowsill. The porch roof was wide; the papers would be at least as safe from the elements as they had been in the stuck-open mailbox.

Leigh's eyes came to rest on the heavy wooden front door, its once-white paint peeling in sheets. She was virtually certain that Archie was not at home—and had not been at home for several days. But she should probably check, just to be sure.

Shouldn't she?

She punched the sorry-looking doorbell. Its casing had fallen off, leaving wires exposed, but she could hear its muffled ring from inside.

She waited exactly ten seconds. Predictably, there was no response.

"Not home!" she said aloud, attempting to sound cheerful to herself. Perhaps Archie had left in a hurry, not knowing how long he would be gone. He could have left out several days' worth of dog food, figuring he would return before it ran out.

Her lips twisted ruefully. To the owner of a corgi, the mere thought of such a plan was preposterous. Given an infinite supply of food, her Chewie would never move again. He would simply gorge himself into oblivion. When and if he regained consciousness, he would cheerfully repeat.

No, Archie was a helpful, gregarious man with many equally helpful, dog-loving friends. He absolutely would have asked someone to care for Wiley. And he probably would have called to check up on him as well.

On impulse, Leigh's arm reached out. She put her hand on the metal doorknob and turned.

Her breath caught. The door was unlocked.

It creaked loudly on its hinges as she pushed it open barely an inch, then stopped. Surely Archie would lock up his house if he knew he were leaving?

"Archie?" she called uncertainly, throwing her voice through the crack. "It's Leigh Koslow. Are you here?"

She put her ear closer. No hearty male voice answered her call. But she could definitely hear something. Professional voices, canned music.

The television was on.

"Mr. Pratt?" she called again, her voice squeaking like a child. "Are you all right?"

There was no reply.

Leigh's heart pounded. It was no use pretending anymore. Archie Pratt couldn't possibly have deserted his house, his truck, and his dog with no word to anyone, leaving his door unlocked and his television on. He must never have left at all.

Which meant he must still be here.

Had he injured himself somehow? Fallen down the stairs? Had a stroke? Could he be in bed with a bad case of flu?

"Mr. Pratt!" Leigh called again. Her hand on the knob shook a little.

No response. If Archie was ill, wouldn't Wiley have stayed with him? The Pack said the dog went in his house and came right back out—that he didn't want to be here.

Her hand pushed the door open another quarter inch, then stopped.

"Leigh Koslow!" she told herself sternly. "Get a grip on yourself. You are *not* cursed, do you hear me? It's all in your mind!"

Of course. It was in her mind. And in the official files of the homicide division of the Allegheny County police department. The City of Pittsburgh's homicide squad, too. Oh, and the state police. In law enforcement circles, the name Leigh Koslow was synonymous with one thing: bodies. It didn't matter who or what killed them; it was Leigh who found them. Never mind that she didn't want to, that she never even tried. Corpse echolocation was her cosmic destiny. For one happy decade while the twins were growing up, she thought she'd been given a reprieve. But this summer, it had started all over again.

"Archie?" she called, trying one more time.

Please. Just a groan. A moan. Anything.

Silence.

Leigh's stomach churned. She tried not to be superstitious. Really, she did. But why, oh why, did *she* have to be the one checking up on Archie? Seriously, how good an idea was that?

I think he's dead, Scotty has whispered.

Did she have no concern for the poor man at all?

She closed her eyes and swore.

Chapter 2

"You're being ridiculous!" Leigh's cousin Cara proclaimed between heaving breaths. "Honestly, how silly!"

Leigh pushed her cousin forward another pace toward the farmhouse door. She was still trying to catch her own breath, after having rousted Cara from work in her home office—precious "adult" time they both considered inviolate ever since Leigh bought the house next door and the women had agreed to trade off child care. She steadied herself and planted both hands on her hips. "Archie Pratt is a genuinely nice person, and I happen to like him very much," she defended hotly. "If my being ridiculous is what it takes to keep the man alive, then *fine*—call me ridiculous!"

Cara's blue-green eyes rolled. "All right, all right," she soothed. "I'll go in first."

"I'm staying here," Leigh asserted, crossing her arms. "If you need me to call 911, just yell."

Cara threw her cousin another exasperated look, but turned and put her hand on the knob. "Mr. Pratt?" she called, knocking briskly with her other hand. "It's Cara March. Are you home?"

They waited. There was no response.

"It's open," Leigh reminded.

Without hesitation, Cara opened the door.

Leigh watched, heart pounding, as her cousin disappeared inside. "Mr. Pratt?" Cara called again.

Leigh's ears strained to hear a response. All she heard was the television. Impatiently she moved forward to stand just outside the doorframe. "Cara?" she urged, "What is it? What do you see? Is he there?"

Her cousin, maddeningly, took her sweet time in answering. "He's not here or in the kitchen. I'll check his bedroom. I'm guessing it's over here..." her voice trailed off.

Leigh turned and paced a bit. She gnawed on a fingernail. She checked her phone to make sure the battery was charged. She paused with one shaky finger hovering over the nine.

"Leigh?"

She jumped. Cara stood in the doorway. "Do you know if he used the upstairs?"

"I have no clue," Leigh answered. "Did you see—"

Cara disappeared inside the house again.

Leigh groaned in frustration. She waited another minute, then moved slowly toward the open door. Cara had said Archie wasn't in the front room, hadn't she? Leigh crept forward and poked her head inside.

Her nose was met by the mingling aromas of must, dust, and burned coffee. The room was shabby and cluttered; about what she would expect for a middle-aged bachelor who was generally either puttering outside or away in his pickup. But the floor was a disaster, strewn liberally with the recognizable shreds of cardboard, paper, and plastic that had once sheathed snack crackers, boxed macaroni and cheese, dehydrated potatoes, and instant soup. Someone—and she had a pretty good idea who—had led a full-out assault on Archie's food pantry.

Leigh jumped as she heard a banging noise from the back of the house. As if on cue, the culprit in question bounded in from the kitchen and danced around her ankles, his flailing paws scattering the litter in all directions. "Down, Wiley!" Leigh ordered, sensing the animal's clearly telegraphed intentions of leaping onto her person. The lanky black mutt seemed to be some combination of Labrador and hound, but his attitude was all puppy. "Been a little hungry lately, have you?"

The dog continued to prance in circles around her as Leigh made her way through the front room to the kitchen. The farmhouse's tired-looking vinyl floor was scratched, pitted, and buried even deeper in waste than was the front room. A small, box-shaped television sat on the countertop, hooked up to a digital converter box and tuned to a free local channel. The one small table was empty except for a single, quarter-full coffee mug; on the floor beneath lay an overturned glass, one fork, and the shards of a broken breakfast plate. The pantry door hung open, its former contents spilling out into the room like a cornucopia.

"He's not in the house," Cara announced, returning down a narrow staircase and joining Leigh in the kitchen. "I looked in every room." Her eyes remained fixed on her cousin, even as she raised a practiced knee to forestall Wiley's attempt at a crotch sniff. "And my guess would be that he either left in a hurry in response to some emergency, or else he didn't intend to leave at all."

Leigh drew in a shuddering breath. "He couldn't be... you know..."

"Stuffed somewhere?" Cara finished without a blink. "No. I've looked in all the closets, under the beds, everywhere that would be feasible. It's a small house; the attic door looks like it hasn't been opened in years. Have you looked around outside? In the cellar?"

Leigh raised an eyebrow.

Cara let out a breath. "We'll have to do it now, then. Did you see this?" She pointed to the kitchen countertop along the far wall. A well-used coffee maker sat with its glass carafe still on the warmer, stained brown and bone dry. The red brew light was on.

"Whatever was left has all evaporated," Cara said soberly, wading through the trash to switch the machine off. "We're lucky it didn't start a fire."

The women stood in silence a moment, looking at each other.

"I'd guess we'd better look around outside," Leigh agreed.

The women proceeded out the back door and into the yard. With Leigh sticking close to—but always behind—her cousin, they systematically checked the farmhouse cellar, the detached garage (which was filled with so much junk it couldn't possibly house any vehicle larger than a scooter), the skeletal shell of the old barn (which was empty except for several decades' worth of bat guano), and the tool shed (whose notable lack of tools shed some light on Archie's deficits as a carpenter). For all his hound blood, Wiley proved no help whatsoever; once they left the vicinity of the house his interest waned and he took off again in the direction of Leigh's place. The women finished their sweep by walking along the creek and looking for any disturbances in the brush along the woods, but they saw nothing unusual. Archie's truck wasn't locked, but according to Cara his keys were in his bedroom, sitting on the dressing table alongside his wallet.

"I think you should call Maura," Cara said when their search was complete. "Not that there's any evidence of foul play exactly, but... well, maybe they can locate a family member who should know?"

Leigh nodded gravely. Maura Polanski might be her best friend since college, but the career policewoman, now a respected detective in line for promotion to Lieutenant, was less than enthusiastic about Leigh's "abilities" in the field of homicide. More accurately, she had threatened that the next time Leigh's name appeared in one of her investigative reports, it would be as the victim *of* said homicide, perpetuated by the detective herself.

Then again, Maura threatened a lot of things. And her bark was always worse than her bite. Besides, Archie's situation was different. Wasn't it?

"I'll call her," Leigh agreed as the women set off walking home along the creek. "But I'm not looking forward to it."

Cara smiled. "Don't be silly. You're merely doing your neighborly duty, aren't you? Besides—"

"Yoo hoo!" a loud, screechy voice called to them from the back of the Browns' house. "You two come on up here and tell me what's going on! What're you looking for? Did the kids lose something?"

Leigh and Cara glanced up at the personal care home's generous wooden deck, where an elderly woman in an athletic pantsuit stood hanging over the rail, supporting herself with one hand while holding a pair of high-powered binoculars in the other.

"Looks like we're busted," Cara whispered. "Maybe we should have been more discreet?"

Leigh shook her head. "Wouldn't have mattered. Her crime sensing makes me look like an amateur." She cupped both hands around her mouth. "We'll be up in a minute, Mrs. Rhodis!"

The older woman leaned out even farther. "Say *what?*"

"Oh dear," Cara responded hastily, turning toward the house. "Let's get up there before she vaults over the rail!"

Leigh hustled in kind. Sadly, her cousin was not exaggerating. Arthritis may have rendered the eighty-something-year-old Adith Rhodis barely able to walk, but her mind was still sharp as a tack—and more dangerously inquisitive than ever. The woman was so bored at being homebound that she could find intrigue in anything from a distant plume of smoke to a half-eaten box of breakfast cereal. And where there was no mystery to be found, she would happily create one.

"I saw you girls looking in the bushes out there!" Adith beamed when the two had finished climbing the steep wooden stairs that led up to the Browns' back deck. "What are you after?"

Leigh smiled at her friend's latest performance-ready, moisture-wicking warm up suit, this one in midnight blue with shiny white racing stripes. Adith had hung onto her prized collection of seventies-era polyester housedresses and pantsuits well into the new millennium, but after losing fifteen pounds to Emma Brown's healthy cooking, her longstanding love affair with double-knit had been forced to evolve. Leigh had been as happy as anyone to see the retirement of the olive-green zippered dress and burnt orange skorts, but Adith's new penchant for athletic-fit spandex did take some getting used to.

"We didn't lose anything," Leigh said carefully, giving the answer she had prepared while coming up the steps. We were just poking around at Archie's place to see if we could find out where he went. He's gone out of town, apparently, but whoever was supposed to be taking care of Wiley hasn't done the best job."

Adith gave a wince. "Oh, Lordy. That was probably Lester. He's been down with a nasty flu bug this week. But he's perked up a bit today."

Leigh and Cara let out a mutual sigh of relief.

"Of course!" Cara said cheerfully. "I forgot that Archie and Lester were such good friends. We should have come and asked Lester where he was to begin with."

"Well, you can ask him now," Adith offered, opening the door to the screened porch and ushering the women on through it and into the Brown's communal sitting room. The modest, yet cozy room featured an assortment of unmatched furniture chosen to be comfortable without being difficult to get out of; the decoration was decided by the residents' own tastes. The fireplace mantel sported pictures of various loved ones, including Adith's late husband Bud, while the long wall was dominated by a giant print of a Civil War battle and a yellow canary in an antique bird cage.

"Lester!" Adith yelled loud enough to wake the dead. "Miss Leigh and Miss Cara are here to see you!" She eased herself into one of the chairs with a grunt, at which point a miniature apricot poodle materialized from nowhere and popped into her lap. "Hello, Pansy love," she cooed. "You knew I was coming back in, didn't you?"

Leigh couldn't resist a chuckle. Adith had maintained at least one of a dynasty of poodles as long as anyone at the Koslow Animal

Clinic could remember—all of which were named Pansy, and all of which (according to Adith) were possessed of psychic abilities. When advancing arthritis had forced Adith to sell her house on the Ohio River Boulevard and seek daily assistance, Leigh had been delighted to recommend her neighbors' care home, knowing that the Browns not only understood the bond between older people and their pets, but were genuinely happy to accommodate it.

A stout, balding man appeared in the doorway to the kitchen wearing a plaid flannel bathrobe and a painfully red nose. "Oh my," he said sheepishly, "sorry you ladies had to see me like this, but I didn't much feel like getting dressed today. Can't believe how long it's taking me to kick this danged virus!"

"Don't apologize," Cara said quickly. "We're sorry for intruding, but we were worried about Mr. Pratt. We didn't know he had gone out of town and Wiley's been a bit out of sorts."

Lester looked from one to the other through tired, bloodshot eyes. "Archie's left town? He didn't tell me. I wondered why he hadn't called back, but I felt too rotten to go over and find out."

The sick feeling returned to Leigh's stomach. She and Cara exchanged an uncomfortable glance. "His truck is parked at his house," Leigh explained. "But he isn't at home now, his mail hasn't been picked up in days, and Wiley hasn't been fed."

Lester blinked back at her for a long moment, digesting the statement. He and his wife, both practical nurses who had spent many years working in hospitals and nursing homes before launching their five children from the nest and opening up their own business, were practical about most everything. "Arch wouldn't leave like that," he said finally. "Not without telling anybody. He must be sick in bed. Probably caught the same thing I've got. I'll get dressed and go on over—"

"I already searched the whole house," Cara explained quietly. "He isn't there."

Lester's cheeks reddened. "That can't be. We've got a meeting of the 102nd on the day after tomorrow! That's why I was calling him. We got a bunch of potential new recruits at Antietam, and he was supposed to..." his voice trailed off. "Are you *sure* he's not just laid up sick over there?"

Leigh's head swam a moment as she tried to place the references, but the giant battle scene on the wall to her left soon jogged her memory. Archie Pratt, a Civil War buff of the first order, was the chief organizer of a local unit of reenactors, a group to which he was forever trying to recruit everyone in the neighborhood—and probably everyone he met. The women's husbands had both politely declined, despite Archie's impassioned pleas that Leigh's husband Warren was the spitting image of Major General George McClellan.

In Lester, however, Archie had found a true devotee. "He's not at his house," Leigh confirmed. "But maybe if he was feeling ill, he could have gone to stay with a friend, or a relative?"

Lester raised a hand to his chin and rubbed at it thoughtfully. "I can't think of anyone. His family's all from Hershey or thereabouts. And he knows Emma'd be only too happy to run him down some soup or whatever he needed."

A sudden prickle swept down Leigh's spine. But after casting a glance over her shoulder, she sighed. Adith Rhodis was standing all of two inches behind her, breathing down her neck.

"I don't mean to alarm anyone," Cara said smoothly, darting a concerned glance over at Adith. "But wherever Archie went, he didn't take his wallet. I saw it sitting on his dresser; his driver's license was in it. And his keys were there, too."

Lester's mouth dropped open a bit. His face paled. "Well… that's strange."

"Archie didn't have any…" Leigh faltered. "I mean, he wasn't afraid of anyone in particular, was he? Having an argument with someone?"

"Of course not!" Lester defended. "You know Archie! He can get along with anybody. Always has. Everybody likes Arch!"

"Of course they do," Cara agreed. "There's no need for any of us to think the worst" —she threw a hard glance at Adith— "but I think we should probably contact the police, don't you?"

Lester considered another moment, then nodded glumly. He pulled a handkerchief out of his pocket and wiped his red nose. "I can do that."

"There won't be much they can do though, will there?" Adith piped up, her bright eyes burning. "They're not going to believe… you know… all the circumstances. With the farm and all."

The others turned to her with blank stares. "What circumstances?" Cara asked.

Adith's lips puckered. "You know what I mean!" Her scratchy voice dropped to a whisper. "The G-H-O-S-T!"

Lester groaned. "Now, Adith, you know better than to bring all that up. Bunch of nonsense, all of it."

Adith's eyebrows arched. "Archie didn't think so. And he's the one missing, ain't he? Well, let me tell you something." She pointed a bent finger. "The spirits aren't to be trifled with. That soldier had his reasons for haunting the farm he settled, and just maybe poor Archie went a bit too far with his poking around in the past—"

The poodle exploded in a fit of frenzied yapping.

Adith smirked. "See there," she crowed. "My Pansy knows. There's something afoot here that goes beyond what meets the eye."

The dog began to jump on and off her mistress's chair, her barks now interspersed with a high-pitched whine. Adith's expression changed slowly, her frown lines deepening to a look of genuine concern. "And I'm thinking," she said hoarsely, "it may be *E-V-I-L.*"

Chapter 3

Detective Maura Polanski unfurled her solid, six-foot two-inch body from the driver's seat of her department-issue sedan and fixed her ex college roommate—and friend of over twenty years—with an exasperated glare.

"Don't look at me like that!" Leigh protested. "I told you already, there's *no body*. We're all just worried about Archie, and since it's kind of a weird situation, I thought it might be better if I called you than for one of the other neighbors to dial 911—"

The policewoman held up a hand. "I get the picture, Koslow." She cast a glance around the area in front of Archie's house, where Leigh had walked to meet her. Maura's voice, for once, didn't sound gruff so much as tired. "When was the last time anyone saw or spoke to Mr. Pratt?"

"Lester Brown, who lives two houses down, talked to him here at his house Monday night," Leigh explained. "And Archie didn't mention going anywhere. Lester tried to call him on Wednesday and then again yesterday, but his machine picked up, and the message Lester left was never returned. So Archie could have been gone as long as four days."

Maura's gaze fell on the O'Malley's house. "Did you ask the nearest neighbors?"

Remembering her unpleasant conversation with Scotty earlier, Leigh frowned. "Well, yes and no."

Leigh described the exchange, explaining also the pile of mail on Archie's bench. "We tried not to mess with anything inside," she found herself saying as the detective walked carefully across the creaky porch and opened the front door. "But we didn't think of it as being a crime scene. I mean… it's *not* a crime scene. Right?"

Maura stepped inside the front room and closed the door behind her.

Leigh moved away and began to drum her fingers on the wooden porch railing. She started to lean against it, but when the whole structure wobbled, she drew back. What *had* Archie been doing to "fix up" the house all these years? According to Cara, he had moved in eight years ago. From what Leigh had seen earlier, he certainly hadn't spent that time obsessing over interior design. Some seemingly random spots in the house had been missing drywall, exposing bare insulation.

After what seemed an eternity, Leigh heard a door slam. She walked around to the back of the house and encountered Maura gazing out over the various outbuildings with a scowl. "Doesn't look good, Koslow," she commented, her voice flat. "Was the coffee maker on when you and Cara got here?"

Leigh nodded, impressed by the detective's nose for detail. "And the television."

Maura's eyes met hers. She let out a sigh. "I'll let the guys know; they'll send somebody out. But this isn't my area, as you know. It's General Investigations. And I've got to be honest with you—without any clear signs of foul play, and when you're dealing with someone who's of sound mind, a missing adult isn't going to get top priority."

"I see." Leigh studied her friend carefully, her own frown deepening. Maura was never in the best of moods on the all-too-frequent occasions when Leigh summoned her on "official business." But today, something else was amiss. Maura's baby blue eyes were bloodshot, with puffy lids and dark circles below. Her complexion seemed blotched and uneven, and although her broad shoulders often slumped when she was relaxed, her posture today seemed uncharacteristically weary.

"Maura, are you feeling all right?" Leigh asked tentatively. "You look... really tired."

Maura's eyes avoided hers. "Yeah," she confirmed. "I am a little behind on sleep."

"Is there—"

"I'm going to walk around and check out the grounds before I go," Maura interrupted, turning away. "I'll meet you back here in ten if you want a ride home."

Leigh shut her mouth. Within seconds Maura had disappeared around the corner of the garage.

Fretting anew, Leigh decided to give her friend some space. She wandered off in the direction of the tool shed and sank down on its front step. Archie's unexpected disappearance was disturbing enough. But a somber, tired-looking Maura Polanski who had been in Leigh's presence for more than twenty minutes without once either blowing her top or cracking some sarcastic joke was *not* the Maura Polanski she knew and loved. What could possibly be the matter?

An odd sound met Leigh's ears, and her eyebrows lifted. She was certain she had heard it—a very high-pitched murmuring squeal, familiar, yet out of place. She was silent a moment, listening. Then she heard it again. It seemed to be coming from below.

She stood up and looked down. There was nothing below. The step she was sitting on was a concrete block. She opened the door to the tool shed and stepped inside. It looked exactly as it had earlier in the afternoon—barren, dusty, and unused. The sounds had disappeared.

Leigh let out a frustrated breath and returned to her step. Her mind was going. Period. Maura wasn't the only one behind on sleep—she herself hadn't gotten eight hours straight in at least a week. She owed that to the crackpot who ran Rinnamon Industries, with whom her advertising agency had so foolishly embroiled itself, despite knowing his reputation. The man went through advertising firms like she went through leftover Halloween candy, chewing up copywriters as fast as their proposals could be wadded up and hefted into the nearest trashcan. He had turned down six of her ideas so far... she had been working on the seventh when she had fallen asleep in her hammock this afternoon. Which would never have happened if she hadn't already sat up half the night trying yet again to make pottery crocks sound "traditional, reliable, and sensational" at the same time.

Her left temple began to throb.

No sooner had Leigh closed her eyes than the high-pitched squeaks started up again. This time she rose and attempted to follow the sound. It seemed to stay with her as she rounded the corner of the shed, but she saw only a primitive stone and clay-chink foundation covered with sprawling weeds. As she moved around the next corner, however, her gaze halted. Midway along the back wall lay a set of slanted wooden doors, one loose on its hinges and hanging askew, both half covered by the overhanging bushes.

"A cellar?" she mumbled out loud, suddenly embarrassed that neither she nor Cara had recognized the rotting planks for what they were when they had walked this way earlier. But in their defense, they had been distracted by what had looked like a trampled spot in the weeds nearby, and besides—who would expect to find a cellar under a tool shed? But a cellar door it definitely was, and the foundation under the building, she realized, was very old. Much older, in fact, than the wooden structure built atop it.

She moved closer to the doors. The squeals grew louder.

Her pulse rate increased. She *knew* that sound. But what was it?

Her hand moved to the door that hung askew. It was barely connected to the doorframe, hanging by a single screw anchoring one rusty hinge. A quarter of the original door was gone entirely, rotted off to leave a sizable hole.

She started to pull the door to the side. Then she stopped.

"Maura?" she called feebly. The detective was nowhere in sight.

Leigh cursed under her breath. Should she… or shouldn't she? The sounds she heard weren't particularly frightening. In fact, for some odd reason they made her think of—

At last, a light bulb flashed in her weary brain.

She grabbed the doors with both hands and lifted them open.

The dim light of early evening shone through the opening, illuminating little more than the top few of a flight of stone steps leading away beneath. But the fierce growling that now echoed upward confirmed Leigh's suspicions.

"What you got, Koslow?" asked Maura, who had appeared behind Leigh's right shoulder.

Leigh turned around and held out a hand. "Do you have a flashlight on you?"

Maura reached down and unclipped the mini LED attached to her belt. "Be careful," she said, handing it over. "Sounds like you're not too welcome down there."

"You think?" Leigh flipped on the light and leaned down into the opening. She cast the bright white beam down the empty stairs and then swept the space beyond.

From the floor of the stone cellar, in the midst of what appeared to be a pile of rags, gleamed two bright eyes and a set of sharp white teeth. The growling intensified.

"It's all right," Leigh soothed, making no move to go closer.

Maura leaned in for a look of her own as Leigh swept the light beam over a medium-sized white and brown spotted mongrel. The dog looked pitifully thin and wore no collar. At least half a dozen newborn pups wriggled at her side, squeaking and squealing like a symphony.

"Is this Mr. Pratt's dog?" Maura asked.

"No," Leigh replied, her eyes perusing the uniformly black pups. "But under the circumstances, I'd say she has a pretty good case for child support."

The mother dog's growls turned to a snarl. She sprang to her feet, dislodging the unhappy pups and causing a cacophony of even louder squeals.

Leigh shut off the beam, and the women backed away.

"You didn't see anything else down there, did you?" Maura asked as she stood up.

"It was pretty dim, but there was no sign of Archie—or any other human—if that's what you mean," Leigh answered as she replaced the door, leaving an opening equal to what had been there before.

"How long do you think the dog's been down there?"

Leigh considered. "Less than a week, for sure. Probably only a day or so. The pups were tiny."

Maura blew out a breath. "Well, we'll leave the animal control to you and the shelter. I can't see that the new arrivals have any bearing on Mr. Pratt's disappearance."

"No," Leigh agreed. "That door has been rotted away for a while. The dog was probably sniffing around for a sheltered place to have the pups and just wandered in." Something incongruous pricked at the back of her mind, but she couldn't seem to identify it. "I'll bring some food and water over for her; she must be starving. But we shouldn't try to move her right now. Can you tell the officers—"

"I'll make them aware," Maura replied, her voice sounding tired again as she set off toward her car. "You want a ride home?"

Leigh considered. Her house was within easy walking distance, but her friend's demeanor continued to bother her. "Sure," she replied, falling into step beside the detective as they rounded the tool shed. "How's Gerry these days?" she asked conversationally, inquiring after Maura's husband of eleven years, who was a lieutenant with the city police force.

"He's good," Maura responded dully. "Been gone a couple days now, though. The department sent him to a conference in Minneapolis for a week." The detective stopped short suddenly, her gaze on the ground. "Did you see this?"

Leigh looked down. The ground next to a maple tree had been recently disturbed. It was only a small area, maybe a foot across, filled with relatively fresh, upturned earth. "Archie's dog, Wiley, is a digger," she said with a shrug. "I imagine Archie has lots of damage to undo. I've seen refilled holes like that all along the creek, even in our yard."

Maura's brow furrowed. "Let me get this straight. Mr. Pratt has a dog—an intact male, evidently—who wanders all over the neighborhood digging holes. Then Mr. Pratt himself goes around with a shovel, putting the dirt back in?"

"Well, he—" Leigh's own brow furrowed. The idea did seem pretty lame, now that she thought about it. Wiley *did* dig holes... she had seen him do it. But Archie had never mentioned anything about it to her, much less seemed apologetic. And why would the man bother to fill in holes in his own yard, when old farm machinery lay rusting by the garage and his front porch was falling in?

"I don't know," she answered finally. "I guess I haven't given it much thought."

"How long have you been seeing these holes?"

Leigh felt suddenly sheepish. "Oh, a long time. The kids started noticing them when we first moved in. We always just figured it was Wiley."

Maura harrumphed. "Sounds a little fishy to me," she proclaimed. "You sure you know who's doing the digging?"

Leigh felt even more sheepish. When her and Cara's offspring got a scheme into their heads, there was little she wouldn't put past them. Particularly not with her deceptively innocent-seeming daughter Allison as their secret mastermind. Leigh didn't doubt for a moment that her own impression of the kids' "finding" the holes could be an illusion they had intentionally planted in her feeble brain years ago. She could no longer even remember how it had all started; since the holes had always been filled in, she hadn't wasted precious energy worrying about it.

"Yeah," Maura said, her mouth drawing into the closest thing to a smile she'd shown all evening. "I can see how sure you are."

"No comment."

"Try to find out," Maura suggested as they reached her sedan. "I doubt it has any more to do with Mr. Pratt's disappearance than his surprise litter of dependents, but you never know."

Leigh opened the passenger door and sat down with a plop. "No," she agreed, an uncomfortable feeling plaguing her middle anew. "You never know."

Chapter 4

"Warren," Leigh asked her husband as she watched through her front window while Maura's sedan drove away. "You know those funny holes that keep popping up out by the woods all the time? The ones that have been dug and filled in already?"

Warren lowered the newspaper he was reading. "You mean the ones the Pack are digging?"

Leigh looked at him ruefully. "What makes you think the Pack are doing it?"

He blinked back at her, puzzled. "Well, who else would?"

"But we've been seeing them for years!" Leigh protested. "The kids were only kindergarteners when we moved in."

Warren shrugged. "They were younger than that when Matthias decided to dig them all to China and cracked the septic line."

Leigh sighed. Maura, Warren and herself had been friends since college, a trio of free spirits who had dubbed themselves "the three Musketeers." But while she and Warren had a complicated history of being friends-only for a ridiculously long period of time before she fell madly in lust (an oversight she bitterly regretted), Warren had always enjoyed an easy platonic relationship with Maura. And often as not, he was more in tune with the policewoman's way of thinking than was Leigh herself.

Case in point: now.

"You don't think Wiley could be digging the holes?" Leigh asked.

Warren raised an eyebrow. "And filling them back in?"

"No! I mean…" she gave up. "Oh, never mind. If the Pack are the ones doing it, why? What are they looking for?"

He returned to his paper. "No telling."

A blur of red streaked through Leigh's peripheral vision, and she turned her head. Her son Ethan, whose unruly crop of cherry-red hair always gave his movements away, had just slipped into the kitchen from the back patio. She didn't need to ask why. The Pack were out playing in the yard; the bag of chocolate chip cookies she had bought earlier was in the pantry. "Ethan? What are you doing?"

He appeared in the doorway. "Looking for something," he said coyly, punctuating the words with his best lopsided, easy-going smile.

Leigh resisted the urge to grin. He looked just like his father when he did that. "I said two cookies each," she reminded. "I believe you're at quota."

The boy's smile faded. "You didn't say three each?"

Leigh held firm. "Not a chance."

Ethan began to slink back outside.

"However," Leigh continued, watching him stop and turn toward her hopefully. "I'll allow one more each on one condition. I want to know everything *you* know about the holes that have been popping up all over the neighborhood ever since we moved in here. And I do mean *everything*."

The boy's face flushed. He looked suddenly uncomfortable. "Um... well..." he glanced over his shoulder toward the patio. "I'm not sure I can really..."

Leigh tapped her foot.

Ethan straightened. "I tell you what, Mom. I'll take your offer back to the others and we'll conference about it. Okay?" He twirled around and disappeared.

Leigh cast a glance at her husband, who was grinning broadly. "Your *offer?*" she repeated. "*Conference* about it? He's ten and a half years old! Where do they get this stuff? Do you give them lawyer-speak lessons when I'm not around?"

Warren chuckled and raised his paper again. "I'm a recovering politician, not a lawyer."

"Same difference," Leigh accused, dropping onto the couch beside him. "When they were infants, yes, I kept wishing time could go into hyperdrive. But all I wanted was for them to conquer the toilet and feed themselves! Clearly, my punishment is having elementary-age children who talk like a combination of a used-car salesman and Mr. Spock."

Warren frowned at her over the Business section. "Don't be dissing Spock."

Leigh's eyes rolled.

The patio door opened and the four children entered and

marched single file into the living room, where they stood facing Leigh and Warren, their expressions serious.

Leigh's anxiety increased. Whatever was coming, it wasn't good.

And this was the second time today.

"Aunt Leigh?" Mathias said importantly. Warren lowered his paper again.

"Yes?" she answered.

"Ethan says you wanted to know about the holes. Funny thing is, we've been talking about that all day. Ever since we got worried about Mr. Pratt. We took a vote, and we decided you should know. It might be important."

The other three nodded in agreement. Leigh tensed. "What might be important?"

Mathias gave a nod to his sister, and Lenna stepped forward. She extended one skinny arm and held out a single sheet of folded paper.

Leigh took it. "What's this?"

"It's a treasure map," Lenna answered proudly. "I found it by the creek."

"We kind of swore each other to secrecy," Ethan explained. "But now, with Mr. Pratt missing..."

"We can't rule out a connection," Allison finished. "So we thought you and Aunt Mo should know."

Leigh unfolded the paper. Warren leaned in and studied it over her shoulder.

It was one of the most bizarre "maps" Leigh had ever seen. A photocopy, clearly, as white showed around the dog-eared corners of the yellowed and creased original. Various shadowed lines were visible along the edges of the paper, indicating any number of previous reproductions. The map itself had boxes that looked like buildings, squiggly lines that looked like creeks, and at the right hand edge, parallel lines that looked like railroad tracks. An assortment of smaller circles and squares could be trees or rocks—or anything. Across the whole map, radiating out from one of the large squares like spokes, were five straight lines. Each line had a series of Xs on it at different points along its length, some closer together than others. The only lettering consisted of two nearly illegible words sitting inside a jagged oval with an attached arrow pointing to the source of the spokes. This label said merely: "The

Guide."

Warren whistled.

"I don't get it," Leigh said. "What are these straight lines supposed to mean?"

"We don't know," Allison answered. "That's what's been so annoying."

"What makes you think it's a treasure map in the first place?" Warren asked reasonably. "It could be a survey of some kind. Albeit not very well done."

The Pack looked at each other. "Well," Mathias began, his tone implying patience with his rather slow elders, "if there wasn't any treasure to find, why would anyone be digging?"

Leigh and Warren exchanged a glance. The squiggly line through the middle did resemble Snow Creek. And the one along the right could be the creek that fed into it on the other side of Cara's farm. If so, the map would include the very spot in which they were currently sitting. "When did you find this?" Leigh asked.

"Last week," Lenna answered. "It was lying on the ground next to the wooden bridge. You know—the little one that Mr. Brown drives his lawn mower over."

"But," Leigh blurted, "I've been seeing those holes for years! What were you digging for *before* you found the map?"

The Pack's faces registered surprise. It was Allison who responded. "Mom," she said with forbearance, "*We* aren't the ones digging the holes."

A moment of silence followed, during which Leigh was grateful her daughter refrained from adding the obvious, "Duh."

"I mean," Allison continued, "we've dug a few since we found it, but that's different. We figured the person who dropped this map must be the same person who's been doing the digging all along. And why would they bother if they weren't looking for something important?"

"That's why we think it might have something to do with Mr. Pratt going missing," Mathias finished. "Because the treasure *must* be really valuable!"

The doorbell rang.

"Grandma's here!" Lenna called with a little hop, making for the door.

Leigh's own heart felt anything but light. She looked from the indecipherable map to her husband's equally perplexed face. "You think it's possible?" she whispered.

Warren drew in a breath. Then he shrugged. "It does look like this area. And if the Pack isn't doing the digging..."

"We should let Maura and the police know," Leigh finished.

He nodded in agreement.

"Grandma, we found a treasure map!" Lenna said excitedly, opening the door. Leigh's Aunt Lydie, who was coming over to stay with Mathias and Lenna while Cara and Gil went on a weekend trip to Lake Chautauqua, responded to the news with her usual unflappable calm.

"Did you, dear?" she said with feigned interest. "Can I see?"

Lenna bounced over and yoinked the paper from Leigh's hand. "Look here!" she explained excitedly, holding the paper up to her grandmother and pointing. "Allison says this is Snow Creek. And this is the little creek by our house. See?"

Lydie's brow furrowed. She studied the map a moment, then cast a glance at Leigh and Warren. "Where did this come from?" she asked, her interest no longer feigned.

Leigh explained. Lydie buried her nose in the map, walked backward over to the recliner, and sat down.

Leigh allowed herself a twinge of hope. Lydie, who had raised Cara as a single parent working two and sometimes three jobs, had gone back to college in her fifties and earned a double major in accounting and history. With luck, maybe she would have an edge on understanding chicken scratches and confusing symbols.

"What do you think, Grandma?" Lenna persisted.

Lydie's lips puckered. "Well, I think the original map—the one this is a copy of—must have been old. Quite old."

"Why?" Leigh asked.

Lydie pointed to the right edge of the paper. "Well, for one thing, it shows the Harmony Railroad Line. I don't know when the actual tracks were taken up, but the line stopped running in the early thirties. And then there are the trees. I'm guessing this cross-hatch pattern is forest, based on what's on the hill behind Cara's farm. Those are older woods, with big oaks. But look at the far left, where there are plenty of trees now. This map shows nothing. People tend to forget that all the flat areas around here used to be farmland. Most of the trees you see now are relatively young maples and evergreens that have grown up since the area went residential."

Leigh sat up. Her aunt had also done some graduate work—in historic preservation. "How old do you think the original map might have been, then?"

Lydie cocked her head. "Well, I'm no expert on maps, you understand. But if I had to guess, I'd say no later than the early thirties. Probably earlier."

The children's eyes widened. "That's almost a hundred years old!" Mathias exclaimed. "Wow!"

"Don't make me feel older than I am, young man," Lydie said drolly. "The early thirties were only eighty some-odd years ago, thank you very much."

"Still," Ethan chimed in. "That's *old!*"

"I found it!" Lenna reminded.

Allison crept quietly to her great aunt's side. "Can you understand the lines, Grandma Lydie?" she asked. "It's strange that there are so many Xs, don't you think?"

Lydie's brow creased further. After another moment she shook her head and rose. She handed the map back to Leigh. "I'm afraid I can't help you there. Makes no sense to me. You kids ready to go?"

"Almost," Mathias said meaningfully, staring at Leigh. The other three children were staring at her as well.

"Yes?" she asked, perplexed.

Mathias cleared his throat, his tone all business. "I believe the contract was for one more cookie each?"

"The *contract?*"

Warren laughed out loud.

She smacked him with the map. "Fine. One more cookie each."

The children turned in unison and headed toward the kitchen. "But don't make your grandmother wait too long," she added. "And from now on, could you please make an attempt to talk like normal ten year olds?"

Mathias spun around on a heel. "I'm thirteen!" he said indignantly.

Leigh sighed. "So you are, as of last month. Duly noted."

He nodded smugly and rejoined the others.

"Could I see that map again a moment?" Lydie asked, stretching out a hand.

Leigh complied.

Lydie adjusted her glasses, the lines of her face creasing deeply in concentration. "I wonder what 'The Guide' is. I'm not familiar with the buildings down that way. What do you think the arrow is pointing to?"

Lydie held out the map so that Warren and Leigh could take another look.

A heaviness crept into the pit of Leigh's stomach.

"That's Archie Pratt's house," she answered.

Water sloshed over the side of the bucket Ethan was holding, drenching Leigh's shoes for the second time today.

"Sorry, mom," he apologized. "You want me to carry it in for you?"

"No," Leigh answered quickly. "The dog is going to be upset enough about one person going in."

"Maybe I should go," Allison piped up. She was standing behind Leigh's elbow, holding a heaping bowl of dog food. "Animals like me, you know. Grandpa says it's because I'm not intimidating."

"You also haven't been vaccinated against rabies," Leigh reminded. "And I have." *Thanks to client nutcase #453,* she thought uncharitably, remembering the man with the silver nail polish and George Washington wig who had sworn up and down that his outdoor cat had been vaccinated every year since kittenhood and was only stumbling around because his crazy neighbors were trying to poison them both with nerve gas. The cat hadn't bitten her, but just holding the animal for five minutes had earned her a one-way ticket to vaccination land. That was a long time ago, when she had been subbing as a vet tech at her father's practice, and she doubted seriously that she was still immune. But her daughter wouldn't know that.

"It's probably worn off by now," Allison said with a pout.

Leigh did not respond. She looked at the opening to the cellar under Archie's tool shed, but could barely see it in the dark. The days were getting shorter all too quickly. "Warren?" she called. "Where are you with the light?"

"Right here," he answered from a few feet behind her, turning the beam back on her and the children, where it had been until just before Ethan bumped into her.

"What's up?" Leigh asked. She knew he had insisted on accompanying them because he was concerned about Archie's disappearance, not because he "needed some exercise" as he had claimed. The children weren't fooled, either. Not only because the seasoned ex-politician never broke a sweat, but because he was about as comfortable in the great outdoors as Daniel Boone at a Star Trek convention. Leigh had only convinced him to move into a place as countrified as this by tempting him with the ultimate man-toy—a riding mower.

"Sorry," he responded, not answering the question. There was something odd in his voice, and Leigh made a mental note to ask him about it later.

She reached down and pushed the broken cellar door to the side. Then she slowly opened the other one, leaned in, and listened. There were no squealing sounds this time, but the low growling began right on cue. "Okay," she instructed. "Warren, you shine the light down the stairs. Allison, give me the bowl. I'm going to set it down right at the bottom—close enough for her to smell it, but hopefully *not* close enough she'll feel obliged to warn me off. If I start to run back up, don't stand there staring—get out of the way. She might follow me. Got it?"

"Got it, Mom!" Ethan said enthusiastically. "When do I take the water down?"

"I'll take the water down," Leigh corrected, "if she reacts all right to the food. Otherwise we'll leave it here. For now, just set it on the ground. All right. Here goes."

She took the food bowl from Allison, inhaled, and started down the narrow stone steps. The growls grew louder. She began to talk soothingly to the dog, keeping her movement slow and steady. When she descended the last step, the dog seemed ready to rise again, but much to Leigh's relief, the animal instead lifted her nose into the air and sniffed. "That's right," Leigh said with a smile. "You get it now. *Food.* You remember the good stuff, don't you?"

Looking at the mother dog from a closer vantage point, Leigh was not at all sure that the dog did remember. The mongrel was painfully thin, with nearly every bone showing through her short coat of once-white, filthy fur. As Leigh set the bowl down on the ground the dog lifted a threatening lip, but the gesture was clearly half-hearted, and her growling had ceased. "Good girl," Leigh praised. "Now let me get you some clean water. We both know you're thirsty, and Snow Creek's a long walk for a mother in your condition. Right?"

Leigh made her way back up the stairs, where Ethan eagerly handed down the pail.

Water splashed all over her shoes again.

"Sorry, Mom," he repeated.

She carried the bucket down the steps and placed it by the food bowl. The mother dog hadn't moved, but lay still as a statue, staring longingly at the bowls. Leigh took a quick look around. With the light beam centered on the stairs, she couldn't see much more than she had been able to earlier in the day. But she did see what had struck her as out of place. On the dirt floor not far from the dog's nest of rags lay a large, bright-yellow plastic flashlight.

The dog began growling again.

Leigh took the hint.

She recommenced her cooing and moved slowly back up the stairs. Once out, she turned around and began replacing the doors.

"Good job, Mom!" Ethan praised.

Warren kept the light on the doors, and no sooner had Leigh moved the broken one back into position than she heard a familiar sound from below. She peeked through the hole to see the dog already at the food bowl, wolfing down the kibble.

"Success!" she whispered happily. The children gave a silent cheer. She stood up and allowed them each a chance to peek down the hole. While Warren continued to hold the light in position, she took a few steps away around the corner of the shed, where she could just see the dim outline of Archie's truck in the same position as before. Her gaze swept hopefully toward the farmhouse, but no light shone from within. She exhaled with a sigh and pivoted back toward the others, then stopped cold.

What was THAT?

Her pulse began to hammer. Her eyes scanned the area by the side of the garage, the area where just a second ago she had sworn she saw—

Leigh gave her head a shake. No. She was losing it. The moonlight was dim; she could barely make out the buildings. Besides, was her long distance vision not deteriorating every year, along with the rest of her body?

The area was dark. Nothing moved.

But something *had* moved. Hadn't it?

Her shoulders gave a shiver.

"Leigh?" Warren called, shining the light her direction. "You ready to go?"

"Absolutely," she answered, moving quickly to his side. "Our work here is done."

"But we'll keep feeding her," Allison corrected. "Won't we, Mom?"

"Of course we will," Leigh replied. *But only in the daylight.*

"Are you all right?" Warren asked quietly, eyeing her with suspicion. The man always could read her like a book.

"I'm great," Leigh answered, almost certainly unconvincingly.

I didn't really see a human figure slipping around the corner of the garage. Particularly not a tall one with a funny long coat…

"You sure?" Warren pressed.

"Positive," Leigh answered.

… and no head.

Chapter 5

"Take this one," Randall Koslow suggested, pulling the thirty-pound bag of premium puppy food off a stack in the clinic basement and hoisting it over one narrow shoulder. "I'll carry it out for you."

Leigh knew better than to argue. Her father might be pushing seventy, but his rail-thin arms were deceptively strong—testament to a lifetime of lifting the dead weight of unconscious dogs on and off of surgery tables.

"Let her eat as much as she wants," he instructed as they walked, referring to Leigh's latest stray. With his sister-in-law and now his daughter on the board of a bustling animal shelter, he was more than used to donating both supplies and his professional time to the cause. "Make sure she has water and keep everyone else away from her. If she's smart enough to find shelter out of the wind and the rain, I'll suspect she'll manage just fine."

Leigh nodded. Her father had always been a staunch advocate for getting strays off the street, neutered, and adopted. But she knew that he harbored a secret respect for the wiliest among them, whose determination to remain independent thwarted even his best efforts.

"Thanks, Dad," she responded, opening the door for him.

"Oh and by the way," he said dryly as he reached the top of the concrete stairs leading up to the tiny parking lot, "your mother is looking for you."

Leigh cringed. Over the years she and her father had perfected the art of covert communication where one Frances Koslow was concerned. Their conspiracy was never discussed; it was simply understood. Randall's actual message was as follows: *Your mother has become obsessed with some new triviality with which she plans to harass you, potentially at some length. You have roughly six seconds to prepare. Godspeed.*

Leigh reached the top step and saw exactly what she expected to see: Frances Koslow herself, giant handbag in tow, marching down the steep brick street, heading straight for them with determined strides.

Leigh's mind raced. What was it this time? Frances hadn't looked so vexed at her only daughter since discovering that her sainted son-in-law ironed his own shirts.

"Can I have your keys?" Randall asked, holding out his hand. "I'll go drop this in your trunk."

Translation: *You'll be tied up here for some time, and I have to get back to work.*

Leigh complied.

"And where have you been, young lady?" Frances spouted as she approached. "I've been calling all morning!"

"I have my cell phone," Leigh offered, knowing the reminder to be pointless. Frances also had a cell phone, but reserved it strictly "for emergencies," a policy she believed the rest of the world should be equally obliged to follow. The failure of anyone to answer Leigh's home phone, which Frances had probably been calling every five minutes for the last hour, was no mystery. Lydie had arrived bright and early to take the Pack on a Saturday field trip to the Heinz History Center, and when Leigh had left Warren was out playing in the yard (a.k.a., "mowing the lawn"). "Everyone's out," she explained, attempting a casual, cheerful tone. "What's up?"

Frances's lips drew into a frown. Levity in the face of calamity was not appreciated. "You know perfectly well what's up!" she retorted, hands planted firmly on her hips. "A neighbor of yours has been violently abducted, snatched away from within inches of my own grandchildren, and not only do you take no steps whatsoever to protect them, but The Family is not even informed!"

Leigh blinked. She should have seen this coming. Whatever she and Warren hadn't told Lydie last night, Mathias and Lenna undoubtedly had, and although Leigh's aunt was the most unflappable of women, she had the tiresome habit of sharing absolutely everything with her twin sister.

Leigh cleared her throat. "First off, all we know is that Mr. Pratt is not at his house; we have no evidence that he was 'abducted,' violently or otherwise. Second, I called Maura last night and the police are investigating. Third, the children have been told in no uncertain terms that they are not allowed anywhere near Frog Hill

Farm without supervision until further notice. And fourth, correct me if I'm wrong, but is there any member of the extended Morton clan who does *not* know this entire story already?"

Frances' lips pursed, confirming that she had already called every relative on her speed dial, and probably half her address book as well. "Your Great Aunt Eliza didn't pick up," she answered tonelessly. "Which is a good thing, because she probably would have had another heart attack."

Leigh sighed. "The situation is perfectly under control, Mom." She did not bother to add the admonition "don't worry," as she had given up on that phrase in the eighties.

"And what exactly do you plan to do about the holes?" Frances persisted.

Leigh's eyebrows rose. "What do you mean?"

"The children could step in them and twist an ankle!"

Metal keys were pressed into Leigh's hand; she turned to see her father slipping surreptitiously back down the basement steps behind her.

"The holes have been filled in already," she answered.

"Dirt settles."

Leigh glanced at her watch. "Sorry, Mom. Gotta run. I… um… promised to bring home food. Wouldn't want anyone to starve."

Frances' jaw tightened, and Leigh crowed internally. Her mother would, of course, assume that Leigh was referring to Warren. And as important as publicly lecturing one's grown daughter on the propriety of family communication was, nothing trumped a wife's duty to feed her (perfectly capable) husband.

Leigh smiled.

Frances glowered back. "We will continue this discussion later."

"See you then!" Leigh said cheerfully, even as her feet took off at a jog. She reached her car, jumped in, started the engine, and pulled out on the street within seconds—half fearing to see Frances trailing behind her in the rear view mirror, holding out some cleaning implement. But her mother had disappeared, most likely down the clinic's basement steps.

Godspeed to you too, Dad.

Warren was still on the mower, cutting a new symmetrical pattern into their already short, long-dead grass, when she returned home and headed out to Archie's with the new bag of dog food and an extra pail loaded in the back of the kids' old wagon. She took the short route along the creek and trundled as quickly as possible past the Brown's house. If Mrs. Rhodis happened to be looking out the back, Leigh would have no hope of escaping detection. But mercifully for the neighborhood, the woman also watched a lot of television.

This time, Leigh got lucky. She made it all the way to Archie's tool shed without seeing or hearing a soul. Although, she thought wistfully as she glanced at the still-unmoved truck, she would really, *really* liked to have seen Archie himself.

Less so the headless specter in the funky coat.

Stop that! Leigh chastised as her coward's heart began to race. *You didn't see a thing.*

She had questioned Warren late last night, asking him why he had left Ethan to bump into her in the dark while shining their flashlight into the woods. His response had been nonchalant: he'd heard leaves crackling, but saw nothing, so figured the sound came from a squirrel or a bird. Leigh had bitten her lip and stayed silent. No way was she ending such a day by making wild accusations about headless trespassers. Her rationality got questioned enough as it was, thank you very much, and although she did *not,* repeat *not,* believe in ghosts, anything one step away from a corpse was something worth avoiding.

She hadn't seen a thing.

She parked the wagon behind the tool shed and pulled opened the cellar doors. The sound of happy squeals drifted up loud and clear, and she smiled. "Guess Mom's milk has a little more punch to it this morning, eh?" She carried the bag down the stairs and set it on the floor. The mother dog did not growl, but watched her descent with an intent, hopeful look. As Leigh opened the top of the bag and scooped a heaping helping into the empty bowl, the dog's thin white tail gave one shy, appreciative thump. "Progress," Leigh said with a grin. "I bet you're a very nice girl when you're not defending your offspring with your life. But take some advice—stay away from the Wileys of the world. Men like that never commit."

Leigh knew that the charming canine Casanova was, even as she spoke, unhappily being confined by Lester, who was worried that the hound might take off in search of his missing master. But she doubted that the new mother gave a hoot about Wiley, or any other handsome face. The dog had eyes only for her food.

"There you go. Breakfast! I'll bring you some fresh water now, all right?" Leigh cajoled, rising to her feet.

The light in the basement went suddenly dim; a figure blocked the head of the staircase.

"Whatcha doing?" an overloud, taunting voice demanded.

Leigh tensed. Scotty O'Malley was quite possibly the last person in the world she would choose to have discovered the hidden den... headless ghosts included.

"Stay where you are," she ordered. "This is—"

"Cool!!! Puppies!!!"

Scotty launched down the stairs three a time, coming to land at Leigh's feet with a plop that send a cloud of dust into the air. "Can I have one? How big are they going to get?"

"Stop!" Leigh demanded, making a grab for him. "Don't go any closer! She's—"

But the boy paid no attention. Eluding her outstretched hand with ease, he barreled straight for the dog and litter, mouth open and fingers grasping.

He did not make it to the puppies. The mother dog was on her feet in an instant. Standing over her offspring with a wide-spaced stance, she snarled viciously and snapped her teeth in the air.

Scotty screamed at the top of his lungs, pitched back with his arms wheeling, and fell flat on his bottom. He let out a string of profanity (laced with liberal use of a certain four letter word which—in Leigh's humble opinion—no eleven-year-old should be allowed to speak), clawed to his feet again and made a rush for the exit. He scrambled up the stone steps in double time, his high voice reverberating with each jerky motion until he disappeared through the hole above.

Leigh didn't move. Despite herself, she was impressed. She couldn't remember ever having heard anyone (standup comedians included) make such creative and frequent use of that particular word in such a short span of time. And the boy had been in motion, too.

Predictably, his absence lasted exactly five seconds. Then his pale face poked over the entryway again.

"You should watch your language," Leigh chastised. "There are children present."

"She's a wild dog!" he accused, his voice still shaky.

"She's only protecting her puppies," Leigh defended. "See, she's fine now."

The mother dog had indeed lain down again, though she continued a low warning growl with an occasional lift of her lip in Scotty's direction.

"You'll have to stay out of here," Leigh continued, not altogether anxious to disabuse the boy of his fear. "She needs complete quiet and solitude for at least another three weeks." Leaving the resealed dog food bag on the floor, Leigh picked up the empty water pail and moved slowly up the stairs. When she reached the top, Scotty stepped back out of the way to let her pass.

"She bit me!" Scotty protested, trailing after Leigh as she carried both the old pail and the new one toward the tap at the side of Archie's house. "I'll tell my dad… and he'll shoot her!"

Leigh restrained herself. "And I'll tell your dad that I watched the whole thing, and that the dog didn't get within a foot of you." She could only hope that Scotty's words were bluster, given that Joe O'Malley was well known for his devotion to the care and feeding of guns. "Just stay away from her and her puppies, and you'll be fine," she ordered.

Leigh turned on the tap and began to fill the first pail. She noticed that Scotty had stopped trailing her and was standing perfectly still about ten feet away. His eyes were scanning the area behind Archie's house, his expression anxious. Leigh made an effort to relax her already taut nerves. She didn't want to be anywhere near the corner of the garage where she had seen… nothing… but the dog needed fresh water and using the tap was a whole lot easier than hauling liquid all the way from her house. She finished one pail and started on the second. Scotty still hadn't moved or spoken. The kid was creeping her out.

"There's dead people here, you know," he declared.

Leigh's teeth gritted. How *did* the little twerp know exactly how to get to her?

"There is not!" she retorted, sounding no older than he was. Chagrinned, she cleared her throat and regrouped. "I told you yesterday, Mr. Pratt is not here. Nobody's here. No humans, and definitely no ghosts."

Scotty sucked air loudly through his crooked teeth. "Says you!

Mr. Pratt said there is. He said Old Man Carr drowned to death right here in Snow Creek, and his ghost still haunts the place, because he was *murdered!"*

Leigh had visions of the entire contents of her pail raining squarely over the urchin's head, but she suppressed them. Her unfortunate personal history with the M word was not his fault.

"Mr. Pratt did not tell you that," she argued calmly, despite the chill that seeped into her bones. "No one was murdered."

Scotty frowned. "Well, they never knew for sure. So he could have been, for all you know. Face down in the crick, all bloated up and everything. He could have been there for *days*. Could have had an Indian arrow in his back... and the fish ate it out of him!"

Leigh took in a deep breath, then let it go. There were so many things wrong with that claim, she didn't know where to begin. But she had to admit, the boy had her intrigued. Mr. Pratt had clearly told him *something*. Could it be important?

She bit. "Who was Old Man Carr, exactly? You mean the Civil War soldier?"

Scotty nodded with enthusiasm and took an unconscious step toward her. "He fought at Gettysburg. You know, the big battle where, like, *everybody* died! Except he didn't, he was a hero, because he was one of the guys who nailed the rebel dude with the hat—right as he came over the wall. *Pow!"* The boy banged a fist into his palm with relish. "And then Carr, he comes here and builds that house right there," he pointed to the building behind Leigh, "and then he turns into an old man and does boring stuff and all until somebody murdered him. And now he haunts the place, because he's like *so* mad that no one treated him like a hero and everyone thought he was crazy when he was really just old and wanted to hide all his money so the government couldn't get it!"

Leigh's eyebrows rose. What Archie had actually told Scotty, God only knew. But the last part was definitely intriguing. "He hid his money?" she asked.

Scotty nodded. Then he seemed to reconsider. "Well, they say he was paranoid... you know, when you think everyone's out to get you. But somebody *was* out to get him, else he wouldn't have got murdered, would he? You think Mr. Pratt got murdered, too?"

Leigh suppressed a scream. She picked up the full buckets and began walking in earnest. It was broad daylight. There were no such things as ghosts. Archie Pratt was *not* dead and certainly had not been murdered. She could not legally strangle Scotty O'Malley no matter how much he irritated her. Furthermore, she had a dog to water.

"Are you scared of being murdered?" Scotty probed, following so close behind her that he clipped one of her heels. "I wouldn't mind being murdered if it meant I could become a ghost. Then I could scare the—"

"Language!" Leigh barked.

Scotty snickered. He clipped her heel again. "I'd scare *everybody*. Just like the headless dude. But I'd be better at it. I wouldn't just slink around empty buildings and stuff. I'd come after people. I'd show up right in their bedrooms… or their *bathrooms!*"

Leigh reached the tool shed and set down the buckets with a slosh. "Don't you have somewhere else you have to be?"

He shrugged. "Not really. Is Allison around?"

"No," *Thank God.* "Where do you see these supposed ghosts?"

Leigh's jaws tightened. She hadn't intended to ask that.

Scotty cocked his head and rotated it around comically. "Like, everywhere back here. Tool shed. Garage. Behind the house. You name it, ghosts haunt it. Scared away all the other owners, didn't you know? Or maybe they were murdered, too. I wouldn't come out here at night if I were you!"

No worries.

"Later!" Without another word, much less any explanation, Scotty took off at a run. He reached the creek and halfway attempted to jump over, instead landing squarely in the middle of it. Leigh could hear him cackling with laughter as he splashed. "Maybe there's a body in here right now!" he yelled cheerfully. "Yo, fish! Did you eat the head off?"

Praying for forbearance, Leigh picked up the buckets once more and headed down the cellar steps. The kid was a loony. She should pay no attention to anything he said.

They say he was paranoid… wanted to hide all his money…

What had Archie really told Scotty? Could the happy-go-lucky teacher/insurance salesman himself have been searching for something the old man left behind?

Leigh stopped at the bottom of the steps and set down the pails. She refilled the food bowl that was empty again already, smiled at the now-placid mother dog, and hardened her resolve. If there were any truth behind Scotty's story, Archie's best pal Lester Brown would know. And if it had anything to do with Archie's mysterious disappearance, she was going to make darned sure the police knew it, too.

Chapter 6

"Lester ain't here," the gravelly voice said curtly. "Adith's knocked out on her meds and Emma's down in the kitchen feeding the baby. What do you want?"

The face of Pauline, Adith Rhodis's roommate at the personal care home, was fixed into a disapproving frown, as it had been every time Leigh had ever seen her. According to Adith, the woman had started scowling the day prohibition was repealed, and hadn't stopped since. While that seemed a stretch, even given Pauline's impressive age of 97 years, Leigh could well imagine that Pauline's sour disposition had begun well before her first social security check arrived. She was, quite simply, a "glass half empty" kind of gal.

"I just wanted to ask Lester a question about the man who built Archie Pratt's house," Leigh responded. "It can wait. Unless you think Emma might know?"

Pauline snorted. "Emma don't care about that stuff. Harvey would, though. Lord knows he's got nothing better to do." She turned her back on Leigh and walked away with her cane, leaving the door open. Pauline was never without the bamboo cane, although its purpose was a mystery. It barely touched the ground as she walked, and she seemed to have no trouble getting up or sitting down. Nor did she have trouble standing, as was made clear when she stopped in the hallway, raised her cane high in the air, and banged it violently against a door. "Har-*vey!*" she yelled. "Get your nose out of those books and come bore this woman to death with your fool stories!" Then she turned on a heel, walked through the door of the room across the hall that she shared with Adith, and closed it behind her.

No sound came from behind Harvey's door, and Leigh looked around with indecision. Adith must have taken whatever despised medication it was that made her sleepy, or she would have appeared by now. And the infant in question must belong to their mutual neighbors; Leigh knew that the baby-adoring Emma was only too happy to play grandma whenever Nora needed to get out for a while.

"Mr. Perkins?" she called out tentatively through the still-closed door. "Don't bother getting up if you don't want to. I can always come—"

The door swung open. Leigh was met by the pleasant smile of a thin, frail-looking man in his early eighties. Harvey was bald except for a wispy fringe of white hair that wrapped around the back of his head from ear to ear; his forehead was dominated by an impressively large liver spot. "Good day, Mrs. Harmon," he said politely, with all the decorum that would be due if her arrival had been heralded by a British butler instead of a thwacking cane. "Is there something I can help you with?"

Leigh smiled back. She had always liked Harvey, though she saw very little of him, as he spent the vast majority of his time alone in his room with his cat and his books. According to Adith, he had spent his life running the family hardware store and was never able to go to college. But he was a born intellectual, and both Lester and Archie frequently praised his acumen as a local historian.

"I hope so," she responded. "I'm curious about the man named Carr, who settled Frog Hill Farm. Scotty O'Malley was telling me stories about him that supposedly came from Archie Pratt, but I'm not sure how much of them to believe."

Harvey studied her for a long moment, his expression thoughtful. "Please," he said finally, extending a hand in the direction of the sitting room. "Come and sit down."

Leigh complied. The room was empty except for Pauline's canary, which hopped from one perch to another with an occasional chirp. The cheerful bird seemed an odd choice of pet for someone like Pauline; Leigh had always thought a hawk would be more appropriate. Or perhaps an iguana.

"So, if you don't mind my asking," Harvey began as he eased into a chair opposite Leigh. "What brought about your interest in Theodore Carr?"

Leigh considered. "Several things, actually. I'm worried about Archie, as we all are. And with nothing much else to go on, I can't help wondering if something odd has been going on over at that farm. Not that I believe in ghosts, of course!" She amended quickly.

Harvey's thin lips drew into a smile. "Nor do I. But you are correct in supposing that Frog Hill has a somewhat… *colorful* past associated with it. A past about which Archie has always delighted in telling stories. Whether the history of his farm has anything to do with his disappearance…" Harvey's voice trailed off a moment, lost in thought. Then he shook his head. "That, I couldn't say."

Leigh leaned forward. "Could you tell me about Mr. Carr? Is it true that he might have been" —she nearly choked on the word—"murdered?"

Harvey tented his bony fingers and took a slow, theatrical breath. Leigh couldn't help but wonder how much he watched PBS television. For a man who never went to college, he bore a suspiciously strong resemblance to a host of *Masterpiece Theater*. "Theodore Carr fought in the Union Army during the Civil War. He was one of the 71st Pennsylvania Volunteers, a regiment recruited from the Philadelphia area. Archie has always been fascinated with the man's history, and I admit to developing more than a passing interest myself. You see, Mr. Carr's regiment played a pivotal role in the Battle of Gettysburg."

Leigh knew from the tenor of that statement that she was supposed to be impressed, and she endeavored, by facial expression, to oblige. In reality, she had retained from her school days only the most rudimentary knowledge of the Civil War, which fell well short of specifics on any particular battle. That Gettysburg had gone badly for the South, she knew from *Gone With the Wind*. Beyond that, she didn't plan to stick her neck out.

"I've helped Archie with his research, as I rather enjoy genealogy," Harvey continued. "Not that the two men are related, but the same methods apply. We learned that after Theodore was mustered out of the army, he married and moved to the Harrisburg area, where he purchased a modest parcel of farmland. The couple had two children that survived infancy, a boy and girl. The girl married young; the boy never married. In 1905, shortly after Theodore's wife died, he sold that farm and bought Frog Hill. He moved here with his son, who was by then an adult, and the two men worked the farm together until Theodore died, twenty years later."

Leigh nodded. She suspected she had heard much of this before, from Archie himself, but at the time she'd had no reason to pay attention. "And how did he die?"

Harvey's clear blue eyes studied hers. "A much-asked question. His death certificate says 'cause unknown.' That's a little unusual, even if he was eighty-two years old and no autopsy was performed. But there was an interesting footnote on the same line of the certificate that said, 'dementia.' None of which proves anything in particular; but as I told Archie, it does support the prevailing oral legend, passed down amongst various neighbors over the years."

"Which was?" Leigh prompted.

Harvey cocked his head thoughtfully to the side. "All we know for certain, from the local newspaper reports at the time, is that Theodore had a habit of 'wandering' and had been missing for two days before his son located his body in the creek. The police speculated that Theodore either fell in and drowned or had a heart attack and fell in afterwards; there was no mention of an investigation for foul play. But according to the local scuttlebutt, Theodore had suffered a slow mental decline for years, such that by the time of his death he had become excessively paranoid, refusing to allow anyone onto the property. Even neighbors he knew well were threatened if they attempted to 'trespass.' His behavior cut both men off from the community; and his son, who apparently was never well liked in the first place, was criticized for allowing the menace to continue. Theodore's death offered the critics additional fodder—speculations of neglect, or perhaps even patricide."

Leigh suppressed a shiver. "Missing for two days? It doesn't sound like the son was looking very hard, if his father was right there in the creek. I'm surprised the police didn't investigate, at least for neglect."

Harvey shrugged. "You have to remember, Frog Hill Farm was considerably larger then; the Carr's parcel extended some distance upstream. It extended downstream too, past your own house. And we don't know exactly where Theodore was found or at what point during those two days he fell in."

"I suppose," Leigh said uncertainly, trying hard *not* to imagine Theodor Carr's body floating in the creek behind her house.

"Regardless of whether the police suspected foul play," Harvey continued, "the local rumor mill remained abuzz about the incident for years. Theodore's son eventually suffered dementia himself, and was admitted to a nursing home. Thereafter, the farm was occupied by a long string of short-term occupants whose hasty and inauspicious departures brought about the 'ghost stories' Archie himself so delights in propagating. When Theodore's son died, in the 1950s, the estate was subdivided and the parcels sold for residential development. The idea of a vengeful 'soldier ghost' who chases away intruders has always seemed to amuse Archie, although I can't pretend to understand why."

Leigh had a feeling she might. "Scotty said something about Mr. Carr hiding his money before he died," she explained. "I don't know if Archie actually told him that or not, but..." she paused a moment, not sure how much of her suspicions she should share. Maura had promised to pass along the information about the map and the holes to the police who were investigating Archie's disappearance, but Leigh was skeptical that anything would come of it. The relevance of a neighborhood treasure hunt was questionable at best, even if Maura had presented the idea with enthusiasm. But on the phone this morning Maura had once again seemed distracted and anxious, worrying Leigh on a whole new front, even as the detective reminded her that Archie's case would not be a high priority for the General Investigations squad.

The issue did, however, rate top priority with Leigh, whose children roamed the same neighborhood as a mysterious treasure hunter at best and a potential abductor at worst. She needed answers. Why shouldn't she confide in an amiable, knowledgeable elderly man with a mind like a steel trap?

"Mr. Perkins," she asked directly, "do you know of any reason why anyone would think that something of value was buried on or around Frog Hill Farm?"

Harvey's clear blue eyes blinked. Then his gaze left her, fixing on some distant point above her shoulder. After a long moment, he looked back at her, his expression intent. "Why do you ask?"

Leigh took a breath. It was a fair question, and she answered it. She told him about the map the children had found and the years of unexplained filled-in holes, and she watched as he leaned forward in his seat with rapt attention.

"I had no idea about the digging," he said finally, his tone disturbingly breathless. "Do you have this map with you?"

Leigh shook her head, happy that she could honestly say no. Harvey's obvious interest in her question made her wary. "Do you believe Theodore Carr buried his money before he died?" she asked.

"No," he answered shortly. "I don't believe either of the Carr men had two dimes to rub together. They were small farmers; there's nothing in their history to suggest they did more than scratch out a living. However…"

His gaze returned to the spot above Leigh's shoulder. This time she turned, wondering if Mrs. Rhodis had awakened and was creeping up to breathe down her neck again. But there was nothing behind Leigh other than the painting on the wall.

"It *is* possible Theodore Carr could have had something else of value," Harvey continued, his voice wistful. "Something of very great value. At least… to some of us."

The house had gone oddly quiet. No baby gurgles echoed up the staircase. The canary had tucked its head under a wing. Leigh's spine prickled. "Like what?"

Harvey's eyes met hers with a twinkle. "Are you familiar with Pickett's Charge, Mrs. Harmon?"

"Regrettably, no," she responded. "And please call me Leigh."

Harvey nodded at her politely. Then, with measured slowness, he moved to stand before the large framed painting. Leigh had looked at the print many times, but her eyes now studied it more closely. Like much art depicting battle scenes, it was simultaneously romanticized and gory. Soldiers were everywhere: some dead, some alive, many somewhere in between. Arms, legs, and weapons mingled in gruesome disorder. Clouds of smoke hung thick in the air, though the immediate subjects of the painting could be seen clearly. There were cannons on spindly wooden wheels, and Confederate and Union flags raised high above the melee. None of the men were on horseback, but one prominent figure stood out from the rest. He forged ahead of the Confederate line, lofting a sword high into the air with a hat perched on its tip.

Harvey pointed at the figure in question. "Brigadier General Lewis Addison Armistead," he announced with reverence. "Battle of Gettysburg, July 3rd, 1863. The weather was hot. The task, impossible. General Lee ordered all fifteen thousand troops in Pickett's division to charge across an open field and break the Union lines. A mile and a quarter they marched, straight into enemy fire. Two thirds of them fell upon the field. But General Armistead would not turn back. He pushed ever forward, holding his hat high before friend and enemy alike. And he did reach the stone wall at the other side, charging bravely over it and penetrating the Union lines just as he was commanded. But tragically, only a handful of men had survived to follow him. And no sooner did he reach that wall than he himself was shot down—with a wound that later proved fatal."

Harvey cleared his throat and returned to his chair. "Our friend Theodore Carr was a witness to this, one of the single most catastrophic events in the bloodiest war in American history. When Armistead stepped over that wall, the 71st volunteers were there to face him. One of their own bullets could have killed him. We don't really know." He leaned toward her again, his voice dropping in secretive fashion. "What we do know is that one of those Union soldiers left that blood-soaked battlefield with a little… shall we say… souvenir."

Leigh leaned forward herself. "Like what?"

Harvey smiled. "The sword of Brigadier General Lewis Addison Armistead."

Leigh's eyes fixed again on the figure in the portrait.

"That particular soldier," Harvey went on, "turned the sword over to a superior. Nearly half a century later, at a reunion of the survivors of the Philadelphia brigade and Pickett's Division, the sword was ceremoniously returned to the South. It resides to this day in the Museum of the Confederacy in Richmond."

Leigh's brow furrowed. "Then what—"

Harvey raised a hand. "The sword was found and returned. Armistead gave his personal effects to a messenger before he died. But one significant item was never recovered." His eyes lifted to the portrait again.

Leigh's gaze followed. "You don't mean… his hat?"

Harvey nodded gravely. "The stuff of legends, my dear. This painting is hardly the only one depicting this epic scene. Whole books have been written on the Battle of Gettysburg. Poems penned. Movies shot. Every year thousands of people gather in the very spot where it occurred to reenact the entire scenario. Civil War enthusiasts scour flea markets and estate sales, looking for precious relics: A frock coat. A haversack. A rifle. A belt buckle. The artifacts market is robust and still growing. The hat of General Armistead, were it ever to be recovered and authenticated, well..."

"The Holy Grail?" Leigh suggested.

Harvey tented his fingers again. "Quite."

Leigh sat back and took a breath. "And Theodore Carr was there. But surely that's not enough for anyone to think—" she broke off at Harvey's crooked grin.

"Oh, I daresay there's more," he continued. "Although frankly, until you mentioned someone digging, I didn't give it much credence, myself. There's another legend—a much less well known one—unique to the Civil War buffs in this area. When I joined the county historical association in the sixties the ranks were still abuzz about how, some years before, a newcomer had started asking questions about how much the general's hat might be worth, where it could be sold, that sort of thing. The members became suspicious that this person might actually know something of the hat's whereabouts, that it might even—joy of joys!—have found its way to the Pittsburgh area. But the man disappeared; and when an attempt was made to trace him, it was clear he hadn't given his real name. It was all quite mysterious, but nothing ever came of it, and personally I dismissed the whole notion of the hat's existence as wishful thinking. Now... I have to wonder."

Leigh bit her lip. She didn't care for the way this discussion was headed. She didn't care for it at all.

"When Archie asked for my help in researching the man who had settled Frog Hill Farm, I was happy to oblige," Harvey explained. "Archie has a deep and genuine interest in the Civil War, and he was practically giddy at having purchased the house of a legitimate war hero. I thought that's all there was to it. But now that you mention a map..." his voice trailed off.

After a moment's thought, he gave his head a shake, then resumed. "It was all a very long time ago. I do recall now that amongst the various rumors about the hat, there was talk of this mystery man having a paper of some sort—some documentation proving that the general's hat was indeed salvaged from the battlefield. But nobody I knew ever actually saw such a paper. And most of us figured that even if the man did have some sort of document, it was probably a hoax."

Harvey's blue eyes glimmered. "I don't recall Archie ever mentioning General Armistead's hat to me, at least not specifically.

And I have no evidence to give you that would link the man with that particular quest. It's just… a possibility."

Leigh's voice quavered. "Do you know if Archie was aware that a Civil War veteran had built this farm *before* he decided to buy it?"

Harvey considered. "I never thought about it before. I always assumed that Archie's interest came about after he moved in and heard the stories about Theodore Carr. But now that you mention it, it is possible that Archie bought the farm because of him."

The accidental idiom hung in the air between them.

Leigh attempted to dismiss the macabre thought.

She failed.

Chapter 7

The doorbell rang. Leigh jumped a foot.

Footsteps sounded on the staircase, and in a moment Emma Brown emerged from the hall door to the kitchen, sleeping infant in tow.

"Hello, Leigh," Emma said pleasantly as she glanced into the sitting room. "I thought I heard you up here. I would have popped up earlier, but the little peanut had other ideas!"

Leigh smiled back. Emma was short and round, with soft light brown hair, merry brown eyes, and a deep voice that was as big as her heart. "No problem," Leigh responded. "Looks like you've worked your usual magic."

Emma chuckled. The baby, who had an unruly mop of flaxen hair and was wearing a Pittsburgh Penguins onesie, was so limp Emma had to adjust her position to keep his head from lolling over her arm as she walked. "He ought to be tired," she answered good naturedly, heading towards the front door. "As little sleep as he gets when the sun's down!"

Leigh heard the front door open.

"Oh my, God!" a young woman's voice rang out in a stage whisper. "What a beautiful sight! Emma, you are a miracle worker."

The door closed and the two women walked down the hall to join Leigh and Harvey in the sitting room.

"Hi, Nora," Leigh greeted cheerfully, attempting—perhaps unsuccessfully—to keep her expression from revealing just how ghastly the young mother looked. The ordinarily bright and perky Nora had dark circles under her eyes the size of plums. "I'm so sorry about what you're going through with Cory," Leigh said, rising. "I sympathize, believe me. Allison did the same thing for months."

"Did she?" Nora asked. "You'll have to tell me all your tricks sometime. Derrick and I have lists we go through. Walking, not walking. Ride in the car. Time on the floor. Swaddling. Baby seat on the dryer. None of it works every time. It's always just hit or miss." She sighed deeply, then smiled down at her sleeping baby. "Of course, when he looks as adorable as this, it makes it all worth it, doesn't it?"

Leigh noticed that Harvey was creeping quietly around the women and back toward his room.

"Oh, Harvey," Nora called out, just as he was disappearing behind his door. "Derrick says thank you. For that information on the zoning."

Harvey paused and smiled back at her. "Tell him you're very welcome," he replied. Then he hastened into his room and closed the door.

"Zoning?" Emma asked.

Nora rolled her eyes. "Chickens," she said with exasperation. "Derrick wants chickens. I kept telling him we couldn't have any out here, but apparently I was wrong. Next thing, he'll want a cow!"

Leigh's eyebrows rose. Nora's husband Derrick was a small, wiry man with thick glasses who worked for a bank. Even though he spent much of his time telecommuting from home, his wardrobe seemed to consist entirely of business slacks, button-down shirts, and loafers. In the year or so since the Sullivans had moved in next door, she had never once seen him working outside. Nora mowed their lawn herself, even while she was pregnant.

"You mean you *can* have chickens?" Emma inquired.

"Unfortunately, yes," Nora responded, reaching out her arms to take the baby.

Leigh's teeth gritted. Earth-mother Cara was always talking about wanting fresh eggs. If this tidbit got out, the Harmons would be sandwiched in between two roosters competing to crow the earliest.

"You know," Emma said thoughtfully, pulling the baby back in closer. "He's so snug now. Why wake him up to move him? You go on home and have a nap. I'll bring him over in an hour or so."

Nora's brown eyes shone with elation. "Really? Are you sure? Oh, Emma… I am *so* tired."

"You know, if you had chickens," Leigh threw in quickly, "you'd be even more tired—"

"Oh, I almost forgot to ask!" Nora broke in, oblivious. "Is Archie home yet? Did he make the meeting?"

Emma's face puckered with concern. "No, I'm afraid not. We're really very worried about him."

"Oh, no," Nora said in a whisper. "Derrick was supposed to go today, but he had to work. He said Archie would *never* miss a meeting. I just don't understand it."

"None of us do," Emma answered gravely.

An uncomfortable silence followed.

"By the meeting, you mean the reenactors, right?" Leigh asked tentatively.

Emma nodded. "Lester's with them now. He's asked for their help in finding Archie. Although what they can do, I'm not sure. I only wish there was something more *I* could do. I've called everyone I can think to call... Lester and I went through every page of Archie's address book. Nobody seems to know anything."

"Well if you think of anything Derrick or I can do to help," Nora offered, "you will let us know, won't you? I mean it. Colicky baby or not."

Emma agreed, and Nora turned and headed for the door.

Leigh followed. She was anxious to talk to Lester, but her questions would have to wait. While the other women stood at the open front door discussing baby care, Leigh paused to look over her shoulder and down the hall. Was there more that Harvey would have told her, had they not been interrupted? He had given no indication of it. He had not even said goodbye.

The smallest of movements caught her eye. Harvey's bedroom door, which had been standing open about an inch, was now closing ever so slowly the rest of the way.

"Now, Miss Leigh," Emma said warmly as she closed her front door behind Nora and shifted the sleeping baby expertly to one shoulder. "What did you want, dear? Did you come to see Adith? I'm afraid she'll be drowsy for a while yet. She does hate that new medication, but her doctor insists on it, you know."

"Actually, I came to see Lester," Leigh admitted. "Do you have any idea when he might be back?"

Emma's worry lines deepened. "Not really. Once the regular meeting is over, they're going to stay and come up with a plan to help find Archie. All the men adore him, you know. He's such a sweet soul. No one can understand why—" her voice caught. Her eyes began to tear, but before any drops could fall she plastered on a smile instead. "Oopsie!" she cooed to the baby. "Somebody's got the stinkies! Excuse me, Leigh honey, I'll just be a minute—"

"I'll let myself out," Leigh offered, and with a grateful wave, Emma disappeared through the door to the stairwell.

"Pssst!"

Leigh heard the sound just as she touched the front door knob. Turning back around, she was surprised to see Harvey's hand beckoning to her from his doorway. She stepped closer.

"Please don't leave just yet, Mrs. Harm—I mean, Leigh," he said pleasantly, albeit with a new urgency to his tone. "There's something I'd like to ask you. Would you come in a minute?"

He swung his door open fully and stepped back. Leigh entered.

She had never seen Harvey's private digs before, and she had to admit a sense of curiosity. Adith had informed her that Harvey was quite spry for his years and would be perfectly capable of living by himself if his late wife of forty-plus years hadn't, as Adith put it, "buttered the man's bread till he forgot how to use a knife." Leigh looked around and smiled. It was just as she would have imagined. Wall to wall bookshelves. An immense wooden desk piled high with more books, folders, reams of loose papers covered with longhand, and a half-dozen coffee cups. The desk and a large leather wing chair with matching ottoman dominated the room; a narrow bed covered with rumpled blankets was stuffed into the far corner like an afterthought. Spreading liberally over the chair's seat cushion was a plus-shaped mass of orange fur only vaguely recognizable as a cat. The tabby—which had to weigh well over twenty pounds—responded to Leigh's arrival with the slightest opening of one eye, which, after a second's reflection, it shut again.

"Now, now, Gimli," Harvey cooed with affection, "don't go stressing yourself. Mrs. Harmon is perfectly friendly, I assure you."

The cat remained motionless.

"He's very protective," Harvey said wryly.

"Clearly," Leigh agreed.

Harvey drew a breath, then tented his fingers again. "I feel a bit awkward asking this," he began, seeming rather more excited than awkward, "but I would very much like to take a look at this map you speak of. I do have some experience with cartography; I might be able to help you decipher it."

"I—" Leigh's response stuck in her throat. She had no reason to doubt Harvey's motives, or his offer of help. The idea that such an intelligent, mannered man could be personally involved in any foul play concerning Archie's disappearance was unimaginable. Then again, history had taught her she didn't always have the best imagination.

"I have to work through the detectives," she finished, fudging the truth a bit. "But if they tell me it's okay, I'll bring it over. We could definitely use the help. Thank you."

To her relief, Harvey smiled broadly, revealing no sign of angst. "I will eagerly await your return."

Leigh finished her last bite of leftover meatloaf, which came immediately after her first bite. Despite her protestations to her mother, she had in fact forgotten to make a grocery run this morning, leaving both her husband and herself to forage for lunch on either two-day-old meatloaf or day-old pizza—and Warren had beaten her to the fridge. If Lydie hadn't fed the kids at the History center, Leigh wouldn't even have the meatloaf—she would be reduced to stale pretzels and whatever jelly she could scrape off the sides of the jar sitting on top of the recycling bin.

Lucky for her, she had married well. Warren had been on his way out to the grocery store when she arrived. "I think you should stick around a while in case Mo comes back," he had said with concern. "She dropped in earlier, but she was in a strange mood. Didn't want to talk to me. But she said she was working nearby and would try to catch you later."

Leigh pondered her friend's odd behavior with unease. Maura had always felt comfortable talking to Warren; in fact, virtually all the policewoman's close friends were men. Perhaps that was part of the problem.

Leigh had promised she would stick around and texted Maura to say so, but thus far she had received no response.

"Mom!" Ethan called suddenly from the depths of the refrigerator, his voice tragic. "We have, like, *no* food!"

"I'm aware," Leigh responded, crunching a stale pretzel. "Your dad's at the grocery store now. Didn't your aunt just feed you three hot dogs and two bags of chips?"

"That was, like, an hour ago!" he wailed. "Can I go to Matt and

Lenna's?"

"To raid their fridge?"

"No, to hang out until Aunt Lydie finishes baking her caramel brownies."

Leigh sighed. She had vowed not to make Lydie watch the entire Pack all weekend... but if the woman insisted on baking, she was begging for extra company. In fact, if the aroma of Lydie's famous brownies happened to hit the wind right, Leigh herself would be stumbling to the farmhouse like a zombie.

"Okay, fine," she conceded. "Is your sister going, too?

Ethan shrugged. "She's in her room with that book she bought at the gift shop."

"What book?"

"I don't know," he said, whirling to leave. "Some boring thing about the North Hills."

Leigh's stomach churned uncomfortably. Most mothers would be excited to have a daughter spend her Saturday afternoon boning up on local history. But most mothers did not have a daughter like Allison Harmon.

"She's not still trying to figure out—"

The back door slammed closed behind Ethan just as the front doorbell rang. Leigh cast a wary glance in the direction of her daughter's bedroom as she rose. "Allison!" she called. "Ethan just went over to the farm to mooch some brownies. You can join him if you want."

If Allison made a reply, Leigh didn't hear it. She meant to call again, but as she swung open the door, the sight of Maura's pale, drawn face immediately distracted her.

"Come in," Leigh insisted, stepping back and ushering the policewoman quickly to the couch. "Have a seat." *You look like hell,* she wanted to add, but didn't. Whatever could be wrong?

"I can't stay long," Maura answered tonelessly, dropping onto the couch. "But I wanted to let you know what was happening with the missing persons case."

Leigh held her breath. "Archie isn't—"

Maura waved a hand. "No, no. It isn't that kind of news. I just wanted to let you know that I don't think the guys are planning to pursue the treasure map angle. At least not any time soon. They did a background check on your friend Archie, and he's not what you'd call squeaky clean."

Leigh frowned. "What do you mean?"

The detective let out a sigh. "I can't get into the details, Koslow. It's not even my case. But let's just say forced abduction isn't as near the top of the rule-out list as, say, insurance fraud."

Leigh sat up. *"Insurance fraud?* Archie? That's crazy!"

"Historically speaking," Maura replied, "Perhaps not."

Leigh shut her open mouth.

"Look, Leigh," Maura soothed, "I'm not sure I agree with the guys on this one, to be honest. I think they're making too much of what's on the record and not enough of what's staring them in the face. But I've done all I can do. At least officially. Unofficially, if you find out anything more about that wonky map of yours, I want you to let me know. Anything weird happens in the neighborhood, you let me know. And make sure the Pack doesn't go anywhere near that empty house. *Especially* Allison."

"Will do," Leigh said weakly.

Maura started suddenly to attention.

"What?" Leigh asked, following her friend's eyes toward the back of the house.

Maura rose and, despite her size, stepped with catlike quietness to the dining room window. Leigh rose and followed her. The backside of Allison was just visible through the bushes, slipping covertly away from the kitchen door and toward the promised brownies.

"I should have asked where she was before I started talking," Maura lamented.

Leigh sighed. "It wouldn't matter. She could be a mile away, and if there's something she shouldn't overhear, *presto*. There she is."

Maura chuckled softly. "I foresee a bright future in law enforcement."

"Bite your tongue," Leigh joked. "It's bad enough stressing out over a friend with a dangerous job. As a mother, I don't think I could take it."

Maura's smile faded. "It's tough being a mother, isn't it?"

Leigh's heartbeat began to quicken. Surely all this wasn't about—

"I'm pregnant, Koslow."

Leigh tried to keep her eyes from bugging. A budding warmth

spread rapidly through her veins. "Why…" she stammered. "That's *wonderful!*"

Her friend's miserable expression stopped her.

"I mean… isn't it?"

Maura straightened and pulled away from the window. Her pale face flushed and she resumed her usual bluster. "How the hell should I know?!" she erupted. "We tried for a long time, but it looked like it was hopeless. And then I guess we both just forgot about it…" She paced the room with a stomping motion, making the dishes in Leigh's china cabinet rattle. "Gerry doesn't know yet… he was in the middle of this horrible case, and I wasn't really sure anyway, and then he went out of town… and I don't even know what to think because they're making me take all these tests, treating me like I'm some medical freak show… Hellfire, Koslow! I'm *forty-two freakin' years old!*"

Leigh resisted the urge to smile. "But you're in great shape, Maura. You know you are. You're a total hypochondriac about your heart because of the way your dad died, but we both know your BMI makes me look like Moby Dick. I'm sure everything will be fine."

Maura blew out a breath. "Well, the doctors aren't so sure."

Leigh steeled herself. "What did they say?"

"Nothing yet. They just sent me all over the damn place getting poked and prodded and probed and I don't know what all. I'm supposed to get some results back Monday, but even then, there's no telling what they'll say. Such and such a chance of this, such a percentage risk of that…"

Maura's pacing increased. Leigh fought the urge to go and stabilize her dish cabinet before anything shattered.

"I mean…" the detective continued. "It's insane, isn't it? To even think I could have a baby now, at my age? Who am I kidding? I don't *do* infants… I was scared to death of yours when they were little. And my job! How the hell could I manage a kid when I'm on-call such crazy hours? What kid would even *want* two detectives for parents? Even if everything is all right, I'd be nuts to think it could work out. Gerry's kids are grown now; it's been years since we even talked about having one of our own. What if he freaks out? What if everything *isn't* all right? It's insane, Koslow! Just totally *insane!*"

Maura swore for another full minute, using language Leigh

hadn't heard in some time, including a few colorful phrases usually reserved for occasions involving herself and corpses. When Leigh's ceramic bluebird salt shaker finally reached the edge of its shelf and took a nosedive into the backside of the china cabinet's glass doors, Maura's pacing came to a halt. She went silent and looked at Leigh, her blue eyes moist.

Leigh smiled warmly. "You really want this baby, don't you?"

Maura took a painful-looking swallow, and her voice dropped to a whisper.

"More than anything."

Chapter 8

Leigh walked across her backyard and headed toward the creek. Her head was still swimming from her conversation with Maura, and she wished Warren would come home, but she couldn't wait any longer to do her afternoon check on the mother dog. Ghosts or no ghosts, she had no intention of prowling around Frog Hill Farm after dark ever again. Archie's disappearance was disconcerting enough without thinking about the unfortunate demise of Theodore Carr as well.

Floating in the creek.

Leigh shuddered. It had happened ages ago, she knew, but *still*. She could never look at the creek again without wondering exactly where the man had drowned. The water level was low now, only a couple feet. But in the spring it could turn into a fast moving torrent within hours. When it flooded, she could paddle from her back patio to Cara's front porch in a kayak. It was not too difficult to imagine a frail and feeble old man slipping into its depths accidentally.

No murder need be involved.

She walked dutifully along the bank, keeping her head down. She had not even thought about the accursed account she was responsible for at Hook, Inc. since Archie had gone missing. And she *had* to come up with something soon. How hard could it be to make pottery crocks from an old stoneware company sound exciting? Had she not gotten people excited about foot odor pads? Machine-washable doormats? Disposable door knob covers? Stupid pottery crocks were messing with the wrong advertising copywriter—

She stopped in her tracks. Her eyes widened. Six feet in front of her, in broad daylight, stood a Union soldier. He wore a sack coat and trousers of blue wool, cinched up with a waist belt and shiny buckle. His boots were ankle high, and his dark hair was damp and sweaty beneath his flat-topped wool cap. He made no move to come closer, but simply stood still, staring back at her.

Leigh's blood chilled in her veins. The only coherent thought in her brain was the fact that he had a head.

"Hey there," the soldier said, his accent all Pittsburghese. "Sorry to scare you."

Leigh's cheeks reddened like fire. She looked over the man's shoulder to see several others dressed just like him poking along the edge of the woods upstream.

She was *such* an idiot.

"We're Civil War reenactors," he explained. "We're all pitching in to help out our captain. You know Archie Pratt?"

She nodded dumbly.

"Well, he's gone missing it seems, and we're all a bit worried about him. You live here?" he asked, pointing up the bank to Nora and Derrick's house.

Leigh collected herself and shook her head. "No, I live next door. Derrick lives here. He's in your group, I believe."

The man's brow furrowed. "Who?"

"Derrick Sullivan," Leigh repeated. "Archie recruited him."

He thought a moment. "Oh, right. That guy. Haven't seen him in a while. You know about Arch, then?"

Leigh nodded. "Have you… found anything?"

The soldier shook his head. "Not yet. But we'll do whatever needs doing, you can count on that."

Leigh believed him. Any man willing to dress himself in wool from head to toe in sixty-eight degree weather was responsive to a higher calling. "You always dress up for meetings?" she asked before she could stop herself.

The man chuckled. "Nah. We had a company photo shoot earlier, that's all. Would have changed after, but as anxious as Les was, we all came straight out."

"I see," Leigh said, her cheeks still burning with embarrassment. "Could you tell me where I can find Lester? I need to talk to him."

The man shrugged, gesturing vaguely upstream. "Somewhere by the house, most likely. He was giving out the assignments."

Leigh thanked him, wished him luck, and doubled her pace. She was not in the least surprised, upon passing the Brown's house, to see Adith Rhodis leaning over the deck railing with her binoculars plastered to her face, this time with Pauline, Harvey, and Emma all in attendance and watching the spectacle right along with her. And quite a spectacle it was, with at least a dozen apparent Civil War soldiers—some carrying knapsacks, canteens, and/or shoulder straps with cartridge boxes—combing the creek area as far as the eye could see. Scotty flitted among the men like a pesky gnat, and Leigh saw that his father, Joe, was also in attendance. Also not one of Leigh's favorite people, Joe O'Malley held the singular distinction of being the only reenactor to have stripped off his wool coat, continuing his near-perfect streak of presenting himself to neighbors in a wifebeater. He was also the only one of the men who found it necessary to carry around his rifle, further convincing Leigh that the only reason he had succumbed to Archie's recruitment was to make things go bang.

Mercifully, neither Scotty nor his father paid any attention to her. When she reached the tool shed she caught sight of Lester standing in Archie's driveway surrounded by a cluster of men and gesticulating purposefully. Deciding to give him a few more minutes, she walked around the back of the shed to check on the dog first.

She was relieved to see a hastily scrawled note attached to the cellar doors, stating, "Stay out. Dog inside. -Lester." It wouldn't do at all for the new mother to be disturbed by a procession of strangers. The dog might even decide to bolt and move the puppies, a possibility Leigh feared, but was temporarily helpless to combat. She could of course move the dog and litter by force to the animal shelter, or confine them somewhere else, but the ultimate outcome was unlikely to be any better, because any upset to the mother could cause her to stop caring for the pups. If only everyone would leave them alone for a couple weeks, Leigh speculated, she was sure she could win the dog's trust and make the family's ultimate move to the shelter a safe one.

She descended the cellar steps slowly, shining her flashlight ahead and calling to the dog as she went. She felt a flicker of panic to see the accustomed spot empty, but soon realized the dog had merely moved her makeshift nest to another corner of the cellar—the area most removed from the stairway.

"Tired of hearing strange voices out there, are you?" Leigh questioned, moving smoothly to the food bag and beginning to refill the empty bowl. "I don't blame you. You're one smart cookie."

The dog uttered no growls this time, but did not thump her tail, either. Given the activity outside, her edginess was understandable. Leigh finished her tasks quickly, combining what was left of the water in one pail and then picking up the empty one. But as she was turning to leave, a queer feeling stopped her. She glanced around the cellar to see nothing out of order; the few odds and ends that littered the floor were as dusty and useless as they had always been. But something was missing. Last night, she was sure she had seen a yellow plastic flashlight lying on the cellar floor. Now it was gone. Had it been here this morning? She couldn't remember; Scotty had done too good a job of distracting her. But it had definitely been removed since yesterday.

Who would have taken it? Had Scotty been back?

"No, no, no!" she heard a man's voice shout as heavy footsteps plodded down the stairs. "No one is supposed to—"

Lester halted abruptly when he saw Leigh. "Oh," he said sheepishly, letting out a breath. "Sorry. I thought you were one of the men."

The dog snarled and rose to her feet. Leigh grabbed her pail and hurried Lester back up the steps and outside.

"I know," she told him, replacing the door behind her. "I'm glad you put the sign up. The poor dog's anxious enough as it is."

Lester, who was also dressed in the requisite blue wool, albeit without a hat, pulled a cotton handkerchief from his pocket and wiped his sweating forehead. His nose was still red and his skin was pale. Leigh would have urged him to go home, crawl back into bed, and let Emma feed him chicken soup until he fully recovered—but she knew that wasn't going to happen. Not as long as his best bud needed him.

"I've got the men combing the area," he explained unnecessarily. "If the police missed anything, they'll find it."

"They're very dedicated," Leigh praised. "It's clear they're fond of their captain."

Lester's bloodshot eyes unexpectedly moistened. "Everybody loves Arch," he repeated. "Have you heard anything from that detective friend of yours?"

Leigh shook her head. "Nothing helpful. But I do need to ask you—" she struggled to find the right words. Knowing what information to share with whom and when had never been her forte. "I got the feeling that the police were concerned about something in Archie's background. Something that could make them think he disappeared on purpose. Do you have any idea what that might be?"

Lester's eyes widened; sharp peaks of color rose in his cheeks. "On purpose? *Arch?* That's crazy talk! Like what?"

Leigh feigned a shrug. "Oh, I don't know. Tax evasion? DUI? Insurance fraud?"

At her last words, Lester's breath drew in sharply. "Nah!" he protested. "There's no way that that— I mean—"

Bingo. "Of course not," Leigh soothed. "But it could look bad. What happened, exactly?"

"It was nothing!" Lester protested, taking the bait. "Arch had nothing to do with it! Well, not hardly. It was this woman he was dating. Her car got hit, and she needed money, and she was coming up with all kinds of injuries she didn't really have, and her girlfriend, too, who was in the car with her. Arch wasn't even there, but she claimed him as a jump in. That's what they call it, you know, a jump in. Trying to cheat the insurance company by jacking up the claims. Arch didn't want anything to do with it, but she wouldn't take no for an answer, and of course they all got caught. Arch got a fine and some probation—was lucky she didn't land him in jail. Cost him his job at the high school!"

Leigh's brow furrowed. "But didn't Archie *sell* insurance?"

Lester waved a hand, "Yeah, but that was later."

"He got hired by an insurance agency?" Leigh asked incredulously. "Even after—"

Lester smirked. "You wouldn't think it, would you? Just goes to show, Arch is one hell of a salesman."

Leigh gave her head a shake. "Listen, Lester," she began seriously, "I found out something last night. Something that may be significant."

He leaned toward her, all ears.

"One of the kids found a paper lying on the ground by the creek last week. It's a copy of a map of some sort, an old one. It's difficult to decipher, but it appears to be a map of this area. And when we started thinking about all the holes that keep appearing in the neighborhood... well, we were wondering if the two things are related. Do you know if Archie was searching for anything? Did he ever mention—"

Leigh broke off her next question. Lester's color had gone from ivory to gray. His pupils had stretched to saucers and he had missed at least two breaths.

"Lester?" she asked, concerned. "Are you okay?"

He stared at her, mutely, for another long moment. Then at last he sucked in a breath and, with a shake of his head, plastered an incredibly unconvincing smile on his face. "Oh, sorry. I'm fine. Just can't quite shake this darn flu bug, you know? I was thinking about something else. A map, you say? Nope, haven't heard anything about that. Don't know why Arch would be looking for anything. I'm sure it's nothing. You didn't— Did you tell anybody else about it?"

Leigh hesitated. The fact that Lester was so obviously lying was disturbing enough, but she feared that telling him that the police already knew the entire story could literally give him a stroke. "Is there any reason I shouldn't?" she asked.

"No," he stammered, "I mean, you could, but it wouldn't amount to anything and I wouldn't want to distract anyone from finding Arch, you know?"

"Finding Archie is everyone's top priority, I'm sure," Leigh replied. "Lester, you really don't look well. Maybe you should take a break? Get something to drink?"

"Yeah, I... maybe I'll do that. And if you—" his next words were broken off with an "oomph" as a furry black missile burst around the corner of the shed and propelled two paws squarely into his belly. "Wiley, you demon, get down!" he chastised, albeit not without scratching the dog's ears in the process. "Crazy hound," he muttered. "Got too much energy. Hates being locked up. But I can't let him roam around all day with Arch gone. If anything happened to this mutt..."

His thought trailed off into a spasm of coughing.

"Go home, Lester," Leigh ordered. "You can control operations from there just as well, can't you?"

Lester didn't even try to answer. Still coughing, he nodded, waved her a goodbye, patted his thigh to collect Wiley, and shuffled off toward the creek bridge that led to his own backyard.

Leigh watched him with a frown. That Lester knew all about the supposed treasure map, and might in fact have been the one who dropped it, was a given. What was far less clear was why he refused to admit it. She was certain that he was genuinely concerned about Archie. Did he really not believe there could be a connection?

She turned with her empty pail and headed toward the spigot at the farmhouse. At least her curiosity was assuaged with regard to Archie's criminal past. People had done crazier things for love, and the man had long since paid his debt to society. What could he possibly have to gain by faking his own disappearance? He had never been married, and his blood relatives were apparently few and far between. If he was attempting fraud on a life insurance policy, who would be the beneficiary? That person would have to be in on it with him, and unless the policy were huge, he couldn't come out that much ahead after leaving behind the farm, his truck, and all his belongings. Never mind that a huge policy benefitting anyone other than an heir would be a giant red flag from the get-go. Archie might have proven himself somewhat gullible in the past, but he was *not* stupid.

The police had it wrong.

Which did not make her feel any less creeped out to be standing beneath the window of his abandoned house surrounded by Civil War soldiers.

"What happened to the drywall?"

The man's voice traveled easily from inside Archie's living room through the single-pane glass and out to Leigh's ear.

"Adding more insulation, maybe?" another voice speculated.

Leigh recalled how Archie's living room walls had been open to the studs in several places. She had thought it odd as well.

"Nah," the first voice responded. "Nothing new put in here in a long time. He just tore out the wall and never put it back." There was a moment's pause. "No electrical. Didn't access nothing. He doesn't even *have* cable. Weird."

"Maybe it had a hole in it."

"And over here, too? And look—more in the bedroom. Maybe if it was your house. Bet you knock a few holes in the drywall every Saturday night, huh?"

"Somebody else's walls, maybe," the second man responded with humor. "But Arch isn't the kind of guy you run into in anger management, you know? Some punk could stick a gun in his ribs, and he probably still wouldn't deck him."

"Nah, he wouldn't. Sweet talk him out of the gun, maybe!"

The men shared a chuckle.

"Damn, this place looks terrible. What the hell was he up to, you think?"

"Looks like he was hunting for his Great Aunt Millie's diamonds or some crazy thing, doesn't it? Like he thought something was hid in the walls."

Leigh sucked in a breath.

"Man tearing up his own house?" the second man replied. "I don't know. It'd make more sense if robbers did it. But Lester said the house looks just like it did before. Maybe it was tore up when Arch bought it, and he just never put it right."

"Sounds more likely. Got a bargain, then got used to it. Arch'd rather hang out on a battlefield than put up a bunch of damn drywall any day."

"You got that right."

The men's voices drifted beyond her hearing, presumably as they climbed the stairs. Leigh's heart thudded loudly in her chest. She had seen the missing wallboard herself, but hadn't made the connection at the time. So it was true. Archie *was* searching for something. And whatever it was, Lester knew all about it.

The question was, what could one seemingly innocent treasure hunt—on a man's own property, no less—have to do with his sudden disappearance? Could it all, just possibly, be a coincidence?

Leigh put the pail down under the spigot and turned on the water.

*Coincidence*s.

She believed in them like she believed in ghosts.

Chapter 9

Leigh studied her daughter's small, bowed head. Allison had been curled up in her favorite armchair in the living room for the past half hour, her nose buried in a thin paperback entitled *A History of the Harmony Line*. Warren had offered to take the whole Pack to the season's last Pirates' game, but after Lenna opted for some one-on-one time with her grandmother, Allison had also declined, ostensibly in favor of a "quiet evening at home."

Leigh couldn't help but be suspicious.

"Learning anything interesting?" she asked, absently stroking the geriatric black Persian that had materialized in her lap the second she sat down after dinner. Not to be outdone, her corgi had taken his favored place splayed across her feet. Too bad she had to go to the bathroom.

"Uh huh," Allison mumbled, not looking up.

The doorbell rang. Puzzled, Leigh reorganized her pets and struggled up from the couch. She wasn't expecting anyone. Her mother had just finished harassing her over the phone an hour ago, and most nonfamily guests had the courtesy to call first.

She looked through the peephole to see a harried-looking Emma attempting to calm Mrs. Rhodis, who was practically hopping up and down. Leigh swung the door open.

"Get your driving shoes on!" the older woman cackled with glee. "We're taking a road trip!"

Emma's eyes rolled good-naturedly. "I told her you might be busy, but there was no restraining her from walking over here. Once she wakes up from that medication, she's *up*. Took twenty minutes, but she was determined!"

Adith shuffled in and collapsed onto the couch. Mao Tse hissed and fled. Chewie, who had trotted off on Leigh's heels when she rose, now sat back down on her feet where she stood. "Road trip?" she repeated.

"If you're busy, I can go home and bring the car around to pick her up," Emma offered.

"Oh, my girl's never too busy to untangle a good mystery!" Adith chirped.

Leigh frowned. *As if.* "What are you talking about?"

Adith straightened herself on the couch and took in a dramatic breath. "I found a witness," she announced. "A real live witness to the goings-on up at Archie's place way back when. A woman who's *seen* the evil. And she's going to tell us about it tonight!"

Leigh looked from Adith to Emma, whose shoulders shrugged. "She's been tying up the phone for hours, that's all I know."

"It's called 'networking,'" Adith said proudly. "I learned that on the TV. You 'leverage your contacts,' you 'put yourself out there,' and *voila!*"

"What woman are you talking about?" Leigh persisted. "A witness to what?"

"So," Adith continued, oblivious to the interruption, "What I did, you see, was think about who I knew who'd ever lived up around here. And I didn't know anybody, not directly. But my friend Barbara Jean in Bellevue, she knows everybody. And I gave her all the names Harvey had found poking around in the property deeds and such, and she didn't know any of them, but she said her cousin Sally spent her whole life up in Ross, and I figured that was closer, so I gave her a call, and then she had this other friend whose sister used to live in Franklin Park..."

Leigh let her mind wander. She knew Adith well enough to know that everyone in the room was getting the whole story whether they wanted it or not.

"...And that's how I found Dora Klinger!" Adith finished triumphantly, several minutes later. "And get this... she's still alive and got all her marbles, too! At 91! So I told her we'd be up to see her this evening and she said she couldn't wait. *So...*" she looked expectantly up at Leigh. "What are you standing around for? Let's go!"

"She really lived at Frog Hill Farm?" Allison piped up excitedly.

Leigh, who had forgotten her daughter was in the room, felt a flicker of panic. The girl was invested enough in this whole mess as it was.

"For nearly two years!" Adith crowed. "In fact, they were the first owners after the soldier ghost's family sold it off!"

Allison slid off her chair and popped up at Leigh's elbow. "Can I go with you, Mom?"

Leigh tensed. "I didn't say we were going anywhere, and besides—"

"Aw, let her come along!" Adith interceded. "Dora's in assisted living, and you know how old people love to see young ones about. She'd be doing a service! What's the harm?"

Allison blinked her dark, whip-smart eyes up at her mother. "It's okay if you think I shouldn't," she said cooperatively. "I'm sure I'll be fine here at home… all alone."

Leigh sighed internally as she helped Adith buckle into the front seat of the van. She wasn't sure what this visit was supposed to accomplish, but she wasn't going to get Archie any closer to home by sitting around her house worrying, either. Why not help two bored elderly ladies amuse each other for an hour?

Allison slipped into the back seat, paperback in hand. Leigh studied her daughter curiously. Her jean shorts, tee shirt, and flip flops had been replaced with tan crop pants, a lacy white blouse, dress sandals, and a large, pale blue hair bow.

"What's up with the do?" Leigh couldn't help but inquire. The clothing upgrade she appreciated, but her daughter had not voluntarily tied a bow in her hair since she was seven.

Allison gave a shrug. "Old people like bows."

The ride to the assisted living facility was just long enough for Adith to give a full report on her own exciting afternoon, which had included eavesdropping on the reenactors as they made their final reports to Lester. "None of them found a gun, or a ransom note, or anything really good," she lamented. "One of them found a baseball cap they didn't think was Archie's, but it looked like it had been wherever they found it a whole lot longer than a week, so that didn't amount to much. Everything else they found on the ground outside was stuff Arch probably dropped—some coins, a grocery receipt, a pen. Nobody thought it looked like he was planning to leave. More like he was *spirited* off… if you ask me."

"Did anyone mention the state of the house?" Leigh asked, thinking of the conversation she had overheard.

"Oh my, yes," Adith replied. "Lester got real upset about that.

They said it was all tore up, and they couldn't figure out what Arch was doing. Well, Lester, he's so protective you know, he told them Arch was redoing the place, but he just wasn't all that good at it, and besides, he didn't have the time to fix everything. Got him so agitated it started a nasty coughing fit, that did!"

I'll bet, Leigh thought uncomfortably.

"He didn't like it when a couple of them made a big deal out of the holes in the yard, either. Lester, he told them that Wiley liked to dig and it was nobody's business if Arch didn't mind his own dog digging on his own property! Though why he'd get his britches in a knot over that I can't imagine, seeing as how many times he's cursed that dog for digging in his tomatoes!"

Leigh bit her lip. Adith obviously wasn't aware of the whole treasure-hunting scenario, which meant that Harvey had deliberately kept his mouth shut about Leigh's earlier conversation with him. Lester was practically making himself apoplectic with zeal to protect the secret. Even Allison was sitting quietly as a mouse, saying nothing… although for her, that was status quo. The child had a one-way data valve.

Leigh's sense of fairness warred with her better judgment. She was no big fan of secrets, particularly crime-related ones. Getting them out in the open was often the best way to render them innocuous. On the other hand, when talking about one Adith Rhodis, a little information could most definitely be a dangerous thing.

She decided to keep her own mouth shut too, at least for now. Adith could—and no doubt would—harass her about the omission later.

Within half an hour they were ensconced in the second-floor end unit of Dora Klinger, who seemed more than delighted to settle them into her olive green Victorian wingback chairs and treat them to a bowl of hard candy that looked like it had survived the Great Depression. Allison and Adith both managed to politely take a piece, but every lump Leigh attempted to extract was permanently affixed to the mother lode.

"I couldn't believe it when Adith called," Dora exclaimed as she lowered herself into a mechanized lift chair. Well-preserved for her age, with an unruly tuft of thick, snow-white hair covering her head like a mop, Dora's animated eyes gave the impression of one tough cookie. Her long limbs suggested she was once a tall woman, but her stature was now reduced by the prominent hunch in her back. Getting around even this small, one-room apartment was probably an ordeal for her, yet she had insisted on rising to meet them and ushering them in. "I do love meeting people from the old neighborhood, but I wish it was under better circumstances. To think that Mr. Pratt has disappeared! I never liked living at that farm, myself. Always had my suspicions about it. But hearing this from Adith now, and thinking back to what I saw back then… it gives me gooseflesh!"

Adith leaned forward in her chair, eyes bugging. "Ooh, tell us all about it! You thought the place was haunted, didn't you?"

"Every place is haunted," Dora responded knowledgably. "It's only a matter of whether the spirits are friendly or not."

Leigh restrained her eyes from rolling. Why exactly was she here?

"Excuse me, Mrs. Klinger," Allison said politely. "When did you live at Frog Hill Farm?"

Dora's dark eyes rested on the girl with a smile. "Why, many years ago, child. My husband and I bought the farm back in 1958, when the houses you ladies live in were just being built. Five acres, a couple of outbuildings, and a crumbling wreck of a farmhouse—that's what we got. I didn't care for it from the beginning, what with the bridge and the flooding and all, but Bert—that was my husband—he liked his privacy, and we couldn't afford much else, so there we were. Little did we know!"

"You bought the farm from Theodore Carr's son?" Allison asked.

Leigh tensed. *How did Allison know—.* She stopped herself with a head shake. Any question beginning with that phrase was better left unanswered.

Dora beamed. "What a clever child you are!" she praised. "And such a pretty bow!"

Allison slid her eyes toward her mother and smiled smugly.

Saints preserve us, Leigh thought, borrowing a quote from her own mother. Most ten and a half year-old girls would be embarrassed to use their small size to their advantage, but Allison had the ruse down to a science. Both twins had both been born prematurely, but while Ethan came out ready to roll, Allison had required four agonizing weeks in the neonatal intensive care unit and had always been the smallest child in her grade. Nevertheless, blessed (or cursed, depending on your perspective) with her grandfather Koslow's ageless visage, Allison could—with a flip of her short hair this way or that, or an adjustment in clothing, posture, or eye wear—pose for any age between six and twenty. At present, she was shooting for "young, innocent, and adorable."

At least two of them were true.

"We bought the farm from a man named Trout," Dora answered. "But he wasn't the son of the soldier, he was the grandson, a nephew to the man who had just died. Mr. Trout was trying to sell off and settle everything. He gave us a good price because of the shape it was in… while his uncle was still alive it had been let out as a rental, and it was all run down. Of course, we didn't know then why none of the renters would stay in it!"

"Well, I can tell you that right now," Adith chortled. "Spooks! The place is crawling with them. My Pansy knew it from the beginning, that's why she always turns her head to the left and sniffs when she's on the deck. Never to the right, mind you. *Always* to the left!"

Dora threw Adith a derisive glance, and Leigh hid a grin. It looked like Dora had heard all about Adith's clairvoyant poodle over the phone already. It also appeared that even among believers, some paranormal claims were deemed more legitimate than others. "Yes," Dora drawled critically, "*Well*. In any event, the renters didn't last. And no sooner had the ink dried on our deed than we started hearing the stories."

Adith leaned forward further.

"There were rumors, you see, that the man who'd lived on the farm for the last fifty years, Tom Carr, had murdered his own father. That was supposed to have happened way back in the twenties, but the neighborhood was still abuzz about it, because Tom was a loner and everybody thought he was touched in the head. Nobody visited the farm; people didn't let their kids play anywhere near it. Getting the man into a nursing home was a terrible mess, I heard. Nephew had to go through the state and get him committed or some such. Bert and I knew all that when we bought the place, but Bert, he never had the ESP, not even a touch, so it didn't bother him. Me, I was leery from the beginning." Her voice dropped to a whisper. "When bad things happen in a place, bad energy *lingers*."

"Oooh," Adith crooned. "Ain't it so, ain't it so! Can I use your bathroom?"

Dora cocked one thin eyebrow, then waved a hand dismissively. "Of course, of course. Help yourself. Now, as I was saying…" she faltered.

"You were telling us about Theodore Carr's son," Allison prompted sweetly. "And the rumors about him? Strange things he did, maybe?"

"Yes," Dora continued, granting Allison an indulgent smile. "Tom was a queer bird. They said he was unfriendly even before his father died, and afterward, he became a recluse. Most likely, his father's vengeful spirit was what drove him to madness. Now Tom, he didn't die at the farm. But unlike what some may tell you, a spirit *can* travel, if they've got a mind to."

Leigh stiffened. Over Dora's shoulder, she could see Adith prowling around in the bathroom, first popping open the vanity and now peering into her hostess's medicine cabinet. She tried to catch Adith's eye with a glare, but as Leigh was directly in Dora's line of sight and Adith was paying no attention, a discreet reprimand was impossible.

"And from the moment I stepped foot on that farm," Dora continued, "I sensed not one, but two centers of energy… and both were as vile and hostile as anything I'd ever felt before!"

Leigh's cheeks flared red. Adith was pulling pill bottles off the shelves, unscrewing the lids, looking inside…

"Of course the nephew, Mr. Trout, he was the nicest man you'd ever meet," Dora digressed. "He knew his uncle had problems, and he seemed to feel pretty bad about the way things had gotten with the neighbors. Once he took control out there, he did what he could to get the place put right. But some things you can't just pick up and haul away on a truck. And *evil* is one of them."

Leigh squirmed in her chair, trying to catch Adith's attention, but the woman was oblivious.

"Do you know if either of the Carrs left a journal or… anything like that?" Allison asked.

Dora's lips twisted in thought. "I don't remember Mr. Trout mentioning such a thing, but we wouldn't know—I'm sure he removed all his relatives' personal property when his uncle went in the home, before the renters moved in. Why would you ask?"

Leigh breathed a sigh of relief as Adith at last exited the bathroom.

"Theodore Carr led a really interesting life, being a Union soldier and all," Allison answered. "I like local history. I'm reading *A History of the Harmony Line* right now."

Dora's wrinkled face beamed. "Why, how nice! I used to walk down the creek and pick blackberries along where the tracks used to be. I remember one time..."

Leigh tuned out as, instead of returning to her seat, Adith took a U-turn into the bedroom area. With Dora's attention temporarily turned to Allison, Leigh frantically gestured for Adith to cease and desist, but the older woman merely grinned at her and proceeded to examine the contents of a chest of drawers.

"Well, he buried his father's body right there on the property, you know," Dora was saying as Leigh tuned back in. "You could do that back then if you wanted—no law against it. Just have to mark it clearly and tell people when you sell."

Leigh's attention shifted back to Dora. "Theodore Carr is *buried* at Frog Hill Farm?"

"Of course," Dora responded. "Hasn't anyone seen the stone? It was downstream from the house a ways, by a little willow tree, near the edge of the woods."

"But there isn't any gravestone!" Allison interjected. "I'm sure there's not. We would have seen it."

Dora shrugged. "Well, it was just a little flat thing. Probably got moved."

But did Theodore? Leigh thought grimly. The thought of an unmarked grave on the property was disturbing. Surely *that* wasn't what the map led to?

But if the "treasure" was buried with his body...

Leigh fought a shiver.

"Is that why people thought it was haunted?" Allison asked. "Something to do with the grave?"

"Oh no," Dora said defensively. "It was much more than that. Lots of farms have family graveyards. But an evil presence... that's something else. There are signs. Clear signs, if you're able to read them. And I can. Floating lights in the wee hours... those are the orbs, you know. *Harbingers.*"

"Ooh! I love orbs!" Adith exclaimed, pausing in her analysis of the top drawer to retrieve a brassiere she'd sent dangling over the side. "I've seen 'em myself, out by the creek!"

Dora did not appear to hear the voice coming from directly behind her, which under the circumstances was fortunate.

"I know a boy who sees floating lights," Allison said quickly, seemingly as anxious as her mother to distract attention from Adith. "I always thought they were probably just fireflies. Or maybe somebody with a flashlight."

Dora's lips turned down into a scowl. "Now don't be a cynic, my dear. You sound just like my Bert. Flashlights, indeed. They may look indistinguishable from ordinary lights, but when you have The Sight, you know. You can *feel* it."

"Amen to that!" Adith added, putting one hand on Dora's mattress and attempting some sort of squat.

"From the very beginning, I saw the orbs," Dora insisted. "Always in the wee hours. I had trouble sleeping, you know, so I was up while Bert snored away. The renters saw the same thing. Lights, sometimes sounds along with them, disappearing well before dawn. Not in one place, but all over. When the place was empty, the ghosts got bolder. Vandalism… that's what really scared the renters away."

"Vandalism?" Leigh repeated. Adith had all but disappeared from view as she painstakingly lowered herself to hand and knees, presumably to look under the bed.

"Oh, yes," Dora insisted. "We heard about all sorts of things. Belongings moved, but never stolen. Tools, shovels, that sort of thing. Poltergeist activity, of course. Windows left open, doors ajar. Coins dropped, but no money ever taken, which only goes to prove it wasn't people doing it!"

Adith remained out of view. Leigh's jaws clenched.

"It happened to us, too, but Bert wouldn't believe it. He always said I left things out of place and didn't remember. But I knew. The spirits at that farm were *disturbed*. Whether Tom killed his daddy I don't know, but they say insanity runs in families, so who could swear that he didn't? Either way, it's clear they both still haunt the place. Misery and unhappiness… and hostility. That's what I sensed. And I don't mind telling you it scared the living daylights out of me."

Adith's gray head at last popped back up, and Leigh breathed a sigh of relief. But her respite was short lived. Adith had to struggle to pull herself up by hanging onto the bedframe, and as she rose she accidentally caught her shoulder under Dora's bedside commode. Leigh watched in horror as Adith unknowingly pulled the entire contraption off the ground, the pot swinging square against her backside.

"Well, what the—" Adith swore like a sailor as, to add insult to injury, the potty lid flipped down on the back of her head.

Leigh was halfway out of her chair, but Allison was quicker. "Excuse me, Mrs. Klinger," the girl said loudly, covering the vulgarity spewing from behind, "But could I use your bathroom, too?"

"Why of course my dear," Dora answered, still mercifully oblivious. "Now, as I was saying…"

Allison leapt to Mrs. Rhodis' rescue as Leigh pretended *not* to see the octogenarian flapping her arms and spinning in circles while the potty seat's rubber feet careened dangerously close to an antique lamp.

"Bert didn't believe a bit of it, of course, until he started having to make weekend trips to Steubenville to take care of his folks. There I was, first time all alone, just me and the chickens, and I wake up in the dead of night to find some man—dead or alive I never knew—rattling on my back door! Well, I got up and turned on the lights and he disappeared quick as he came. Happened more than once after that—every time Bert left town."

Leigh relaxed slightly as Allison succeeded in freeing Mrs. Rhodis, then replaced the commode where it belonged and scooted dutifully off toward the bathroom.

"Now isn't that just like a man!" Adith chirped, returning to her chair and the conversation as smooth as butter. "Never believe a thing you say until it bites 'em on the nose. Then they say 'why didn't you tell me!'"

"Indeed," Dora nodded. "He said it was all in my head, until his mother passed and we went to Steubenville for the funeral. That was the first time we were *both* gone from the farm, and when we came back, even Bert had to admit someone had jimmied the back door open. He knew because I'd made him lock it himself."

"That's thinking," Adith praised.

"Well, after that, he told me to wake him up next time I saw those lights bobbing, and I did, and he went running straight out there with his shotgun. Said he didn't see anybody running away, but of course he wouldn't. Never did admit the place was spooked, but he did decide right then and there to pull up stakes and sell it—and that's what we did."

"The time someone broke in," Leigh asked, her trepidation growing again. "Did they take anything?"

Dora shook her head. "Not a toothpick. But we did find something strange afterward. One of the stones in the cellar wall was loose. It had been chiseled all around, like someone wanted to take it out. Bert said that was fool nonsense, the mortar was just old, it was crumbling everywhere and a lot of the stones were loose, but I knew better. It was a *sign*."

"A sign of what?" Adith asked breathlessly. "The apocalypse?"

Dora scowled with disapproval. "Of course not! A sign that the evil spirits were staking their claim. They didn't want anyone else to live in that house. Ever." Her scratchy voice lowered to a growl. "*Or else.*"

Leigh thought of Archie, and despite herself, a wave of goose bumps crept up both her arms.

"If you ask me," Dora continued, "I'd guess poor Mr. Pratt must have seen something he couldn't quite handle. I expect he'll come back when he's ready. And when he does, he'll put that cursed place right back on the market—you see if he doesn't!"

The toilet flushed.

A few seconds later, Allison emerged. "You have a nice bathroom, Mrs. Klinger," she flattered. "I like the ocean pictures."

"Why thank you, dear," Dora answered. "It seems quite" —she stifled an obvious yawn— "*popular* tonight."

Taking the cue, Leigh rose, thanked their hostess profusely, and readied the trio for their exit. Dora graciously showed them out, thanked them for an evening's conversation, and urged them to come back for another visit any time. She warned them all to be on their guard around the farm and made Adith promise to keep her updated about Archie.

The second they were out of earshot, Adith practically burst. "You can trust what she says, I can tell you that!" she assured proudly. "No psych meds at all, not even a sleep aid! Just something for thyroid and blood pressure. She had her vitamin D and the bone meds, but nothing heavy for pain—just over the counter stuff. Now, if she was on the narcotics I'd be a little wary, but with a profile like that her mind's good to go!"

"*That's* why you were snooping in her medicine cabinet?" Leigh asked incredulously, "To assess her mental state?"

"Well, of course," Adith said innocently. "Why else would I?"

"And her underwear drawer?" Leigh accused.

Adith's lips pursed. "Some people keep their drugs in their undies."

"You missed half of what she was saying!"

Adith waved a dismissive hand. "I'd heard it all on the phone already anyway."

Leigh's face grew hot. "Then why on earth did you insist I drive you out here on a Saturday night?"

Adith gave a shrug, her merry eyes sparkling with mischief. "Some stories, you really need to hear firsthand. Besides, she sounded lonely. When *I'm* old, I can only hope three such young and gorgeous ladies will want to spend a Saturday evening chatting with me."

Allison let out a giggle.

"So, are you convinced now?" Adith asked, looking at Leigh intently.

"Convinced of what?" Leigh grumbled.

Adith frowned. "That the farm is under the evil influence, that's what! That Archie's gone missing because of the spooks!"

Leigh hesitated. She didn't believe in the supernatural elements of Dora Klinger's tale for a second, and despite all appearances to the contrary, she'd always suspected that Adith didn't really believe in such nonsense, either. But it was getting harder and harder *not* to link Archie's baffling disappearance to the mounting evidence that for the last half century, *someone* had been searching for *something* at Frog Hill Farm.

Oh, Arch. What have you and Lester gotten yourselves into?

"There's evil out there, all right," Leigh agreed soberly. "But given the choice between an orb and a flashlight... I'd rather run into the orb."

Chapter 10

The Sunday morning sun shone bright and pleasantly warm for the season, even at the ungodly early hour at which Leigh found herself heading off for a quick check on the mother dog and pups. She hadn't slept well. Again. Warren and Ethan had returned quite late after the baseball game went into extra innings, and although Warren had dropped off immediately into peaceful slumber, Leigh had continued to toss and turn for hours. Giant pottery crocks had danced in and out of her vision, all dull and boring as dirt, except that a few had tiny black puppies hiding inside, and one had a baby in a police uniform. When her mind's incarnation of Theodore Carr had shown up in blue overalls and started firing at the crocks with a rifle, she had jerked awake in a cold sweat.

Being up and fully conscious was better. Even if she was exhausted.

Listening to the birds chatter and admiring the maple leaves just beginning to turn color, Leigh could hardly believe that anything bad could happen in a place as peaceful as the banks of Snow Creek. She smiled as she passed the low spot in the Sullivan's yard, where every spring she and the children would collect hundreds of wood frog and toad tadpoles from the dwindling rain pools, raise them in myriad tanks on her sun porch, then watch as they hopped back into the wild. She was thinking about the herons that inevitably staked out the same spot—and not watching where she was going—when she stumbled, nearly twisting her ankle.

She looked down to see another recently dug and filled-in hole. But this one hadn't been filled in so well, with mounds of dirt still piled nearby while the turned-up earth in the hole sank well below the grass line.

Amateurs.

Leigh's brow wrinkled. Was the current digger the same person or persons who "haunted" the farm in Dora Klinger's day? Certainly not if Archie and Lester were the culprits. She didn't know the men's exact ages, but even if they were older than they looked, they couldn't have been more than toddlers in the days when Dora had intruders rattling at her door.

No, it seemed far more likely, if less pleasant to think about, that the mysterious map of which the children had found a photocopy must have been in various hands before theirs, and before Archie's as well. It might even be the rumored "paper" that came to the attention of Harvey's historical society back in the sixties. Then again, it might not. The search could be for something far more sinister than a Civil War general's hat.

Oh, hell, Leigh berated herself. She was starting to think just like Dora.

She spent the rest of her walk attempting to soothe herself with the blissful ambiance, but her anxiety was too deep-rooted to shake. Lester was a good and decent man, but he was not the brightest bulb in the ceiling. He might *think* he was helping Archie's cause by staying silent about the search, but Leigh would have to convince him otherwise. And soon. The police would need the whole story to get Archie home safe and sound, and that couldn't happen quickly enough—for any of them.

She reached the tool shed and leaned down to pull aside the cellar doors. Her arms stopped in midair when she realized the doors were already open, with the loose one flung wildly askew. She froze a moment and listened.

No sound met her ears.

Her heart beat rapidly as she pulled her small flashlight out of her back pocket and brandished it in front of her. The steps were well illuminated with sunlight, but she knew that dark corners remained below.

"Momma dog!" she called out, her voice quavering slightly. "Has someone been bothering you?"

It's probably just Scotty again, she told herself. He couldn't resist sneaking another peak at the puppies, and of course he would forget to close the doors again afterwards.

There was nothing to panic about.

She took a steadying breath, held out the flashlight, and started carefully down the stairs. "Momma dog?"

The cellar was silent.

The near side of the room where she had first seen the pups was empty, and her heart skipped a beat. Only after several seconds' panic did she remember that yesterday the dog had moved the litter to the far corner.

Calm down, you idiot, she chastised. *Everything is fine.* She forced herself to take the last few steps at a quicker pace, then spoke again to the dog as her flashlight illuminated the newer nesting spot.

"I should have known you—" her voice broke off.

The mother dog and her litter were gone. They had been replaced with the prone figure of a man.

And he wasn't moving.

"No!" Leigh exclaimed out loud. She cast her flashlight quickly around the remainder of the room, but there was nothing else to see. "No, no, *no!*"

She centered the beam back on the man, her heart pounding against her ribs. He was curled away from her, facing the wall. Nevertheless, he looked familiar.

Trembling like a leaf, she forced herself closer. She shone the light full on his face.

It was Lester.

Her heart fell into her shoes. She stood as if frozen, staring in horror at the paleness of his damp skin, a stark contrast to the oozing ribbon of blood that began at his temple and streamed down over his eye and across his cheek.

The cool stone walls of the cellar felt suddenly claustrophobic. Like an animal trapped in a hole she panicked, whirling around to seek the exit and run up and out and as far away as she could get…

She had gone halfway up the steps before her brain caught up with her.

Oozing blood? *Damp* skin?

She stopped and turned around again. Was there really some cosmic rule that every horizontal person she came across on the ground, near the ground, or inside a major appliance *had* to be dead?

Not Lester. Please.

She stretched out a shaky hand and shone her beam on the figure's chest. To her amazement, his ribcage jiggled slightly. Then it let loose with a full-fledged cough.

"Oh, thank God!" Leigh exclaimed, reaching the man in two strides. She patted his warm cheeks, and his eyelids promptly fluttered. "Lester! Lester, wake up! Can you hear me?"

Lester moaned. His lids opened only halfway, revealing bloodshot eyeballs that rolled in their sockets. The lids shut tight again.

Leigh put her fingers in the hollow beside his Adam's apple and was relieved to feel a decent pulse. She examined his face more critically and could see that despite the blood, the cut on his temple was neither deep nor serious. Whether it had been delivered along with a concussion was another matter.

"Hang on, Lester," she said soothingly. "You're going to be just fine. I'm going to get some help now, okay? I promise I'll be right back."

Lester made no response, but his breathing and pulse remained steady.

Leigh made a beeline for daylight and didn't stop until she was fully under the clear blue sky. She pulled out her cell phone and dialed 911. She might or might not have been able to get reception in the cellar, but regardless, she felt safer above ground. The valley, creek, and woods looked as bucolic and innocent as ever. The only beings up and moving at this hour were her and the birds.

She requested an ambulance immediately but refused to stay on the line, as she needed to reach Emma and did not want to leave Lester alone. The Brown's phone rang four times before a bleary-sounding Emma picked up, her voice hoarse with sleep. "Hello? Leigh?"

Caller ID was a wonderful thing. Leigh was sure that if Emma's phone had read "private caller" or nothing, she would never have stirred at all.

"What's wrong, honey?" Emma asked with a yawn. Then her voice seemed suddenly to sharpen. "Is it about Archie?"

"No," Leigh responded, wondering if Emma usually woke up alone. "It's about Lester."

"Lester?" Emma repeated, sounding bleary again. "He's around here somewhere. You want me to fetch him?"

"I'm with him already," Leigh explained. "At Archie's tool shed. I'm afraid he's been injured."

Emma's voice snapped to full alertness. "Injured? What? He was sleeping right here... I mean..." there was a pause. "Where did you say he was? Is he all right?"

"I'm sure he's going to be fine," Leigh assured. "But he has a bump on the head and he seems to have passed out. I've called an ambulance and I'm waiting for them here behind the tool shed. He's—"

"I'm coming!"

The line cut off.

Leigh cast a nervous glance back at the entrance to the cellar. Her fingers itched to push Maura's number on the speed dial, but she refrained. It was wretchedly early, and she knew that the detective had been on duty last night. Maura had asked to be kept informed, true, but under the circumstances Leigh refused to interrupt her friend's sleep *and* jack up her stress level without a darned good reason. Despite every instinct in Leigh's body screaming foul play, she couldn't be certain that Lester had been assaulted. The man was sick as a dog and had been for days. He could have snuck out in the middle of the night, overexerted himself, passed out, and hit his head falling down.

The township police were already on their way; she would let them and the EMTs figure it out. She took a deep breath, collected what little courage she possessed, and headed back down the cellar steps.

Lester was groaning slightly as she entered. Feeling guilty at having left him, even for two minutes, Leigh hastened to his side. He had rolled over on his back and was pawing at his head with one flailing hand.

"Emma's on her way, Lester," she reported. "And the ambulance will be here any minute."

His mumbling coalesced into words.

"Arch," he muttered, his low voice filled with angst. "Who's… nobody knows… somebody… I have to… I've got to get… Arch… maybe I can… don't want you hurt… can't be hurt… everybody loves Arch…"

Even as Leigh strained to understand, she worried at his agitation. His body rocked from side to side, and clammy sweat beaded up on his brow. His forehead felt feverish.

"Just lay still," she ordered. "You shouldn't be moving your head around."

"My head!" he exclaimed suddenly, reaching for his temple with his hand again. "Damnation! What the—" he launched into a stream of curses that could only make Leigh smile. Now *that* was a healthy man's reaction to waking up on a hard dirt floor with an aching skull.

But all too soon, the mournful mumbling began again. "I'm trying… I am, I'm trying… hang in there, Arch… I won't… don't worry…"

He continued with more of the same, and as Leigh continued to gently shush him, one word suddenly jumped to her attention.

"Harvey…"

"What, Lester?" she asked quickly. "What about Harvey?"

"He knows, Arch… He knows…" Lester's hand flew up to his mouth, making his next words indecipherable. Leigh gently pulled the hand away.

"Lester," Leigh asked, not at all certain he could hear her. "Do you know who hurt you?"

"Steal it!" his voice became suddenly clearer. For the first time his eyes opened fully and his gaze, though still unfocused, showed real fear.

"Don't trust…" he said fiercely, *"anyone!"*

Leigh tapped her feet nervously on the carpet of the Brown's sitting room. One of the women in Adith and Pauline's bedroom was snoring like a freight train, but otherwise, the house was still and quiet as death. It was a metaphor Leigh could do without.

Emma, who could generally be counted on to remain calm in a crisis, had been near hysterical when she reached Lester's side after having run across the backyard and creek in a nightgown, robe, and slippers. She couldn't understand how he had gotten there, since he had been in bed asleep when she retired for the night. His fever had spiked again last evening, and she had dosed him up with over the counter meds and tucked him into bed early, worried that he might be coming down with pneumonia.

Had he been sleepwalking? Was he delirious with fever? Emma had had no other explanation to offer the EMTs or the police except that he might have gone to check on the stray dog. Why he would do that in the middle of the night while sick, however, she had no clue.

Leigh had deftly managed to avoid talking to the police in front of Emma, busying herself instead with running to the Brown's house and fetching the woman's purse and a change of clothes so that she could ride up front in the ambulance and accompany her husband to the hospital. Having something constructive to do had helped soothe Leigh's own panic. She had overheard the EMTs describe not one, but *two* head wounds. She had also heard that Lester was running a fever of 103, which made it entirely possible that he had passed out first, then hit his head falling down, perhaps stumbling repeatedly.

It was also possible, she thought grimly, that he had been deliberately struck and *then* fell and hit his head, or even that he had been struck twice. But how could anyone tell? The stone walls of the cellar were roughhewn, and although the floor was primarily dirt, it had plenty of natural stones embedded in it. The only loose object she had seen near Lester was his own lightweight flashlight, but that was little comfort. If he had confronted someone, that person could have conked him on the head with their own, heavier flashlight, or a shovel, or any other convenient tool—and then fled with it in hand.

Leigh stared down at the phone numbers Emma had scribbled on a piece of notepaper borrowed from one of the policemen. The residents at the personal care home could not be left alone, and Leigh had agreed to call in one of the Browns' regular relief staffers. But the first two on the list had not been available. One was already working another job, and the other was out of town and couldn't make it back until afternoon. The third and last name on the list was Nora.

Leigh sighed. Nora was a nursing home aide by profession and had moonlighted for the Browns for years, even before she moved in next door. But Nora's working overtime had come to a halt after the baby was born, and this morning seemed a particularly lousy time to resume it. Every time Leigh had opened her door to put her corgi in or out last night, she had heard little Cory screaming.

"Oh, I hope you don't have to call Nora," Emma had said worriedly. "She's been so overtired lately. But if the others can't make it, you'll have to. I don't like to bring in strangers."

Leigh really had no choice. Emma's directions had been explicit, and the home was a business that needed coverage by someone officially trained in direct care, which Leigh was not.

She picked up the Brown's landline and dialed. The phone rang interminably, until at last an answering machine picked up, interrupted almost immediately by Nora herself. "Emma?" she said with alarm. "What's wrong?"

"It's Leigh," she corrected. "I'm really sorry to wake you up, but I'm afraid it's an emergency. Emma's on her way to the hospital with Lester, they need someone to stay at the home, and no one else is available until this afternoon. I know it's—"

"Oh, no!" Nora exclaimed. "Of course I'll come over. I knew Lester wasn't right when I saw him yesterday! I told Emma he needed to slow down or he was going to make himself even sicker! Oh, my. Did his fever go up? Can't he breathe?"

Leigh jumped in as soon as she could. Once Nora got going, the woman seemed able to speak without breathing herself.

"He got a head injury somehow," Leigh offered simply. Whatever details Emma chose to share later, Emma could share herself. "He got out of bed with a fever and they don't know if he passed out and fell down or what, but he was unconscious for a while, so—"

"A concussion?" Nora effused. "Oh, how awful. Emma must be frantic!"

"Well, she's—"

"I'll be over in three minutes," Nora continued, her voice bouncing as if she were moving around as she talked, "Derrick's home all day so he can watch the baby. Emma doesn't like calling in the temps, and I don't blame her, Pauline's so tricky about her meds, and I swear she's been teaching Adith how to—. Oh! Where are my… Did I not finish that load of laundry?! I thought I—"

"Nora?" Leigh broke in. "I'll stay till you get here. Thanks." Not meaning to be rude, but in no mood to listen to the sleep-deprived young mother's stream of conscious narration of the dressing process, Leigh hung up. Perhaps, after taking care of a colicky baby nearly 24/7 with a reclusive husband whose helpfulness was questionable at best, spending a quiet day with three elderly people would be a relief.

She returned the phone to its cradle, then rose and walked to one of the back windows. Most of Archie's place was out of view, thanks to the trees, but there were a few open spots visible near the tool shed, and she could see parts of the farm's driveway. The ambulance had left a while ago, but the township police lingered still; she could see them intermittently as they wandered the grounds around the shed. As she watched, another sedan cruised down the lane. It was a unit from the county police force—most likely related to the missing persons investigation. She could only guess what the two teams of detectives would make of this latest mishap. Would the county begin to take the treasure-hunting angle seriously? Or would they focus on Lester's fever and write the whole thing off as unrelated?

She might find out for herself soon enough. The police had made clear when she left that they would be coming over to the Brown's house later and would question her there.

Fabulous.

Leigh stepped away from the window and plopped down on one of the high-seated chairs. Not even Pauline's canary was fully awake yet. It startled when she sat, but then blinked at her with disinterest and stuffed its head back under its wing.

"It's okay," Leigh said wryly. "I get that a lot."

Her gaze wandered to the battle scene covering the far wall, and her stomach flip-flopped. Harvey's musings had been interesting, but she hadn't really believed them. That is, she hadn't really believed that a Civil War relic could bestir enough interest to cause actual... well... *mayhem*. The idea was too farfetched. Digging for gold, jewels, or cold hard cash was one thing; risking one's life and liberty for a historical conversation piece was another.

Still. The facts were beginning to fit together far too neatly to be ignored. She held out a reluctant hand and counted them off. One: Archie was a certified Civil War enthusiast who knew all about Theodore Carr's history when he bought Frog Hill Farm eight years ago. Two: Somebody had been digging for something in the neighborhood for at least the five years she had lived in it. Three: Somebody had been searching for something on or around Archie's house as far back as the 1950s. Four: The children had found a treasure map of the area that appeared to be from the 1930s, at the latest. Five: Archie and Lester were almost certainly working together to find this mysterious something when Archie disappeared.

Were they getting close?

She replayed in her mind Lester's feverish ravings, and the

memory made her feel no better. *I'm trying... I am, I'm trying... hang in there, Arch... I won't... don't worry...*

What exactly had Lester been trying to do? Was he attempting to find the treasure himself last night, and if so, how would that help Archie? Did Lester think that his friend had been kidnapped for ransom?

Did he *know* that he had?

The thought induced another spurt of stomach acid. Surely not! Lester had recruited his entire reenacting company to scour the area for clues... would he do that if he was trying to keep things quiet and cover up the fact that he was hiding a ransom note?

Maybe. If he thought his buds could help him either track down the culprits or find the desired object... without involving the police.

Leigh sprang up from her chair. "Lester, Lester," she muttered miserably. "Please tell me you're not that dense."

Don't trust... His words came back to her. *Anyone!*

Leigh buried her face in her hands.

The doorbell rang. She hurried toward the sound, grateful for the interruption. She swung open the door to admit Nora, who had apparently managed to find clean clothes after all.

Makeup and a hairbrush, not so much.

"I got here as quick as I could," Nora said breathlessly. "Cory's still asleep, thank God. He should be out for a while, after last night." She walked straight back to the sitting room and glanced around. "Commotion didn't wake them, huh? I'm not surprised about Pauline and Harvey, but Adith always seems to know when something's up—even when she's sound asleep!"

Leigh grinned. Nora did know her patients, at least.

"Did Emma leave instructions about the meds?" Nora continued. "I know a couple things have changed recently, but I don't know exactly how. Adith's schedule is off from the others now and I'm not sure about Pauline's new compression stockings—"

Leigh was rescued by the ring of the landline. Nora stepped over to check the ID and swiftly picked up. "Emma!" she gushed. "How is Lester? How are you? Are you okay? What's happening?"

Leigh listened as the one-way conversation unfolded.

"Well at least he's awake, that's good... well, does he have a concussion then? Oh... I see. How long do they think... an MRI?

Oh, because of the fever… oh, I'm sure it's not that serious. Has he said why he… The TOOL SHED?! Why on earth… That's crazy! Oh, well, maybe he's still just confused… that'll make him groggy, I bet… well, he'll just have to take it easy! Don't you worry about a thing here, it's about time Derrick had Cory alone to himself anyway, and I could use the change of pace. But you need to tell me" —she hunted around for a pen and pad— "What is Adith's new schedule? And what do I do about Pauline's—"

Leigh gave her mind permission to wander. Unfortunately, the place it wandered to was no more pleasant. She could not remove her eyes from the image of one particular soldier in Harvey's gruesome painting. He was in Union garb, lying on the ground with a bloodied leg. His face was screwed into a grimace. His hands clutched his rifle, which he appeared to be aiming squarely at the man lofting a sword with a hat on its tip—General Armistead.

Theodore Carr was there.

Could a moth-eaten, 150-year-old hat really be that important? Could it possibly be worth enough to someone to—she cringed at the thought—commit violence?

Nora hung up the phone and faced her. "Lester's gone in for an MRI," she reported. "His head wounds don't look serious, and they think his concussion is mild. But his having a fever at the same time means they have to rule out some kind of bleeding… I'm not sure what that's about. But Emma thinks he'll probably be there all day, and maybe even overnight for observation. Did you know he was out at Archie's place?!"

Leigh nodded. "I did, actually. I was checking on the stray dog."

Nora shook her head. "He must have been delirious. Either that, or he was taking one of those new sleeping pills. I hate those things. Why, we had one woman at St. Mary's, she—"

Leigh's patience wavered. She had nothing against the nurse's aide, but Nora had the kind of mouselike metabolism that rendered her incapable of functioning without either her body or her mouth—or both—in motion at all times. "Did Emma say if Lester was able to explain what happened?" Leigh interrupted.

Nora shook her head. "She said she asked him, but either he didn't answer the question or what he said didn't make sense, I'm not sure. He's definitely awake and talking, though. That's a good sign."

Leigh nodded in agreement. Lester's return to consciousness was a very good sign.

His unwillingness to talk about what happened last night was not.

The front doorbell rang again. "Who could that be at this hour?" Nora asked.

"Most likely it's the police," Leigh answered without enthusiasm. "They talked to Emma already but they said they had a few questions for me, too."

"I didn't know the police came out!" Nora responded, seeming concerned. "Why would they?"

Leigh considered a moment. The officers had come, no doubt, because of what she'd told the dispatcher—that she'd found Lester on a neighbor's property unconscious with a head wound of unknown origin. Put that way, the more sinister possibilities were obvious. But she did not want to unduly alarm Nora, or anyone else in the home. And she was pretty sure she'd just heard the floorboards creak in Harvey's room. "I think it's routine with an accident," she said blandly.

"Well, I'll get out of your way then," Nora offered. "I need to go down and start breakfast, anyhow. Just yell if anybody needs anything."

Nora headed down the stairs to the kitchen, and Leigh moved to open the front door.

"MRS. HARMON?" A friendly looking younger officer with frizzy blond hair inquired.

Leigh winced slightly. Of the various policemen on the scene, why did she have to get the loud talker? His tone was perfectly pleasant, he just spoke as though the entire rest of the world was deaf.

"That's me," she said more quietly than necessary as she ushered him in. "The residents are still sleeping."

"GOOD FOR THEM!" he said merrily. "I WOULD BE TOO, IF I COULD!"

Leigh directed him to the farthest possible corner of the sitting room, then closed all the doors she could close.

"What is it you'd like to ask?" she said in a near-whisper.

The officer crossed his legs and flipped through a notebook. "COULD YOU JUST RUN THROUGH FOR ME HOW IT WAS

YOU HAPPENED TO COME UPON MR. BROWN THIS MORNING?"

Leigh considered a more direct rebuke, but decided it was pointless. The floorboards in either direction were already creaking. She took a deep breath and gave as succinct and unremarkable an accounting of her discovery as she possibly could, knowing that almost certainly every pair of ears in the house was now listening.

Even Pauline's canary had awakened.

She finished her prepared tale and looked over at the young officer with dread. She could not be nearly so vague once he started asking pointed questions.

The officer flipped his notebook closed and stood up. "OKAY, THAT'LL DO! THANK YOU VERY MUCH, MRS. HARMON."

Leigh's eyes widened. He couldn't possibly be serious. Didn't he want to know whatever she knew about a possible relationship between this incident and Archie's disappearance? Had the county officials told him it was her children who had found the treasure map? Didn't he care what her first impressions were when she found Lester unconscious? Exactly what Lester had muttered when he was still delirious?

Evidently not.

"THE COUNTY BOYS MIGHT HAVE SOME QUESTIONS LATER," he shouted as he headed toward the door. "BUT I DOUBT IT. THEY'VE GOT YOUR CONTACT INFORMATION IF THEY DO. YOU HAVE A NICE DAY NOW, MS. HARMON!"

Leigh uttered a bland farewell, then watched as the policeman walked out the door and around the corner toward his cruiser, which was parked in Archie's driveway. She didn't know whether to be relieved… or worried. It certainly did not sound as though the county detectives had pushed the idea of a connection between Archie's disappearance and Lester's concussion, much less discussed the possibility of hidden treasure. Perhaps they were still focused on the fraud idea. Perhaps they considered a sick neighbor's passing out on Archie's land to be irrelevant.

Leigh wished she could believe that, too.

But there was little else she could do about her theories except wait to talk to Lester. Maybe if he were honest with her—and the police—they would all have a better idea of what had happened to Archie and how dangerous the situation might be. In the meantime, it was just as well that not every warm body in the neighborhood knew that something valuable might indeed be buried on Frog Hill Farm.

She closed the door and turned around. Pauline, Adith, Harvey, Nora, and an apricot poodle stood clustered in the hallway six feet away, staring at her with widened eyes.

Pansy sneezed.

Chapter 11

"Wiley, settle down!" Leigh chastised. She felt sorry for the dog, who was not used to leash walking, but she preferred not to dislocate an elbow. She had barely managed to extricate herself from the human mob in the Brown house in one piece. "Momma dog!" she called without conviction, cupping her hand to cast her voice out into the woods. "Where are you?"

No response was forthcoming, which was entirely expected. She wasn't worried about the mother dog and litter having being "stolen," much less "spirited away," as Pauline and Adith, respectively, had hypothesized. Leigh found it infinitely more likely that the protective female had put up with one too many intrusions and had voluntarily decided to move her family elsewhere. She was probably holed up nearby, hoping the gravy train of free food would continue.

Whatever slim chance Leigh might have had to lure the stray out of hiding was no doubt ruined by the presence of the wildly hyper "poppa dog" currently slobbering on her shoes. But she could not leave Wiley at the Browns all day with only Nora there to care for him. The nurse aide would be busy enough just preventing Adith from sneaking out to examine the tool shed for "remnants of evil."

Leigh's phone buzzed in her pocket, and she pulled it out with a sudden feeling of remorse. Warren would be awake by now, no doubt wondering where the hell she was.

"Hello?" his crisp, professional voice greeted. "Is this Ms. Leigh Koslow Harmon?"

She smiled. She always did melt at the sound of his voice. "It is."

"This is Warren J. Harmon the Third," he continued formally. "I was looking over my mortgage documentation, and I noticed your name listed as co-signer. So I was wondering, might you be planning to actually occupy said residence at some time?"

Leigh's smiled widened. "I'm sorry, Warren. I slipped out to feed the dog—I didn't think I'd be gone so long. I'm walking Wiley home from the Brown's right now… It's kind of a long story."

"That would be the usual scenario."

"Are the kids up yet?"

"Ethan's still zonked, but Allison is reading a book in her room."

"Is it that new one about the history of—"

"Uh huh."

Leigh muttered a curse. Why couldn't her daughter be reading a nice, safe adventure novel? Or some reference book about ponies? At this point, she'd settle for a boy-band magazine. Anything that got Allison's too-sharp mind off the problems at Archie's place.

"Have you heard from Mo since your talk yesterday?" Warren asked with concern. Leigh had filled him in on Maura's situation, at Maura's request. Now all three of them were anxiously awaiting the results of her tests—and the still-clueless Gerry's imminent return to town.

Leigh responded in the negative, pushed Wiley's paws off her waistline, and hung up with a solemn vow to be home in a matter of seconds. She lifted her chin and took one long, last look around. She had not gone back into the tool shed's cellar, but she was determined to return later—with Warren or somebody else—to put more food outside for the mother dog.

Leigh tried to envision the scrappy canine carrying each of the six puppies, one by one, up the cellar steps and out into the woods. Improbable as it seemed, she knew that wild animals made such moves on a regular basis. But the process would take some time. Had the mother dog moved the pups after Lester became unconscious, or before he arrived? Had someone else been in the cellar before him?

If so, and Lester surprised them there…

Leigh exhaled a nervous breath. If only the dog could talk, she would make the perfect witness. Who exactly had been down in that cellar lately, and why? Who had left the yellow flashlight? Who had taken it away again?

Was the tool shed even depicted on the children's map?

Leigh couldn't remember. She could only picture the one scrawled square depicting Archie's farmhouse, the one that was labeled "The Guide."

"Come on, Wiley," she urged, giving the dog a tug in the

direction of her own house. "It's breakfast time. Then you can wreak havoc with your buddy Chewie for a while."

Leigh's empty stomach rumbled at the thought. She could use a little breakfast herself.

After that, she had a date with a map.

Leigh stuffed the last bite of crumbling, still-warm blueberry muffin into her mouth and practically moaned with delight. "Aunt Lydie," she said a moment later, licking her lips. "You should babysit for Cara more often."

Lydie grinned. "It's not hard to make Matt and Lenna happy, considering what their mother feeds them." She finished drying off the skillet she had used to fry the mountain of bacon which the Pack (with a little help from Leigh and Warren) had just wolfed down and put it away in the cabinet.

Leigh chuckled. The statement was as close to a criticism of her only daughter as Lydie ever made—yet another distinction between her and her twin sister Frances. "I'm sure," Leigh said wryly, "that Matt and Lenna actually *prefer* tofu bacon and wheat bran. They just didn't want to hurt your feelings."

Lydie lifted one eyebrow and smirked. "Undoubtedly."

Leigh studied the view out Cara's kitchen window. The Pack were hanging out on the adult-sized swing set next to the barn. Ethan and Matt were playing fetch with a still-hyper Wiley. Lenna and Allison had their heads together, talking and trying to distract the resident springer spaniel, Maggie, from interfering with Wiley's game. Leigh intended to keep an eye on all of them this time before saying anything even halfway "interesting."

"I brought the map," she announced. She joined her aunt in sitting at the table and handed over a folded copy. "I was hoping you'd be willing to take another look at it and brainstorm with me. Maybe help me figure out how Archie's tool shed could fit into the picture?"

Lydie's expression turned serious. She was a singularly unflappable woman, as a rule, but hearing that yet another person in the neighborhood *might* have experienced foul play had disturbed her. She took off her glasses and squinted at the map. Then she put them back on again. "I don't know, honey," she said finally, her voice laced with frustration. "The whole thing is just... well, *odd*. If I had to guess, I'd say this map is only part of a puzzle. There isn't one 'X marks the spot,' if you know what I mean. It's as if there's another piece to it that we don't have. Something that would explain what all the little marks on the spokes are supposed to mean."

Leigh drew in a breath. "Do you think that's what it means by 'The Guide?'"

"Quite possibly," Lydie agreed. "But the location of the guide isn't made clear, either. The arrow just points to the whole house."

"Tell me about it," Leigh replied. *And tell Archie,* she thought miserably. From the look of his farmhouse, she wondered if he had spent the last eight years tearing holes in the structure at random.

"What bothers me more," Lydie said with a frown, "is the inaccuracy of it. I don't know what the other farm looks like, but the squares for Cara's place are all wrong. See the shape of the rectangles? It's clear this is supposed to be the barn, but it's not in the right place. Snow Creek Farm never had a barn up there—the hill's too steep, never mind that it's covered with trees that have stood for at least a century."

Leigh suffered a sinking feeling. "You think maybe the mapmaker wasn't as familiar with this farm? Both the father and the son were supposedly anti-social types."

"Antisocial? Hmm." Lydie continued studying the map. "Well, there's no question that it's a map of this neighborhood—with the two creeks merging along the Harmony tracks, and the road and the old woods on the hill all right there. I just don't think it's a very *good* map."

Leigh frowned. "Meaning?"

"Meaning not everyone who wants to draw a map can do a decent job of it," Lydie said practically. "Either he wasn't entirely clear on how the buildings were laid out at this farm, he wasn't good with spatial relationships, or he plain just couldn't draw." She turned the map on its side. "Seems like the creek is pretty crooked, too, in relation to the road."

"Well, if it's drawn so poorly," Leigh asked, "how could anyone possibly find anything it was trying to point to?"

Lydie's eyebrows tented. "Perhaps that's been the problem."

Leigh groaned. "You must be right. The thing has certainly been around long enough, presumably without anyone's finding anything. I just wish it could help us get Archie back home." She rose and went to stand at the window again. Allison remained safely out of earshot. *Check.*

She briefly summarized for her aunt her conversations with Harvey and Dora, and her suspicions that Archie and Lester were working together. "But maybe I'm making too much of the map," she finished. "After all, we really don't know how old it is. Particularly if it's drawn so badly—for all we know it could be something Scotty O'Malley did last week as a joke!"

Lydie harrumphed. "You mean that dreadful little boy who brought his BB gun over here that time? I think not!" She pored over the map with renewed interest. "I'm telling you, this map is *old*. I'd bet my degree on it. How old is your house?"

"1958. I believe all four houses between the two farms were built within a year or two of each other."

"Well, there you go," Lydie continued. "None of those houses are on this map, so we're talking early fifties at the latest. I might be wrong about it being drawn while the Harmony Line was still running… after all, if the Carr men had lived here a long time, they might draw the tracks in even if the actual ones had already been removed. But just looking at what they're calling woods and what they're not, I'd still guess twenties or thirties."

Leigh considered. "I guess I've been thinking that Theodore Carr made the map, when it just as easily could have been his son, Tom. But there's something else that still bothers me. Why wouldn't either of them put their own barn on it?"

Lydie looked again at the area of the map where one solitary square was labeled "The Guide." As Leigh had remembered, there were no other squares around it. In fact, the area to the left of it was essentially blank. All the "spokes" shot out to the right, down the creek and toward Cara's place.

"The tool shed and the garage you mention might have been added after the map was drawn," Lydie suggested. "But you're right, a farm has to have a barn. Why the owner wouldn't draw it on his own map, I can't imagine. Unless it was behind the house in this unfinished section," she pointed to the area upstream from Archie's house.

Leigh shook her head. "The barn isn't to the left of the house, it's right behind it, which means it would definitely be on the map. But look… he drew trees there!"

Lydie's lips pursed. "There's something else I think you have to consider then," she said solemnly.

Leigh's eyebrows rose. "What's that?"

"That this man and his son, both of whom were reportedly 'antisocial' and 'paranoid,' could have drawn this map while not completely in their right minds."

Leigh grimaced. "I do *not* want to hear that."

Lydie smiled sympathetically. "I know."

"But the problem is really still the same, isn't it?" Leigh continued. "Even if the map is worthless, if there are people out there who *think* they can figure it out, it still poses a danger! I just can't figure out the real motivation… what it is that everyone is trying so hard to find."

Lydie shrugged. "Harvey's theory sounds plausible enough to me."

Leigh's eyes widened. "The hat thing? Really? You can't be serious."

"And why not?" Lydie challenged.

Leigh hesitated. From someone like Harvey or Archie or even Adith (who, thank the mighty stars, Leigh didn't think had tumbled onto the treasure-hunting angle yet) she could understand the romantic appeal of searching for a lost piece of history. Her practical-to-the-bone aunt, on the other hand, she would have thought impervious to such drama, history buff or no. "Really?" she said uncertainly. "Treasure-hunting for Civil War relics as a motive for…" She almost said "abduction," but stopped herself. She didn't want to think that way. She didn't want to say "assault" either. "Well," she evaded, "it just seems a little farfetched."

Lydie studied her niece quietly for a moment. Then she rose. "Come here with me," she ordered.

Leigh followed her into Cara's study, where Lydie sat down at the computer and clicked onto a search engine. Within seconds, Leigh was viewing the site of a business specializing in the sale of Civil War artifacts. Handmade flags. Gold corps badges. An inscribed bowie knife. Silver spurs. Drums. Each was priced at thousands of dollars. A few were listed for five figures.

Leigh whistled. "Are you kidding me?"

"Obviously not," Lydie responded, clicking around again. Within seconds she had found another site with more of the same. "You underestimate the ardor of the enthusiasts, my dear. I'm more a student of domestic history, myself, but your friend Harvey is right. Finding a hat that could be authenticated as belonging to General Armistead and recovered at the Battle of Gettysburg would be a major, major event for a whole lot of very interested people."

Leigh bit her lip. It was getting sore again. "How much?" she asked weakly.

Lydie cocked her head to one side. "I'm hardly an expert on the matter. But from what I've seen on sites like this, and from what I know of how passionately many people feel about the Civil War, I would guess it might auction for six figures. Maybe seven."

Leigh's thudding heart dropped into her shoes. *"Seven figures?"* she breathed.

"Uh huh," Lydie confirmed.

When it came to motives for violence, seven figures was anything but farfetched.

Leigh swore beneath her breath.

"Uh huh," Lydie agreed.

Chapter 12

Several hours later, Leigh tromped dutifully to where her mother had parked her latest Taurus, on the street beside Greenstone Methodist in Avalon.

"I think it's foolish myself, mind you," Frances lectured, as she had been doing continuously ever since the service ended. "But you know your aunt Bess. She made me swear I'd get the equipment to you, and I suppose it can't make things any worse."

Leigh had been listening to her mother's opinion about the dangers of Leigh's wild and lawless neighborhood in the suburbs for a good twenty minutes already, and Frances didn't know the half of it… at least not yet. Leigh had begged her aunt not to spew *all* the details of the treasure hunt to her twin, but Lydie would make no promises. Frances had already heard enough about Lester's hospitalization to be sure that armed marauders were stalking her beloved grandchildren—and if it weren't for Warren's stepping in and swearing that the children wouldn't set foot off their own property without supervision, Frances might have insisted on moving into the guest room to watch them herself. But Warren could be believed. As opposed to Leigh, who—to hear Frances tell it—regularly shoved her children outside in weather-inappropriate clothing and ordered them to catch viruses.

Frances popped open the trunk of her car. Inside lay an unusual looking camera and tripod. "Bess would have given you both cameras," Frances explained, "but she went on and on about Ferdinand and some other tomcat she's seen gearing up for a showdown… total nonsense, of course."

Leigh smiled. Her Aunt Bess lived on the edge of a woods that hosted a determinedly feral clan of cats, and Bess loved to spy on them with her favorite toys: a set of motion-activated night-vision cameras. Originally, Bess had planned to send a live feed to a website to raise money for the animal shelter, but since the cats only showed up once in a blue moon, she'd settled for entertaining herself and boring various relatives. "That was very selfless of her," Leigh praised. "Where did she go, again?"

Frances's orange-painted lips turned into a disapproving scowl. "To Myrtle Beach. With a man she barely knows."

"You mean Craig? The widower she met at the benefit? He seemed like a real sweetheart."

Frances's scowl deepened. "He's ten years younger than she is," she huffed. "And Bess has never even met his family!"

Leigh tried hard not to grin. "Well, she is in her sixties. And she has been married three times already."

"All the more proof," Frances proclaimed, "that her judgment concerning the opposite sex is sadly lacking. Now, do you know how to work this thing?"

Leigh lifted the equipment out of the trunk and settled it on her hip. "Sort of. I'm sure I can figure it out."

"Do that," Frances ordered, slamming her trunk lid closed. "You should hide the camera itself, then put up signs all around your property, informing potential intruders that it will be under constant surveillance. You need any help with that?"

"Um, no," Leigh said quickly. "But thanks for offering."

"One other thing," Frances said gravely. "Bess insisted on my giving you this." She dug a small white envelope out of her handbag and handed it over.

Leigh looked at it with raised eyebrows. The flap of the envelope was sealed with actual wax, in which Bess had scratched all her initials, including her middle, maiden, and three married surnames: BMMGRC.

Frances' eyes rolled. "Such nonsense over secrecy! Really, my sister can be the most irritating person sometimes."

Leigh tucked the envelope into a back pocket.

Frances's jaws clenched. "Well, aren't you going to open it?"

"I will later," Leigh replied. "Thanks for the camera. If Bess calls, tell her I promise to use it."

"If Bess calls while shacking up with yet another unsuitable man," Frances muttered, moving to get into the driver's seat of her car, "I'll have a few *other* things to say to her. Of all the..."

Leigh waved and set off down the sidewalk. As soon as her mother was out of sight, she put down the equipment, pulled out the card, and opened the envelope.

Sorry, kiddo, her aunt had written in beautiful, flowery cursive. *I've got nothing to say. Just wanted to mess with Francie. Ha! Take care.*

Leigh laughed out loud and picked the camera equipment back up off the pavement.

Whatever stress her family gave her, thank goodness it could also take away.

The sun was still high in the sky, presiding over an inappropriately gorgeous and carefree-seeming autumn day, when Leigh returned to the scene of… whatever it was that had happened to Lester. But this time, she was not alone. She was not even close to alone.

"Where do you want this?" Warren asked as he walked by her side, toting Bess's camera and tripod.

Leigh considered. "At the edge of the Brown's property, I think. Hidden in their woods and aiming toward Archie's tool shed. I'll ask Emma about it later—I'm sure she won't mind."

"I can help you set it up, Dad," Ethan offered. "Aunt Bess showed me how to do it—I've helped her move it around a bunch of times already."

"Maybe we'll catch somebody digging!" said Lenna with enthusiasm, even as her blue eyes radiated apprehension.

Leigh squelched a sigh. She doubted that Cara's shrinking violet of a daughter wanted to be anywhere near a known site of criminal mayhem—past, present, or future. But Leigh had wanted to show Lydie the layout of Frog Hill Farm, Warren had insisted on accompanying the women, and Allison and Mathias had vociferously demanded the right to help look for the missing mother dog and pups. Good-natured Ethan had offered to stay at the house with Lenna if she didn't want to go, but the girl's ego had ultimately chided her into denying her fear, resulting in a parade of three adults, four children, a camera, and a metal detector that was certain to provide prime fodder for Adith Rhodis' afternoon binocular viewing.

The metal detector had been an unexpected add-on. "What exactly do you plan to do with that thing, Mathias?" Leigh inquired. The device had been a Christmas present from his parents, and she had seen him toying around with it pretty regularly back in the spring, during which he had found a handful of coins, one old pocket watch, and a whole lot of trash. His suddenly renewed interest in the device disconcerted her.

The boy shrugged. "Oh, you never know."

His blue-green eyes, so like his mother's, slid over surreptitiously to meet Allison's brown ones. The two children exchanged an unmistakable look of conspiracy.

Leigh's blood pressure kicked up a notch. "Warren," she said quietly. "Keep an eye on them, would you?"

Her husband's eyes caught hers with equal understanding. "Will do."

"No one is going down in the cellar besides Aunt Lydie and me," Leigh reiterated to the Pack. "You guys stay close to your dad-slash-uncle and don't get out of sight, even for a second. Got it?"

The children nodded impatiently, then moved a few feet away into a private huddle. Leigh noted that Allison carried a pen and note pad.

"I said I'll watch them," Warren repeated, placing a soothing hand on her taut shoulder. "You and Lydie go see what you need to see so we can all get the heck out of here."

Leigh nodded in agreement. She turned to Lydie, only to discover that her aunt had already taken off without her in the direction of the farmhouse. Leigh caught up to find her aunt circling the house's foundation, consumed with obvious interest.

"It's constructed very much like Cara's," Lydie proclaimed as she moved. "Stone foundation, wood frame structure. Cara's was built in 1907, and I'd guess the same for this one, give or take a few years. The Carrs would have built it themselves, then?"

Leigh searched her memory banks for the details of her conversation with Harvey. "I think so. In nineteen-O-something."

Lydie nodded. "The barn would have been built around the same time." She moved to the far side of the house and threw a dismissive look at the garage. "Recent," she proclaimed. "As for the barn—"

"Something going on here?" Boomed a voice from behind them.

Leigh whirled to see Joe O'Malley hastening down Archie's driveway toward them, his son Scotty trotting at his side. Scotty was grinning from ear to ear. His father was not. Dressed in his usual wardrobe of faded workpants and a wifebeater, Joe was unshaven and scowling.

He was also carrying his trusty shotgun.

If Leigh didn't know the man better, she might have run screaming into the hills. But since sighting Joe O'Malley without a gun was only slightly more common than sighting him with one, she did not take his armed state as signifying any mood out of the ordinary. Nevertheless, she cast a glance over her shoulder toward the children, and was gratified to see that they were both close to Warren and well out of the way.

"No," Leigh answered pleasantly. "We've just come to see if the mother dog has returned. All of the commotion this morning seems to have frightened her away."

"Just as well," Joe grunted. "Don't need no rabid dogs around here. Got enough problems in this accursed neighborhood."

"Accursed?" Leigh inquired. Joe didn't ask to be introduced to her aunt, and she didn't offer.

Joe's scowl deepened. "Hell, yeah. Lived here ten years now, been putting up with this damned nonsense the whole time. Archie's taking off is just one more thing. Guy I bought my place from told me this here farm was haunted, and I thought he was a loon. But there's *something* messed up going on out here, that's for damned sure. Noises, lights—"

"They're orbs, Daddy!" Scotty piped up excitedly.

Joe's eyes flickered over his son with a mixture of skepticism and pride. "My boy says he sees things. And my boy ain't a liar."

Scotty looked toward the area downstream where the Pack were, and his eyes took on a sudden sparkle. "Hey! Allison's here!"

He took off at a run.

Leigh squelched a strong urge to snatch the child by the collar and hogtie him to the porch railing.

"My wife saw cops crawling all over this place this morning," Joe continued, his voice turning more sober as his son moved out of earshot. "She called over to the Brown's, and Nora told her Lester had passed out while he was over at Archie's, and that you found him. That true?"

Leigh nodded. She cast a glance over Joe's shoulder toward the O'Malley's, and noted that although trees blocked a direct view from house to house, his wife no doubt would have seen police cars coming and going on the drive and the officers walking about on the grounds.

"Then why all the cops?" he questioned.

"It wasn't clear at first what happened to Lester," Leigh explained carefully. "So when I called for an ambulance, they sent the police out. It's routine."

Joe's gray eyes searched hers for a moment. He grunted. "That's what they always say. 'Routine.' Nothing routine about a man taking off and leaving his dog and everything he owns, that's what I say. Something's going on out here. And I don't like it."

Leigh spied some rare common ground. "Neither do I," she agreed.

"I believe the boy sees lights out here," Joe said slowly. "But I don't believe in no ghosts. That's what they want you to think. They want you to tell people you see floating lights and spooky Civil War figures creeping around, just so no one will believe you—so they'll think *you're* the crazy one. They're clever that way. But I got their number."

He adjusted his hold on his shotgun—an unconscious gesture Leigh could have done without seeing.

"They?" she repeated meekly.

He bestowed her with a tolerant, protective look. "You know who *they* is, don't you?"

Leigh's mind skittered through the likely possibilities. What was popular with the conspiracy theorists these days? Federal agents were always a good bet. But there were other possibilities. Communists? Aliens? Marauding gangs of hoodlums? Anarchists? Devil-worshippers? Second-rate Elvis impersonators?

Leigh played it safe and shook her head.

Joe leaned in close to her ear. "Damned IRS," he whispered.

Bingo.

"Leigh, dear," Lydie said sweetly. "We should finish up out here, soon. I've got to get back and take my medicine."

Joe straightened up and took a step back.

Leigh threw her aunt—whom she knew perfectly well was not on any medication—an appreciative look. "Yes, of course." She turned her attention back to Joe. "Thanks for helping out with the search for Archie," she praised. "We all want him home safe."

Joe assumed an avuncular air. "Yes, sirree. Don't you ladies worry—I'm keeping an eye on this place myself from now on. The whole neighborhood."

Fabulous. "That's a comfort," Leigh lied. "But you should know that I'll be coming by regularly to put food out for the dog. So please don't shoot me!"

She kept her tone teasing, but there was no answering sparkle in the man's eyes. He seemed to consider a moment.

"Maybe you should wear a hunter's vest," he advised. "Just to be on the safe side."

Leigh's response stuck in her throat.

"Come on, dear," Lydie coaxed, grabbing her arm and smiling a plastic smile. "We need to be moving along!"

Joe gave a nod of farewell and turned around. Much to Leigh's relief, he then whistled for Scotty to join him as he headed back toward his own house.

"Charming man," Lydie declared as they rounded the back side of the farmhouse. "How that type manages to procreate in a post-cave world is a mystery to me. And speaking of mysteries," she continued, changing topics smoothly, "you're right about the map being hopelessly inaccurate. The barn should have been drawn in. It's almost certainly the same age as the house."

"And the tool shed?" Leigh inquired, keeping an eye out over her shoulder for any sudden recurrence of her trigger-happy neighbor.

"Also left off the map," Lydie agreed. "Let me see how old it looks."

As Lydie prowled around the unimpressive looking structure, Leigh screwed up her courage and withdrew her flashlight from her pocket. The bag of premium dog food was still down in the cellar. All she had to do was bring it and the water pails up, and then she would be done with the place. She threw a look at Warren, who was watching her from the edge of the woods fifty yards or so away. Lenna and Ethan were up on the hill in the trees, calling for the mother dog in all sorts of imaginative (and clearly counterproductive) ways. Allison stood motionless on the edge of the woods, holding out her pad and pen and watching as Mathias walked in short, straight lines with his metal detector.

What were they up to? Leigh had a sudden image of the crumbling remains of Theodore Carr, buried all too hurriedly in a shallow grave, his rotted wooden coffin a mere yard beneath

Mathias's feet…

Cut it out.

The children were hunting for treasure, not bodies.

She summoned her willpower once more and stepped through the open cellar doors to the stairway beneath, shining her flashlight before her. To her comfort, her Aunt Lydie soon fell into step behind her.

"This is interesting," Lydie commented.

"What's interesting?" Leigh asked, relaxing slightly as each step down revealed more of the cellar to be vacant. When at last she reached the bottom step and confirmed that she and Lydie were the only occupants, her shoulders slumped with relief.

"This cellar," Lydie answered, walking immediately to the nearest wall and running a finger along the stone. "The shed up top isn't as old as the barn, but this foundation is quite old. Perhaps it started out as a root cellar."

"You mean, a separate place to store food?"

"That's right," Lydie explained. "Before refrigeration, most everyone had them. Still," she said speculatively, walking around the room's perimeter. "It's quite a large one. Larger than the building that's on top of it now. Did you notice?"

Leigh had not. What she did notice now, and what shot a pang of angst straight through her heart, was a spot on the far wall that seemed to be missing something. Notably, a good bit of mortar.

She stepped closer and shone her flashlight directly on it.

"Ho there," Lydie protested. "You're leaving me in the dark, dear."

"Sorry," Leigh said, swinging the beam back into Lydie's path until she joined Leigh at the wall. "But look at this. Someone has been chiseling the mortar around this rock."

Lydie ran a finger in the groove to the left of the large, rectangular stone—the largest in the wall. Below the hole, on the dirt floor, lay a distinct pile of lighter-colored dust. "Indeed," Lydie agreed. "But not just here. Look over that way."

Leigh moved the beam across the wall and sighed. So much for thinking that their treasure hunters were actually honing in on their target. The mortar was chipped away in any number of places. One fist-sized stone near the stairs had been removed completely, then set back in. Leigh pulled it out and looked behind it, but there was nothing to see except more hard-packed, naturally rocky dirt, no different in texture or composition than the floor.

"You know, Aunt Lydie," she said dispiritedly, "I don't think anybody knows what the hell that map is pointing to. Including whomever is responsible for Archie's disappearance. *If* the two things are even related."

"You may be right," Lydie said thoughtfully. "But just the same, I'd like to have another look at that map sometime, if you don't mind."

"Be my guest," Leigh answered. "It's back at the house." She handed her flashlight to Lydie, then walked over to the dog's water pails and emptied their remaining contents onto the ground. She then picked up the bag of food and set it on a hip, grabbed the empty pails with the opposite hand, and headed up the stairs.

Good riddance, creepy cellar, she thought to herself, secretly hoping that the mother dog would not in fact return here, but would find herself another shelter nearby—something with a less unnerving aura.

No sooner had Leigh reached the top of the stairs than small fingers clasped the pail handles and tugged them out of her hand. "I'll refill the buckets, Mom," Allison said sweetly, turning away with haste and skipping toward the house.

Warren appeared a few seconds later, the other three children trailing behind him.

Leigh set down the bag and threw him a questioning glance. "How long did she—"

"Ninety seconds, give or take," he said with remorse. "Sorry, I tried. She slipped over just as Lenna tripped on a rock and cried out."

"Did Lenna really trip over a rock?"

Warren's eyebrows arched. "I don't think I want to know."

"I'll help her carry the water," Lydie offered, handing Leigh back the flashlight and heading after Allison.

"Were either of you saying anything... hazardous?" Warren inquired.

Leigh thought back as she watched Allison reach the house and turn on the spigot. The other children were rapidly approaching from the opposite direction. "I don't think so," she answered. The conversation with her aunt, whatever its details, had certainly not enlightened *her* in any way. But with Allison, one never knew.

"No sign of the mother dog or puppies, Mom," Ethan reported. "But Matt found a screw."

Mathias grimaced. "Yeah. Another epic find. Next Christmas I'm asking for the kind that goes deeper. Like... eight, ten feet. *That* would be cool."

"Ooh," Lenna squealed. "Would that find bodies?"

Matt's eyes met Ethan's for only a second, but Leigh caught the tell.

Holy crap. They *were* looking for Theodore!

"Metal detectors can't find bodies, dork!" Mathias snapped. "They find *metal.*"

Lenna's blue eyes grew instantly apologetic. "Oh, right."

"She knew that," Ethan piped up quickly, grabbing Lenna by the elbow and urging her off toward Allison. "Let's help with the water."

In a blink, they were gone.

Mathias lifted his chin and stood his ground, looking uncannily like his self-assured, self-made father, Gil. "That girl says the dumbest things sometimes," he lamented. "Using a metal detector to find a grave. Sheesh! You want me to put some of that food out by the woods, Aunt Leigh?"

Methinks thou doth protest too much.

Leigh picked up the food bowl that Lydie had brought from the cellar and handed it to him, along with the bag. "Sure," she answered. "Go ahead and fill up the bowl, but bring the rest of the bag back. Otherwise the raccoons will clean us out."

"Sure thing," the boy answered, leaving his metal detector and heading off with pride.

Leigh's eyes met her husband's. "Did you see the look—"

"Oh, yeah," he answered.

Leigh didn't doubt his response. Warren always could read her mind. "What do you think the Pack were—"

He cut her off with a quick kiss and an arm around her shoulders. "Seriously, Leigh. Do you really want to know?"

She let out a long, tortured sigh—one that had undoubtedly been shared by countless parents of precocious tweens since the dawn of humankind.

"Hell, no," she replied.

Chapter 13

The parade of people started walking back toward Leigh's house along the creek, and Leigh was surprised when they reached the bridge at the Browns' to see that Adith was not in attendance on the deck. She was even more surprised to see Harvey on the back lawn, walking slowly toward them and hailing her with an outstretched hand and a smile.

"I don't think I've ever seen him outside the house before," Warren commented, putting her own thought into words.

Leigh shook her head. Although Harvey moved about more easily than his frail appearance suggested he could, the farthest she'd ever seen him away from his books and his cat was the front porch. "He probably just wants to ask me more questions about the map," she replied. "But I should see what he wants."

"Should I wait?" Warren asked, casting an anxious glance back toward Archie's place.

Leigh smiled at her husband's attempt at protectiveness. They both knew that when it came to physical danger, he spoiled for a confrontation about as much as Lenna did.

Still, the gesture was sweet.

Leigh assured him she would stay on the Brown's property and then walk home by the road, and Warren, Lydie, and the kids set off without her. She walked uphill and met Harvey in the middle of the Brown's backyard, where he had stopped to rest by Lester's hammock.

"Hello Ms.—I mean Leigh," he corrected. "Lovely day today, isn't it?"

Leigh nodded, although she could not help wondering if, on an average day, Harvey had any idea what was happening in the world outside his room. His lack of interest in the great outdoors was further evidenced by the fact that the giant sweater engulfing his torso clearly belonged to Lester.

"I have a message for you from Adith," he said pleasantly. "She's asleep at the moment, but she wanted me to tell you that she saw the dog you were taking care of."

Leigh's eyebrows rose. "Wiley, or the stray mother dog?"

"The stray," he replied. "The little white one. Adith said she saw her midmorning, pacing around at the edge of the woods. She might have gone back into the tool shed, but Adith couldn't see."

Leigh smiled. "That's good news! I hoped she hadn't gone far. She should get the food we left out, then."

"That's fortunate," Harvey said politely.

"Is Adith having trouble staying awake again?" Leigh asked, not really needing an answer. With everything that was going on in the neighborhood, she knew that Adith would otherwise be out on the deck, binoculars and popcorn in hand, 24/7.

Harvey nodded. "Emma keeps trying to adjust her schedule so she'll be sleepy at night, but the medication seems to affect her differently every time. Last night she was up until the wee hours. By noon she couldn't keep her eyes open, even though she kept saying she wanted to talk to you the minute you got back from church."

The wee hours? Leigh made a mental note. Had Adith seen or heard Lester leave the house?

"But I must confess," Harvey said soberly, "I have my own reasons for wanting to speak with you."

Leigh steeled herself.

"You wouldn't happen to have a copy of that map handy, would you?" he asked hopefully.

Leigh shook her head. "Sorry. I haven't spoken with the police yet." *At least not about that.*

To her surprise, Harvey shook his head. "It doesn't much matter," he said gravely. "The fact that it exists is enough." He paused a moment, scanning the horizon in every direction with pale, troubled eyes. A gust of wind ruffled the crown of white hair behind his ears, and he pulled Lester's sweater tighter around him. "I've been thinking, you see. About how that map came to be lying on the ground."

His eyes moved to hold hers. "Emma has called a couple of times today. She told Nora about an hour ago that Lester's fever is down and his confusion seems to have cleared up. He says that he couldn't sleep last night and went outside for a walk because it was cooler. He heard some sounds coming from the tool shed and decided to check on the mother dog. The next thing he knew, he was lying on a stretcher with paramedics hovering over him."

"I see," Leigh replied tonelessly, studying her shoes.

"I don't believe that story," Harvey said flatly.

Leigh looked back up at him with surprise. "You don't?"

Harvey shook his head. "I think that Lester dropped that map. I think that he and Archie were looking for something together before Archie disappeared. And now, for whatever reason, Lester has gotten even more desperate to find it."

Leigh sucked in a long, slow breath. "That's what I think, too," she admitted.

"What I'm trying to figure out," Harvey continued, "is who *else* has the same map."

"I gave the police the copy the children found," Leigh explained. "I made more copies of it beforehand, though, to hang onto myself."

"You keep them with you, then," he said sternly. "Extras will only confuse the picture."

Leigh studied his troubled face. "Tell me what you're thinking," she urged.

Harvey nodded. "If the item Archie and Lester were seeking is indeed a valuable Civil War relic, it must have come from Theodore Carr. So therefore did the map. The question is, how would a map made by Theodore wind up in Archie's hands? If Carr made the map to preserve the item for his descendants, he would have given it to his son or daughter, and it would then have passed down through the family. But Archie is in no way related to Theodore Carr. I can assure you of that from my genealogical studies."

Leigh caught the drift. "Then at some point, someone in the family must have given a copy of the map away to a friend, or sold it, or something."

"The copy that fell into Archie's hands, yes," Harvey speculated. "It could have passed through several pairs of hands, and probably did, if the history of the farm being 'haunted' since the fifties is true."

"It is," Leigh assured. She gave a brief summary of Dora's story, which Harvey listened to with rapt attention. "Adith told me something about that visit," he said wryly, "but her story bore little resemblance to yours."

Leigh grinned. "I expect not. Focused on the orbs, did it?"

Harvey harrumphed. "My point is, if we could determine who else might have a copy of that map, we will also know who else might be searching for the treasure."

Leigh's expression darkened. "And who might be determined to keep Archie and Lester from finding it first."

Harvey nodded gravely.

Leigh tensed. "You really think it could be the hat of General Armistead?"

At her words, Harvey's eyes blazed with an internal fire. "I can't express to you how valuable such a treasure would be to the faithful. I've been doing some reading since our last chat. The hat would be of gray wool felt, what they call a slouch hat. It would have had a wreath insignia and been worn with officer's cords. I read one account, based on an enlisted man's journal, that claims the general wore two ladies' hatpins hidden under the brim, one to honor each of his late wives. And of course, the genuine article would probably have a hole in the top crown, where the sword punctured through."

Tiny beads of sweat formed on Harvey's brow. Leigh hoped it was from mere excitement and that he wasn't catching Lester's flu, although seeing physical evidence of the man's ardor on the topic was almost as disconcerting.

"It's unlikely such a treasure could have survived in good condition," Harvey said at last, lightening his tone a little. "It would have to be very well preserved. Air tight, without humidity. Not easy to do, perhaps. Never mind the ample evidence we already have that Theodore was not in his right mind when he died."

"But it could have been the son," Leigh pointed out. "Tom Carr could have made the map and buried his father's hat."

Harvey considered a moment. The thought seemed new to him. "I suppose so," he mused. "But why? We know that Theodore suffered from dementia and paranoia; it makes sense that he would hide the hat from whatever imaginary threats he perceived. But would his son feel the same inclination?"

"According to Dora," Leigh explained, "Theodore and Tom were both a little off their rockers at the end. Tom could have been just as convinced the government was out to steal their prize, or UFOs, or the ghosts of Confederates past… whatever."

Harvey nodded. "Good point."

"I just hope," Leigh continued, her thoughts turning suddenly macabre, "that Thomas didn't bury the hat *with* his father."

Harvey's bushy white eyebrows rose. "You mean... in a cemetery?"

"No," Leigh answered. "On Frog Hill Farm. According to Dora, Theodore was buried there."

"I never heard that!" Harvey exclaimed. "I'm sure Archie would have mentioned it."

"He might not know," Leigh replied. "Dora described a small, flat gravestone, but it's not there anymore. The kids have explored all through those woods and around the creek—there's no way they would have missed a gravestone."

"I suppose not," Harvey mused. "Such things are supposed to be disclosed when a property is sold, but... well, people don't always comply. It's possible." He pulled a handkerchief out of a pants pocket and dabbed at his forehead.

Leigh noted that, suddenly, he looked very tired. "Let me walk you back to the house," she offered.

Harvey complied. "I wish I thought the searching was all in good fun," he said, his voice growing feebler as he moved uphill. "An honest quest, if you will. But with Archie gone, and now Lester..." his sentence remained incomplete. He stopped a moment and looked at her. "I know that Lester is lying to the police. He even lied to me yesterday when I asked him, point blank, what he and Archie were up to. But I know why he did it—it's because he's scared. I've known Lester since he was a little boy; his father was a friend of mine. He and Archie are good men, Leigh. It might not seem like it under the circumstances, but I know that they are."

"I know that too," Leigh agreed. "And I think you're right... about everything. But that includes this being a potentially dangerous game. So please, don't feel like you have to do any more. I promise I'll make sure that the officers investigating the case know everything we've talked about. It's their job to sort it all out."

To her surprise, Harvey smiled at her wryly. "You didn't believe me when I first mentioned the hat. You thought it was an old man's nonsense. Are you sure the police won't think you're a little 'off your rocker' too?"

Leigh let out a chortle. "Of course they will. But I'm used to that."

As Leigh walked past Nora and Derrick Sullivan's house on her way home, her heart contracted with sympathy. The baby was crying again. Little Cory had cried as much as any newborn for the first month, but then the testy tyke had kicked it into serious overdrive. He was close to three months old now, and not only were the evening cry sessions still going strong, but he was often fussy all afternoon as well. Before she had kids of her own, Leigh would have blamed the parents. Surely they were doing *something* wrong?

Now she knew better. She also knew that Nora had already made an excessive number of visits to her pediatrician, certain that the baby must have some medical ailment. But happily, little Cory always checked out fine.

His parents, on the other hand, were probably getting close to the brink. Just as Leigh reached the corner of her own yard, the crying stopped, and she breathed easier. She wondered if Nora could hear the crying from inside the Brown's house—and hoped she could not. Listening from afar was probably worse than being there. Besides, Nora had a point. Derrick, like all new fathers, would be well served by some one-on-one time with his son.

Leigh entered her house to find the entirety of the Pack playing some incredibly noisy game in her basement. Cara and Gil were running late in their return from New York state and Lydie had pleaded some unspecified prior commitment, leaving Warren to supervise all four. He was accomplishing this by relaxing in his favorite armchair reading a paperback with a glittering purple light saber on its cover. Both their guest mutt and the resident corgi, energy temporarily depleted, slumbered at his feet.

All in all, it seemed a typical Sunday afternoon.

Leigh fidgeted with her phone, contemplating a call to Maura. She had no way of contacting the detectives from the General Investigations unit directly—she didn't even know who they were. Even if she did, she doubted the effort would bear fruit. The best way to deliver the new information was through Maura… who at least believed that a treasure hunt might be a possibility and who would know how to present the evidence so the theory didn't sound quite so ridiculous. But should she do that *now?*

Maura's husband Gerry was due back from his trip this afternoon. Leigh glanced at her watch. Any minute, actually. Which would make her timing maximally terrible.

She sighed and walked to the front windows. There was no emergency. Not really. Lester was safe in the hospital. No one would be going back under the tool shed—at least not this afternoon. She would give Maura a little more time with her husband, then call her later tonight. The detective probably wouldn't pass along the info until the next morning anyway.

"Warren," Leigh announced without enthusiasm. "I'm going to my brainstorming hammock. Those pottery crocks aren't going to promote themselves."

Warren nodded. "May The Force go with you."

Leigh's eyes rolled. "As always."

"And don't leave the yard."

She offered a salute.

"I mean it, Leigh," he said seriously, lowering the book. "If I look out those back windows and you've mysteriously disappeared, I'm picking up the phone."

"You'd call Maura?"

"No," he answered, his tone grave. "I'd call your mother."

Leigh scowled. "That's dirty pool."

A devilish grin played on his lips. "Indeed."

No sooner had Leigh crawled into her hammock, closed her eyes, and started thinking about pottery crocks than she heard it again.

Baby Cory was screaming his lungs out.

She put her hands over her ears and swayed the hammock.

Look what's new in ancient pottery crockware!

Absolutely nothing.

This isn't your great-grandmother's pottery!

She peed in hers.

It's not just for King Tut anymore!

Even you can be buried with it.

Leigh groaned out loud and opened her eyes. The hammock wasn't helping. Neither was the crying baby. She could stand it no more.

She marched back into her house, informed Warren of her intentions, walked out through the front, crossed her lawn to the

Sullivan's house, and rapped on their door.

After a long wait, the door swung slowly open.

Nora's husband Derrick peered out, holding the door with one hand while using the other to balance his infant son on his shoulder. His typical button-down office shirt was liberally covered with a spit-up rag, which was liberally covered with spit-up. His black slacks seemed to have taken the worst of the eruption, making him look like a reverse Dalmatian.

A very sad, very tired Dalmatian who was lost, confused, and about to wander in front of a speeding truck.

Leigh smiled. "Never fear," she proclaimed. "Help is here."

Derrick blinked at her from behind oversized glasses that magnified his bloodshot eyeballs. The man was nice enough, but Leigh had yet to run into him when she had not in some way been reminded of a rodent. It wasn't just that he suffered from a prominent overbite, which he did, but that he had a curious way of walking with his shoulders hunched and his hands flailing in front of him. It was almost as if he were working at a computer—even when he wasn't.

"Help?" he repeated, dazed.

Leigh clapped her hands together and held them out, talking loud enough for her voice to carry over the continued caterwauling. "I'd love to entertain little Cory for a while. I know Nora's still working and let's face it—you need a break. I am the mother of twins, one of which screamed for most of her infancy. The fact that's she alive and well now and I am not in prison should tell you that I'm eminently qualified for the task."

"Oh," he responded, a light apparently dawning. Slowly. "Oh, that's nice. Thanks."

If Leigh didn't know that the man was employed as a systems analyst, a job requiring no small amount of analytical brainpower, she might be inclined to question his mental acumen. But she knew better than to judge any parent in the throes of sleep deprivation.

Derrick turned and gestured for her to follow him back into the house. She complied, shutting the door behind her.

The room looked like it had been struck by a white and blue tornado. Every surface was covered with baby blankets, baby toys, baby towels, and baby spit-up. It smelled of sour milk and one particularly ripe diaper that was balanced on top of Derrick's printer, apparently having never completed its journey to the covered step-pail in the corner.

Leigh fought back a grin. The room was actually quite well appointed and fundamentally clean... she suspected it had looked much different when Nora left this morning.

Derrick flitted about the room, picking up various towels and blankets from off the furniture, inspecting each with a grimace, then setting it back down again.

Leigh stepped over to the baby's changing table, opened the cabinet door beneath, and pulled out a clean burp cloth. She threw it over her shoulder and held out her hands once more.

"Seriously," she coaxed. "I'd love to watch him for a while. Why don't you take a walk, or a drive to the convenience store? Get some air?" She looked at her watch. "Nora's relief person is due at the Brown's in half an hour. I can stay here till she gets home, if you like."

Derrick's eyes widened. "Oh, no!" he said nervously. "I can't be gone when she gets back. She'd kill me! Look at this place!" Even as he spoke he gently handed over little Cory, whose cries quieted to whining wails at the transfer.

Leigh held the infant in a firm cuddle that had, at one time, been as natural to her as breathing. The baby stopped crying and stared at her.

"How did you do that?" Derrick asked with wonder.

"Don't feel bad," she assured. "It won't last. This is just the novelty phase. He'll start squalling again in a minute. But that's okay. Par for the course."

Derrick took a deep breath and looked around. "Maybe if I just... would you mind holding him while I clean up a bit?"

"Absolutely."

The new father proceeded to stumble around the room, picking up various soiled linens and moving them to other places with no apparent plan in mind. "Have you," he began uncertainly, "heard any more news about Archie?"

Leigh sighed. "I'm afraid not. But I have a friend who's a homicide detective with the county, and I'm hoping she'll light a fire under the investigators pretty soon. I have my doubts about how aggressively they've been looking for him. To them, of course, Archie is an adult of sound mind who has every right to take off without telling anybody."

Derrick frowned. "I suppose so. But still, it doesn't sound like him."

"No," Leigh agreed. "It doesn't. Did—" she cut herself off. She had been about to ask, "Did you know him well?" But the past tense was not acceptable. "Do you know him well?" she amended.

Derrick gave the slightest of shrugs. "I don't get out in the neighborhood much. But I've been to a few meetings of the reenactors."

Leigh glanced idly about the room, half expecting to see more Civil War paintings and memorabilia hung around. But all of the couple's framed pictures were inexpensive prints of landscapes and flowers. "So Archie gave you the bug, too?"

"Excuse me?" Derrick had managed to gather most of the soiled linens into a pile in the center of the floor, but the last few rags seemed to allude him.

Leigh surreptitiously grabbed the one nearest her and added it to the stack. "I mean, did Archie get you interested in the Civil War, or were you already a fan?"

"Oh," he responded, picking up the pile of linens and dropping two. "Not really. I mean, I've always thought history was interesting." He returned in a moment with a plastic trash bag, which he shook open and proceeded to carry around the room filling with crumpled tissues, pop cans, and the occasional used baby wipe.

"Archie tried to convince Warren he looked like General McClellan," Leigh said with a laugh. "But trying to recruit my husband for a reenactment in an itchy wool uniform is a lost cause. Unless it involves the Starship Enterprise, of course."

Derrick laughed out loud—or at least, Leigh thought it was a laugh. It sounded more like a snorting seal. "Oh, that would be funny," Derrick replied, walking past the dirty diaper on the printer for the fourth time. "Now, wearing *those* costumes would be fun."

The question of itchy wool coat versus shiny spandex pajamas seemed like a toss-up to Leigh. But as her husband so frequently reminded her, she was *not* one of the faithful.

Her novelty had evidently worn off. Little Cory started to cry again. She shifted him into a new position and started moving. "So… how many of the events have you participated in?"

Derrick looked at her blankly.

"The reenactments, I mean," she clarified. The baby cried louder.

"Oh. None of the big stuff," he answered. "I was too busy for Antietam. But the Perryopolis Parade is coming up pretty soon."

"Oh?" Leigh said politely, slipping into the adjacent bathroom and wetting a clean rag with cool water. As she began gently sponging the baby's face, his cries ceased. "What do the reenactors do in the parade?"

Derrick shrugged again. "Just march and stuff, I guess." He was watching her intently. "Hey, that's a neat trick! He likes that."

"Just a distraction," Leigh explained. "You have to keep varying your tactics."

Derrick continued his marginal efforts at cleaning up, and for a few minutes, Leigh tended to the baby in silence. Eventually Derrick managed to get the dirty linens corralled and had parked them and the half-full bag of trash by the door to the kitchen. He stood still a moment, then threw Leigh a pointed look. "I was wondering... have you heard any more about how Lester's doing? Nora said he'd probably have to stay in the hospital overnight."

"You know as much as I do, then," Leigh responded.

Derrick's chin lowered. His hands fidgeted with the drawstrings of the trash bag. "He's a really nice guy, Lester," he said awkwardly. "Archie, too. I hope they're both okay."

Leigh could stand it no longer. She stepped over to the printer, picked up the dirty diaper, and deposited it in Derrick's bag.

He appeared not to notice.

Nora, my dear, Leigh thought to herself. *Your husband is one odd duck.*

Then again, who in this neighborhood wasn't?

"I hope so too," she agreed.

Chapter 14

Leigh's living room was dark, illuminated only by the flickering static on the TV that represented the inactive camera feed. The kids were getting ready for bed and Warren had retired uncharacteristically early in anticipation of a long drive to meet a new client the next morning. Leigh alternated between staring at the static and staring at her phone. Should she call Maura, or wait until tomorrow? The detective had asked to be informed. Perhaps a text would be better?

She wondered what was going on in the Frank-Polanski household. She and Warren were both quite certain that Gerry would welcome his wife's news, however unexpected. Still, Leigh feared that any reaction less than sheer, unbridled enthusiasm on his part would send her friend into a complete tailspin. Never mind that handling violence, corpses, murderers, and criminally insane lunatics was all in a day's work for Maura. Facing a first, unplanned pregnancy at forty-two? *That* was scary.

Leigh jumped as her phone rang in her palm. She checked the number.

It was Emma Brown's cell.

"Emma!" she greeted, her pulse beginning to race. "Is everything okay?"

"As well as could be expected, I suppose," the usually merry voice said tiredly. "Lester's asleep, finally. I'm going to leave here and head home in a minute—I've got a friend picking me up. But I'm coming back first thing tomorrow."

"How is Lester?"

"He says he's fine. But then, he's a man." She let out a sigh. "Nothing scary showed up on the tests, and they're saying his concussion is mild. They don't think he was unconscious very long after he hit his head; more likely, he was delirious with fever and just drifting in and out of sleep when you found him. He was pretty dehydrated—never mind how much I pushed the fluids at him."

So, Leigh thought with chagrin, *no one is even considering the possibility of assault.* And why should they, with Lester lying about the whole incident?

Maybe she was wrong. Maybe he did pass out first and hit his head second. She certainly wished that were the case.

"The police questioned him?" Leigh inquired.

"Just a bit," Emma replied. "It looked a little fishy, you know, him being on Archie's property when it happened. But he explained all that."

"Was it just the local police who questioned him?" Leigh continued, worrying even as she spoke that she was pressing too much, "or the county investigators working on Archie's case?"

There was a pause. "I think it was the locals," Emma said uncertainly. "Why?"

Stupid running mouth. "I was just wondering if anyone thought there was a connection to Archie's case. But obviously not." Leigh made an attempt to sound cheerful, reassuring. She did not want to alarm Emma further.

Emma didn't answer for a moment. "Well, I'm calling because Lester made me promise I would. He wants to see you, Leigh. I don't know why—he wouldn't tell me. Well, he did tell me, but it was some nonsense about him needing to tell you how to feed Wiley. Like that mutt wouldn't eat dirty shoe leather! By the way, somebody did feed him today, didn't they?"

Leigh assured her that the Pack was spoiling the dog rotten. "Did Lester want me to come to the hospital?" she asked, her heart still thumping.

"He did," Emma responded. "But I told him no way was I asking you to drive out tonight, and that he needed his rest. Of course he argued with me, but then he fell asleep anyhow. I was thinking he'd be discharged tomorrow morning, but the last doctor that was in here said maybe not—it will depend on whether his fever goes back up. Lester wanted to call you, but they won't let him talk on the phone, or watch television, or anything like that. Still, he's determined to see you tomorrow whether he goes home or not. I told him I'd ask you just to settle his mind."

"I'd be happy to come," Leigh said quickly, mentally revising her schedule so that she could work from home tomorrow. Being a founding partner in an advertising agency did have its perks. "Just tell me when would be a good time, and I'll be there."

Emma said that she would call tomorrow and let Leigh know; only when they were about to hang up did Leigh remember the camera. But how could she ask Emma's permission without upsetting her? A thought struck.

"Well, of course that's all right with me!" Emma replied to her request. "I hope the dog shows up and the kids can figure out where she's got that litter stashed. It's too bad that Lester scared her away like that. But at least the weather's warm, and there's been no rain."

Leigh agreed. The women exchanged pleasantries and hung up.

The television screen flickered suddenly to life. An image of the tool shed in the distance appeared. In the foreground, something moved, then disappeared again. Leigh leaned forward, eyes wide.

Come back!

The figure moved onto the left side of the screen.

"Oh," Allison said with disappointment. "It's just a deer."

Leigh startled. Her daughter was standing behind her chair, not ten inches from her ear. Clad in a cotton nightshirt with running mustangs gracing its front, Allison hopped around and plopped herself down in front of the TV. "We can actually look for the dog if you want," she said pleasantly, with just the slightest trace of a smirk.

Leigh bit back a retort. She really hated getting caught in a lie—even a white one—by a child she tried so hard to teach *not* to tell lies.

Especially white ones.

Explaining to Allison that she had been trying to keep Emma from getting unnecessarily upset on an already trying day would only add fuel to the fire, given that "I thought it might upset you" was Allison's favorite excuse for her own infuriating omissions of fact.

"We *are* looking for the dog," Leigh said firmly.

Allison merely smiled.

They watched together a moment as not one, but four deer stepped out of the woods and began to graze on Archie's lawn. The sight would have been entrancing if it weren't something all the neighbors saw in broad daylight on a daily basis. Archie liked to joke about how he'd once driven three and a half hours up to Potter

County to go hunting on the Wildcat Trail and didn't see a single deer all day, then drove back home to find six of them in his driveway.

"Mom?" Allison asked tentatively. "Are you going to talk to Aunt Mo about the map again?"

Leigh's pulse sped up. Clearly, pretending that the Pack in general and Allison in particular were capable of forgetting everything that had happened at Frog Hill Farm and going on their merry way was fantasy. Allison had always been like a dog with a bone, and finding a decades-old treasure map depicting her own backyard was prime rib.

Perhaps it was best not to fight it.

"Probably," Leigh answered, trying hard to keep her voice from sounding upset, even as her heart pounded against her ribs. "Is there something you think she should know?"

Allison looked thoughtful a moment. Then she scampered off to her room and returned with a copy of the map.

Leigh decided not to bother asking where she had gotten it, since Leigh had given the map the kids found to Maura and had kept her own copies carefully guarded ever since. No doubt the little minx had made and squirreled away multiple copies of her own before even allowing Lenna to show it to the adults.

"I'm not a hundred percent sure," Allison said seriously. "But I think it was Thomas Carr who made this map, not Theodore."

Leigh's eyebrows rose. "Oh? And why is that?"

Allison held out the map and pointed to an irregularly shaped blob drawn at the edge of the woods, downstream from the farmhouse. "There isn't anything else on the map drawn exactly like it," she explained. "And it's right about where Dora said Theodore Carr was buried. Which makes me think it's supposed to be a gravestone."

Leigh studied the tiny squiggle. Despite herself, she was impressed. "That does make sense," she acknowledged.

Allison beamed. "Dora said he was buried near a little willow tree, and there aren't any willows out there. But that doesn't mean anything—the tree could have been cut down, or just died. Mathias didn't find any metal either, but I told him he probably wouldn't. Theodore's casket was most likely made out of wood, so there wouldn't be anything to find unless he was buried with a belt buckle or a watch or something. Plus, Matt's detector doesn't go down very deep. Bodies are supposed to be—" she paused and looked up at Leigh's green face with alarm. "Are you okay, Mom?"

"I'm fine," Leigh forced out, trying really, *really* hard not to dwell on the fact that her ten-year-old daughter's idea of fun was to speculate on the precise location of a long-dead corpse. She swallowed. "You were saying?"

Allison released a small sigh. "It's not much to go on, I know. But since we were thinking that Theodore made the map, I thought it might be important for the police to know that it might not be that old, after all."

"I'm sure you're right."

Allison smiled and rose, folding the map carefully as she did so. "Okay, then. Goodnight, Mom."

She began to skip away, but Leigh stopped her with an outstretched arm. "Allison," she said gravely. "It's very important that no more copies of this map start circulating in the wild. You shouldn't show it to anyone. No one should know that *you* know anything whatsoever about it. You understand?"

The girl nodded.

"And what your father and I have already told you still stands. Under *no circumstances* are any of you to leave our yard or your Aunt Cara's without one of us present. Studying the map is fine. Watching the camera—from the living room—is fine. But your safety is more important to us than anything else involved here. You understand?"

Allison dutifully restrained from rolling her eyes. But Leigh could tell it was a struggle. "Yes, Mom," she answered.

The girl headed off to bed, and Leigh stared motionlessly at the television until the last deer moved out of range and the screen reverted to static again. She stared several more moments before getting up. *You're right, Aunt Bess,* she thought. *This thing is addictive.*

No sooner had she risen to her feet than her cell phone rang. She looked at the ID and picked up quickly. "Maura? How's it going?"

"It's not," the husky voice replied. "Listen, I can't talk long. Gerry's in the shower."

"He's... what? Did you tell him?"

There was a pause. Leigh could vaguely hear the sound of water running in the background.

"Not yet," came the response.

"Maura!"

"I know, I *know,*" the detective moaned. "But I couldn't. Not when I don't know crap about the tests. Tomorrow I'll know something. Then I'll tell him. It'll be better that way. Anyhow, I haven't heard from you in a while, and that usually means you're holding out on me. What's happening out there?"

Leigh released a heavy, pent-up breath. Then, as concisely as possible, she spilled the entire day's load, from finding an unconscious Lester to Allison's theories on the true origin of the treasure map. Surprisingly, the detective seemed eager to hear it. Or perhaps it wasn't so surprising—perhaps Maura was looking for a diversion from her own worrisome thoughts.

"From where I sit, it sounds like you're stacking up some pretty credible evidence, Koslow," she said at last. "Let me think about this. The guys at GI aren't going to pursue Lester's injury as a possible assault when he's saying himself that he was alone when he passed out. *Unless* they can see a motive for Lester to lie. You think you can convince him to come clean? At least about what he was doing down there? That alone should make them take another look at the possibility that Archie met foul play. Money is motive, period. Whether this 'treasure' is real or not doesn't mean jack—as long as the perp thinks it is."

Leigh allowed herself a smile. Good ol' WonderCop. They hadn't promoted her friend steadily up through the ranks for nothing. "I'm going to see him tomorrow, so I'll give it a shot," she promised. "What I'm really worried about, though, and I know it sounds crazy..."

"Yeah?" Maura prompted.

Leigh steeled herself. Some things she didn't like saying aloud. She twisted around to see if Allison were within earshot. She saw nothing. But that meant nothing. She moved quickly to the front door and stepped outside onto the porch.

"What if Archie was kidnapped by someone who wanted the treasure, but didn't know how to find it? Maybe their goal is to force him to find it. Or maybe they've already contacted Lester, and he's trying to find it to save Archie?"

Lester's feverish, mumbled words seemed imprinted in her brain. *I'm trying... I am, I'm trying... hang in there, Arch... I won't...*

don't worry...

"It's not impossible, Koslow," Maura answered. "Which means you should all act like it *is* possible. It's one thing to keep the Pack out of it, but you've got to be careful who you share information with, too. No one besides the police needs to know you have a map, much less that you have any idea what's going on with Lester, or you could be putting yourself at risk. Capiche?"

"Right," Leigh said weakly. How many people had she told so far? Only two outside the family that she could think of, and both were in their eighties.

Like *that* meant anything!

Harvey... Lester had mumbled, practically in the same breath. *He knows, Arch... He knows.*

What did Harvey know?

"Call me right after your talk with Lester tomorrow," Maura ordered. "Try to make him understand that he and Archie will both be safer if he cooperates with the police. You may be able to pick up something just from his vibe. Then I'll take a little walk over to General Investigations and make myself unpopular."

Leigh smiled once more. "Thanks, Maura. And by the way, you can come over here any time tomorrow to talk, if you want. I'll be working at home."

"Thanks," Maura said shortly, making Leigh wonder if Gerry were within earshot. The water had stopped running a while ago. "And by the way—where the hell are you?"

Leigh looked around in confusion. Then she heard the sound her brain must have been conveniently filtering out for a while now. Baby Cory was screaming again.

The time seemed less than opportune for a discussion of infant colic. "That's just the television," she assured.

"Oh," Maura answered skeptically. "Well, goodnight."

"Goodnight." Leigh hung up and pressed the phone to her side.

Another lie.

The parenting experts of the world would just have to forgive her.

Chapter 15

"I understand why you wanted me to go with you the last time you went to Archie's. Sort of," Cara said with a yawn, throwing a windbreaker on over her tee shirt and sleep pants. Leigh had come by immediately after the kids boarded the school bus; her cousin had not yet finished her morning coffee. "But I'm not getting why you need me now."

"Because," Leigh insisted. "I promised Warren I wouldn't go alone. And if he finds out otherwise, he's threatened to tell my mother about the maids."

Cara's eyes widened in mock alarm. "Oh, heavens! No!"

Leigh scowled. "You joke. But if my mother knew I spent so much as one penny of her grandchildren's inheritance paying somebody else to clean my house… even if it *is* my own earnings… you know perfectly well she'd—"

"Yes, yes," Cara held up a staying hand. "Spare me the blood and gore, please. I'd like to keep down my breakfast. But why does Warren not want you to go by yourself?"

Leigh took a breath and brought her cousin up to date on the events of the last forty-eight hours. It took a while. She talked while Cara located her shoes and secured Maggie the spaniel inside the house. She kept talking while they crossed her own yard, where the resident corgi politely escorted them from one end of the invisible barrier to the other as Wiley, hooked up to his trolley line, paced its generous length with wails of misery.

"Can't Wiley come along?" Cara asked, breaking off Leigh's story just before she got to the part about finding Lester.

"No," Leigh responded. "He'll scare off the mother dog. She's got the litter hidden in the woods somewhere and I want to find them. It's supposed to storm tonight."

"Why did she move her litter to the woods?" Cara asked.

Leigh sighed. "Can I tell this in order please?"

"Sorry."

By the time Leigh got to Lester's request to see her at the hospital, Cara's jaunty enthusiasm had been replaced with mother-wolf wariness. She spied the tool shed ahead of them with a frown. "I don't want the Pack anywhere near here."

"Neither do I," Leigh concurred. "They have been warned. And they've all promised to stay in our yards."

Cara's frown deepened. "They have ways of getting around their promises."

Leigh sighed once more. "Tell me about it."

"Did you catch anything on the camera last night?" Cara asked.

Leigh shook her head. "A bunch of deer early on. But around midnight or so, it cut off. I think the battery may be low. That's another reason I wanted to come out here." She cast a glance up at the Brown's deck, but saw no one. Poor Adith. That new medication was seriously messing with her productivity as the neighborhood snoop. Leigh made a mental note to go and visit whenever the older woman happened to be awake today.

"Where did you set up the camera?" Cara asked. "You hid it pretty well if it's out here; I don't see it."

"It's in this bush," Leigh explained, stepping to the edge of the woods. Archie's property wrapped around behind the O'Malley's place and included the bulk of the steep, wooded hill that stretched down to Cara's farm. All of the homeowners' parcels included the creek behind their houses, but from the Brown's on down, the back line also included a little of the woods on the opposite bank.

Leigh frowned. "I'm sure this is where Warren and Ethan put it," she said to herself, pushing aside some leafy branches.

Her heart skipped a beat. The tripod was still there, turned over on its side. Her Aunt Bess's camera lay on the ground nearby, its lens smashed and innards gutted as if it had been bashed against a tree.

She borrowed a few of Maura's swear words.

"What is it?" Cara exclaimed, coming quickly to her side. "Oh, my. That's not good."

"To put it mildly." The cost of the camera didn't matter nearly so much to Leigh as the fact that the destroyed equipment had been so generously and trustingly loaned by her Aunt Bess. And neither of those issues was as disturbing as the thought of how—and why—it had happened in the first place.

"Okay, this really irks me," Cara said sharply, mirroring Leigh's rising anger. Anger which, Leigh had found over the years, made a convenient substitute for fear. "This is no accident. Somebody deliberately sabotaged that camera so you wouldn't see what was going on out here."

Leigh nodded. "Which suggests the question: what *is* going on out here?"

Both their eyes came to rest on the tool shed.

"We'll just take a quick peek," Cara suggested. "See if anything has changed since you found Lester. Something clearly must have."

Cara started to move, but Leigh's feet remained planted.

Cara's eyes rolled. "Oh, for heaven's sake, Leigh. You stay at the top of the stairs and keep a look out, and *I'll* go down. There's no reason to assume the worst. But if we can show that someone's been trespassing at night, don't you think it would help for the police to know that?"

Leigh gave in and fell into step beside her cousin. When they reached the doors to the cellar, she removed her flashlight from her back pocket and handed it over. "Just stand on the stairs and look around," she suggested. "I'll keep watch up here and make sure we stay alone."

Cara nodded, took the flashlight, and opened the doors. As her head of strawberry-blond hair descended gradually below, Leigh surveyed Archie's yard. After confirming again that they were alone, she pivoted to look down the stairs. Cara was standing on the bottom step.

"See anything?" Leigh asked.

"Not a thing," Cara returned flatly. "You want to look?"

Hell, no. "All right. Come back up and I'll go down."

The women changed places.

Leigh took a deep breath and shone the flashlight around the cellar. First quickly, to make sure there would be no nasty surprises. Then once again, with a slow sweeping motion. "Hello, dark and dank," she said aloud, trying to abate her anxiety. "I've missed seeing you lo these last twelve hours. *Not!*"

"Are you talking to me?" Cara called down from above.

"No, just myself," Leigh answered.

"Well, cut it out! I'm trying to listen for footsteps… or whatever."

Leigh was about to declare her examination finished—and sprint back up into relatively less creepy territory—when her flashlight came to rest on the stone she and her Aunt Lydie had examined yesterday. Then, the mortar had been chiseled away from along its left side. Now, the mortar was chiseled out all around.

Leigh moved her flashlight beam to the floor. There was no accompanying pile of mortar dust. Someone had obviously swept that evidence away. There were no footprints anywhere either, except her own. Someone had swept the whole floor, period.

She gripped the mini flashlight between her lips and extended both hands to the corners of the stone block. She got a grip and attempted to jiggle it.

The stone wouldn't budge.

She took the flashlight in hand again and pointed the beam into the cracks where the mortar had been. In its deepest spot, the cavity extended only about two-thirds of the way through the depth of the block. Whatever method this person was using to attempt to loosen the stone, they had a very long way to go.

"Leigh!"

She jumped and whirled toward the steps. "What is it?"

"Come up here!"

Leigh complied. She found her cousin standing a few steps from the cellar doors, looking off into the woods up the hill.

"Is that the dog you're looking for?"

Leigh followed Cara's gaze. Then she smiled. At least one thing was going right this morning. "That's her all right!"

She turned and closed the doors to the cellar, hoping she would never have cause to enter its eerie confines again. Perhaps the next time the mother dog found shelter, she would show a bit more taste.

"I'm going to grab a bowl of food and take it to her," Leigh explained. "Can you stay on the edge of the woods? She'll run off if we both go up."

Cara nodded in agreement.

Leigh fetched the empty dog bowl that Ethan had left out last night, refilled it from the bag of food she had stored in the above-ground part of the tool shed, and began walking slowly up the hill. To her delight, the dog hadn't moved. The plucky she-mutt, who in the daylight Leigh guessed to be a mixture of terrier and spaniel, stood still as a statue, her eyes locked on Leigh. Or, more accurately, on what Leigh held in her hands.

"How are you doing, Momma?" Leigh cooed as she moved closer. "What a smart dog you are to get away from all this craziness." *And how badly I wish you could talk!* "Are your puppies all right? Can I see them?"

As Leigh approached, she looked around and listened for telltale squeals, but no signs of the litter were forthcoming. The dog stood her ground until her pursuer was within about six feet, then she turned, trotted off several paces, and faced Leigh again, her eyes still locked on the food bowl. She licked her lips.

"Okay, fine," Leigh said, setting the bowl down and backing away. "You eat first. Then we'll talk."

When Leigh had moved about ten feet away from the bowl, the dog sprang into action, pouncing on the dish and wolfing down the kibble.

Leigh cast another glance downhill to check on her cousin, and found that Cara had followed her just far enough into the woods so that the women could keep each other in sight. Leigh offered a thumbs-up sign. Cara returned it.

The dog emptied the bowl in a matter of seconds. Then she turned tail and trotted off again. Leigh picked up the bowl and followed, looking carefully at every bush and tangle of thicket that seemed a likely hiding place. "You want to show me those, puppies, Momma? I can help you get them somewhere safe. It's supposed to rain tonight, you know."

The mother dog, seemingly in a charitable mood, wagged her tail slightly. But try as Leigh might, the dog would let her come no closer. After Leigh had followed her back and forth through the trees for nearly ten minutes, it was clear the dog had no intention of leading anything but a merry chase.

"She's laughing at you, you know," Cara said with a smirk as Leigh joined her in resting on a conveniently flat boulder near the wood's edge. "She's probably got those pups a half mile away."

"Probably," Leigh conceded. "I just hope that wherever they are, it's got a roof over it."

The women startled in unison as a loud beeping sound accosted their ears.

"Where is *that* coming from?" Cara asked. "It sounds like a truck backing up." The women rose and walked out into the open. They rounded the tool shed and moved toward the farmhouse to get a better view up Archie's driveway.

"What the—" Leigh was unable to complete the sentence. Backing down the gravel drive toward them was a gigantic green flatbed truck, loaded up with a piece of construction equipment that looked like a giant claw.

Just before it reached the bridge over the creek, the passenger door opened and a man jumped out. Oblivious to the women and their dropped jaws, he proceeded to direct the driver over the narrow bridge and into the wider circle of Archie's drive, taking out a few low-hanging branches on the way. When after many false starts and retries the truck was satisfactorily parked, the man walked over to Leigh and Cara and issued a nod of greeting.

"One of you ladies Ms. Archie Pratt?"

"I'm afraid not," Leigh answered.

The man appeared annoyed. "Well, is he here?"

Leigh shook her head. "Was he… expecting you?"

The man looked at her as though she had the brains of a marshmallow. "He'd better be!" he answered shortly, looking at his watch. "We got other deliveries to make today. Is he coming back soon?"

"I'm afraid we don't know." She looked again at the giant conglomeration of metal, grease, and bright-green paint. "What exactly did Archie buy?"

The man snorted. "Not *buy*, Lady. *Rent.* Not too many individuals need to keep one of these big boys around."

The driver of the truck popped out of the cab.

"Hey, Lou!" the first man called testily. "Renter ain't here. They don't know where he is."

The driver swore, then looked down at a clipboard. "Nah, man! It's all right here. Ordered a week ago today, 9:45am. Archie Pratt, 976 Snow Creek Road. Put a deposit on his credit card—balance to be paid today. Delivery ten to twelve. Don't go telling me he ain't here. I ain't backing that thing down twice!"

"If you don't mind our asking," Cara asked in the fake-sweet voice she reserved for men she deemed not smart enough to tell the difference, "what exactly is… that thing?"

The driver's pique softened a little. He smiled. "That," he answered proudly, simultaneously puffing out his chest and hitching his belt up under his belly, "is a 38 flywheel horsepower,

10,000 pound, practically brand spankin' new compact hydraulic excavator."

Chapter 16

"A *hydraulic excavator?*" Adith repeated loudly, her eyes hidden behind her giant binoculars. She was leaning over the railing of the deck and staring toward Archie's place, never mind that the rental company had hauled the equipment away twenty minutes ago. "And I thought it was a backhoe!"

Leigh said nothing as she leaned on the railing next to Adith, staring out the same direction for no particular reason. Her head was swimming.

Maura had not picked up when she called, but Leigh was certain that her message would be relayed to the other detectives in earnest. If sinking hundreds of dollars into a deposit of rental equipment to be delivered today was not good evidence of Archie's intentions to be home, she didn't know what was. Surely now the police would have to take the possibility of a forced abduction seriously, regardless of whether they cared about the smashed camera and the tinkering beneath the tool shed.

"Well," Adith said merrily, "I suppose it doesn't matter much. They both dig, don't they? Must be the septic. That's the problem with living outside the city, you know—always something going wrong with the septic."

Leigh nodded absently. Archie had indeed been planning to dig for something, but she doubted it was his septic tank. She could only hope the investigators would agree with her and bestir themselves to action, because the larger implications were distressing.

For the last eight years, Archie had contented himself with ripping out drywall and digging up various patches of earth with a shovel. He had concealed what he was doing from the neighbors, not because it was illegal, but because he didn't want any additional competition. Never in all his years of puttering had Archie done anything so drastic as rent an excavator—an action which would be impossible to hide and difficult to explain. Why now?

Perhaps because, at long last, Archie had made a breakthrough. Had he found "The Guide?" If so, for the first time since his quest had begun, he might actually be able to read the map.

Which would all be well and good. Except that Archie obviously *did* have competition for the prize. Competition who was dead set on getting to it first.

"Yoo-hoo!" Adith called, waving a twisted hand in front of Leigh's absently staring eyes. "Where's your brain at, girl?"

Nowhere good. "Sorry. What did you say?"

"I asked if Harvey gave you my message yesterday. He said he would, but you know his type—they can recite the name of every president since Jesus, but they can't figure out how to fry a damn egg."

"Oh," Leigh's mind snapped back to the present. "About the dog. Yes, he told me. Thanks. I saw her myself this morning."

"That wasn't the only reason I wanted to talk to you," Adith said, her voice dropping dramatically.

"Oh, no?"

Adith made a show of looking over her shoulder toward the house. "You never know who's eavesdropping around here. Walls are thin as paper." She motioned for Leigh to lean closer. "I was up night before last, you know. The night Lester went out."

Leigh's eyebrows rose. "You were?"

Adith nodded solemnly. "I'm up half the nights these days, thanks to that danged fool medicine! Doctor keeps telling me the side effects will go away, but it ain't happening yet. I lie there and stare at the ceiling and listen to Pauline snoring like a moose and get so danged bored I can't stand it. So that night I decided I was getting myself up, arthritis or no, and I was getting a change of scenery. And I did. I put on my bathrobe and went out and sat on the deck a bit, and you just guess what I saw!"

Leigh's breath held. "You saw Lester leave?"

Adith frowned. "Well, no. Don't you think I would have called out to him if I had? I didn't know anyone else was even awake… not then. But what I saw down by the creek was clear enough, even without my binocs."

She paused and motioned for Leigh to move closer still. Leigh complied.

"It was them orbs again!"

Leigh tried hard not to sigh. "You mean, the floating lights?"

Adith nodded. "Only one this time. Bobbing along out there by the creek, with one of those hazy, misty glows around it, you know?"

Leigh wondered if Mrs. Rhodis had been wearing her glasses at the time. She decided not to ask. "About what time was that?"

"Would have been around one in the morning," Adith answered. "And I don't mind telling you, it gave me the gooseflesh too, just like Dora said. Pansy knew from the beginning, of course. She wouldn't even come out onto the deck with me. Stayed there at the foot of my bed, she did. Wouldn't come a step closer to those evil beacons!"

Leigh also didn't ask if the dog had been asleep.

"Well," Mrs. Rhodis continued, "I watched that orb float off toward Archie's place, and that was enough for me. So I went back to bed. It was later—and I can't say how much later, because I had drifted off by then—when I heard a door close downstairs. It sounded like the back door, but I didn't think much of it. I guess I thought it was Lester or Emma letting that dog of Archie's out. I was a bit muddled—thought it might be morning, but in thinking back on it, I'm sure it was still pitch dark."

Adith's wrinkled face clouded. "Now I suspect it must have been Lester leaving. I feel real bad I didn't wake up the rest of the way and see what he was up to. Danged medicine!"

"You can't help it if you weren't awake enough to think straight," Leigh assured.

"But I should have known!" Adith lamented. "I should have known Lester was vulnerable!"

Leigh's eyebrows rose. "Vulnerable how? To what?"

"To the lure, of course! The orbs have a power, you know. Dora says they're harbingers, but I'm not so sure about that. I think those little floaty bits of evil have a power all their own. And Lester, he was sick as a dog and all feverish, and that makes your brain weak. If he'd looked out the window when I did and seen that same orb... why, they can turn you smack into a zombie, they can! Led him right out there to the creek, and him not half in his right mind—"

She broke off abruptly, her face paling. "I wonder if that's how the old soldier drowned!"

Leigh straightened. "Let's not let our imaginations run away with us. However Theodore Carr died, it was a very long time ago. I'm more worried about Archie."

Adith bristled. "You think I'm not? *You* may poo-poo the supernatural, but Archie knew what was going on out here, and despite all his good-natured storytelling, deep down, it scared him. Why else do you think he went to Dora? Because he knew he was in over his head, that's why!"

Stop. Rewind.

Leigh gave her head a shake. "What did you say? Archie went to see Dora? When?"

"A week or so ago," Adith said dismissively. "Didn't I tell you that?"

"No," Leigh said tightly. "I'm quite certain you didn't. And neither did Dora."

"No?" Adith considered. "Well, it wasn't a secret, for heaven's sake. She said when I called that she'd just visited with Archie and wasn't it nice to hear from so many neighbors. I told you that Archie asked Harvey if he could come up with a list of people who'd lived at the farmhouse since the Carrs—but Harvey's list just had the names. I don't know how Archie found out where Dora lives now, because I'm pretty sure he doesn't know my friend Barbara Jean down in Bellevue. Then again, you never know who Barbara Jean knows. Why, back when Doc Shepherd's first wife Coreen had her eye surgery—"

"Mrs. Rhodis," Leigh interrupted, "Why did Archie want to see Dora?"

Adith threw her an exasperated look. "Because of the haunting, of course! He wanted to know what she'd seen when she lived there. When I told her he'd gone missing, she was so upset—she seemed quite fond of him. Everybody loves Archie, you know."

"Yes, I know." Leigh's mind drifted back to her conversation with Dora. The older woman had indeed been concerned about Archie's disappearance. Leigh could envision the two of them hitting it off famously, comparing notes on supernatural visitations while Archie casually threw in his actual questions. But what questions were they? And more importantly, what were her answers?

If Archie had talked to Dora a little over a week ago, that meant he had talked to her only a few days before he rented the excavator.

A few days before the children found the map. A few days before he disappeared.

What had Dora told him?

Harvey… Lester's muttered words continued to drum in Leigh's brain. *He knows, Arch… He knows.*

"Mrs. Rhodis," Leigh asked urgently. "Did Harvey know about Archie's visit with Dora? Do you know if Archie came to see him afterwards?"

Adith's brow creased. "Oh, I couldn't say about that. Before he went missing Archie used to pop in here all the time, either to see Lester or to mooch from Emma's kitchen. But if Harvey knew that Archie had already found Dora he sure didn't tell me about it when he gave me the list. Would have saved me about a hundred phone calls!"

Leigh's pulse rate increased. She was getting close to the truth at last. "I need to talk to Harvey," she announced, turning toward the door to the house.

"He ain't here," Adith informed.

Leigh's eyes widened. "What do you mean? He's always here. Does he have a doctor's appointment or something?"

Adith shook her head. "No. A friend of his came and picked him up. He said they were going to the library."

Leigh blinked. "Has he done that before?"

Adith shrugged. "Every once in a while. Harvey's a book man, you know. Doesn't care for computers. When he's got the yen to do some researching he heads off to the Carnegie. At least I think that's where he goes. That's how he came up with the list of farm owners. You'd think Archie could find out that stuff for himself, with his being a teacher once, but he's got no patience for that kind of thing. Neither does Lester. Hell, Emma wanted a recipe for pot pie one time and Lester got on her computer and came back with directions on how to bake marijuana into a graham cracker crust! Then of course Emma went back and found the right thing herself in about ten seconds—"

"Do you know when Harvey will be back?" Leigh asked anxiously.

Adith shook her head. "By dinner, I'd expect. He gets his pills at six. Why are you so anxious to talk to him, anyway? What's he supposed to know that I don't know? He's not even a believer.

Telling me my orbs are *flashlights!*" She gave a derisive snort. "Ridiculous. I ask you, how could an ordinary, everyday flashlight turn Lester into a zombie? Huh? Huh?"

Leigh's cell phone rang. She pulled it out quickly. "Hello, Emma?"

"Yes, honey." Emma's voice sounded considerably more chipper than the last time Leigh had heard it. "I just wanted to see if you could come down and see Lester now. He's asking for you, and it's visiting hours."

Leigh drew in a shaky breath. "I'd love to," she said sincerely. "I'll be right there."

"Hi, Lester," Leigh said warmly, taking a seat by the bedside of the short, stout man she realized now had always subconsciously reminded her of a teddy bear. This realization was made plain by the fact that an actual stuffed teddy bear was propped up on the table beside him, mimicking his roundish figure, protruding ears, and smiling brown eyes to a T. The teddy, however, had a small black nose, whereas Lester's was still swollen and fire-engine red, in colorful but unhealthy contrast to the puffy, blue-black rings under his eyes.

"Hi there," Lester returned. He gestured toward the stuffed animal. "How do you like that? Grandkids got it for me. I think they figure they'll get to keep it for themselves."

"Which they will, of course," Emma added proudly. "Smart bunch of kids, I'd say."

"Sounds like it," Leigh agreed, glancing at Emma. The woman had seemed a trifle miffed ever since Leigh had arrived, which was out of character. Leigh sat awkwardly and watched as the couple proceeded to stare at each other for several seconds without speaking.

"All right!" Emma said finally, gathering up her purse and rising. "I'll leave! But I'm not going any farther than the cafeteria, you hear me? Such nonsense! Men and nonsense…" She was still muttering as she closed the door behind her.

"Sorry about that," Lester apologized. But he did not explain. "I hope it wasn't too much trouble for you to come out here, but I had to ask…"

Leigh moved closer.

"Well, they tell me you were the one who found me. You know, after I passed out."

Leigh nodded. "You don't remember?"

Lester started to shake his head, but winced at the motion.

"Yeah, I know," Leigh said with a smile. "I got conked on the head once, too."

Lester's eyes widened. "I don't think I… I mean… well, what did you see, exactly?"

Leigh wanted to ask questions a whole lot more than she wanted to answer them, but she forced herself to proceed carefully. The fear in Lester's eyes was hard to miss; it was in his voice as well. "I went down to the cellar to feed the dog," she explained. "The dog was gone but you were there, lying curled up on the floor. I didn't know if you were asleep or unconscious at first, but then you started moving. You had a bump and a cut on your head, so I called an ambulance."

"When you… Did you…" Lester stammered. He seemed unable to choose the right words. "You didn't see anyone else around?" he asked finally.

Leigh shook her head. Then she took a chance. "Did you?"

Lester's pupils dilated; his breathing sped up. "Oh, no. I just went to check on the dog too, you know."

Leigh's jaw tensed. The man was about as convincing as a child who insists, through a mouth smeared with frosting, that he never touched the cupcakes. "Was she there when you got there?"

Lester stiffened. "Who?"

"The dog," Leigh replied. Whom did he think she meant?

"I'm…" Lester hesitated again. "I'm not really sure. I can remember walking down the steps to the cellar. But that seems to be the last thing I can remember, until the EMTs were talking to me."

Leigh believed him. "Why did you go down the steps?"

"Well, to see… I told you. I wanted to check on the dog." Fine beads of sweat broke out on his bald forehead.

Leigh exhaled sadly and softened her voice. "Lester, I know you're worried about Archie. I am, too. I also know you didn't go outside and walk across the creek in the middle of the night to check on a stray dog you knew perfectly well I was already taking care of. You went there because you thought that, somehow, you were going to help Archie. Am I right?"

Lester drew up against his pillows. His face reddened. "No, I wanted… I mean, the dog was… why would I do that?"

Leigh tried not to cringe. But she had seen better acting in her kids' kindergarten Thanksgiving pageant. *We Native Americans bring you food. Be thankful for future holiday. We eat now.*

Of course, one could only act so well when the script was ludicrous. And Lester's script was as ludicrous as they came.

Leigh decided to go ahead and lay it on the line. "Lester, please listen to me," she pleaded. "I'm not sure why you think it would be a bad idea to level with the police, but I have to disagree with you on that. If someone has… well, if someone *has* Archie, that's kidnapping. The police know how to deal with these things—they have the experience to handle these situations so nobody gets hurt. You and I do not. Don't you see, that's *why* such people don't want the police involved!"

Lester's face paled. "I didn't say anything about kidnapping!" he insisted, his voice breaking in the middle of the last word. "Why are you talking like that?"

"Because you're not talking at all, so I can only guess at what you're hiding," Leigh retorted. "I told you about the map my kids found. I know you and Archie were looking for something. It's pretty obvious that someone else is looking for it, too. What I don't know is why you thought that going to the cellar of the tool shed in the wee hours of the morning was going to help anything. Can you make me understand?"

"Who else is…" Archie's breathing had become distressingly rapid again. "I mean… what makes you think anyone is looking for something?"

"Who else do *you* think is looking for it?" Leigh pressed.

"I don't know who!" Lester stammered. "I mean… I didn't say anyone was… Oh, hell!"

Leigh softened her voice again. "I'm only trying to help you help Archie," she assured. "If you know who might be trying to keep Archie from finding this… this *whatever it is*, then please, you've got to tell the police. I don't know. I have no clue. I can't tell them anything. Right now they're not taking the risk of foul play to Archie seriously, but they will if you cooperate… all you have to do is be honest with them about what you and Archie were doing and what really happened to you down in that cellar."

Lester's eyes turned away from her. He grabbed a tissue from off his bedside table and dabbed at his sweating forehead. "I don't know, Leigh. I just don't know. Arch said…"

Leigh leaned in. "What did Archie say?"

Lester went mum. He pressed his lips together stubbornly.

"Lester," Leigh said, drawing sudden inspiration. "Perhaps it would help your decision to know that a 10,000 pound hydraulic excavator was delivered to Archie's driveway this morning?"

Lester stared at her a moment. Then he uttered several words no teddy bear should hear. "I forgot all about that," he added.

"Yeah, we figured as much," Leigh said sympathetically. "But now that the police know about both the excavator and the map—"

"Arch was having troubles with his septic, you know," Lester offered.

Leigh raised one eyebrow and looked at him.

After a long moment, he sighed. "I made a promise," he said miserably.

"Archie couldn't possibly have anticipated these circumstances," Leigh reasoned. "Besides, it doesn't really matter what he was after. All that matters is figuring out who else was after it. Does that help?"

Lester made no response.

Leigh took a breath. "Here's what I think. I think that you looked out your window Saturday night and saw a light out by the creek heading toward Archie's place. You went to see who it was, and you followed them to the cellar. But before you knew what happened, they hit you with something and knocked you out—or at least knocked you down. How close is that?"

Lester blinked back at her, his eyes confused. "I didn't see any light," he said softly.

"You didn't?"

His moved his head slowly from side to side. "I went out on my own, like I said. To… to check on the dog. But when I got closer, I heard something."

Leigh's pulse sped up. She was getting somewhere at last. "What did you hear?"

His eyes assumed a distant look. "A buzzing sound. Like a motor of some kind. It was strange. There's no electric down there, you know. I thought maybe... but I don't remember. I wanted to see you so I could ask... what was down there? I mean, when you found me?"

Leigh shook her head. "There was no machine. The only thing I saw on the ground was your flashlight. But..." she hesitated only a moment. "Since yesterday, someone has chiseled out a good bit of mortar from around one large stone."

Lester's eyes widened. "No," he said bleakly, barely above a whisper. Then he repeated, much louder, *"No!"* His hands scrabbled at his blankets and he attempted to swung his feet toward the edge of the bed.

"Lester, don't!" Leigh begged, trying to settle him back on his pillow.

"Do you really think they hit me?" he asked. "Really, honest to God, knocked me out? If they'd do that, what would they do to Arch?!"

"Tell the police," Leigh pressed. "Tell them everything you can. It's the best thing we can do."

"The police!" Lester said derisively. "They think Archie's hiding out to commit *fraud!"*

"Not after you tell them the truth, they won't!"

Lester grunted and leaned back. His face was flushed and he looked terrible, but at least he was no longer trying to get out of bed.

"My head is killing me," he said gruffly. But his sulky pout once again put Leigh in mind of a teddy bear. She felt like a heel.

"I'm going now," she said apologetically. "You rest. And try not to worry. But do think about what I said. Okay? Please?"

Lester grunted again. He closed his eyes.

His head hurt; Leigh could see it in his face. She rose and walked toward the door.

"Leigh?" he called.

She stopped and turned around. "Yes?"

"Thanks. For caring so much about Arch. But you need to be careful. You need to stay out of this. It could be... dangerous."

No freakin' kidding.

"And could you..." he continued. "Would you tell Harvey to stay out of it, too? I worry about that man."

Harvey knows.

"Why?" Leigh asked softly. "Why are you worried about Harvey, Lester?"

Lester closed his eyes again, and Leigh knew she could harass the poor man no further. At least not today.

His voice drifted into a mumble. "Too smart by half, that old man. Can't have… I don't want anybody hurt…"

Leigh slipped quietly out of the room and closed the door behind her.

Neither do I, Lester, she thought to herself grimly. *Neither do I.*

Chapter 17

Leigh was pulling into the elementary school parking lot when her cell phone rang. She swung the van into the nearest spot, threw it into park, and picked up. She had a special ringtone for calls from Maura's office… a wailing siren.

"Hello, Maura?" she said anxiously, wondering if her friend had news from the obstetrician. "What's up?"

"Nothing," the policewoman answered. "At least not with… the results. They're saying midafternoon now. But I didn't call about that. I called to let you know that the guys in General Investigations now officially have a fire lit under them. I'm sorry, Koslow—it was worse than I thought. The chumps hadn't done jack. Archie's description hadn't even been loaded in the databases yet—whole damn thing was stuck in clerical."

Leigh's shoulders slumped. "Oh."

"I got it moving again," Maura assured. "Shouldn't take long to hear back if there's a match in the system."

Leigh didn't want to think about a match with what.

"At least they're open to seeing the obvious now," Maura continued. "They're planning to interview Lester again sometime today. You think he'll level with them this time?"

"I certainly hope so," Leigh said earnestly, rubbing her face with her hands. "But I don't know. Lester's loyal to a fault, and he swore to Archie that he'd keep the whole thing a secret."

Maura did some swearing herself. "That won't help either of them now."

"I know," Leigh agreed. "I'll keep trying." She got out of the van and walked toward the school office, summarizing for Maura on the way her conversation with Adith and her suspicions about Archie's having made a recent breakthrough. But when she reached the office and saw Allison waiting for her, she promptly cut the call short. "I have to go now," she explained. "Orthodontia calls. Allison has an early dismissal."

"Gotcha," Maura responded.

"Was that Aunt Mo?" Allison said innocently as she skipped alongside her mother out the front door and across the parking lot toward the van.

"What makes you think that?" Leigh asked, quite positive she hadn't identified her caller.

Allison shrugged. "I just thought maybe you'd be talking to her. Any developments on the case?"

Leigh tensed. It was going to be a very long orthodontist appointment.

It was a very long orthodontist appointment. The only thing saving Leigh from Allison's continual peppering of questions was the fact that the waiting room was packed and Leigh insisted that discussing the issue in public would be inappropriate. At least the van ride over had been short. Short enough for Leigh to get away with divulging only the merest highlights of her day, focusing on her finding the mother dog and the delivery of the excavator—which she was certain Allison was bound to hear about anyway.

To Leigh's surprise, her daughter did not immediately resume the interrogation when the appointment was over. As they got back into the van Allison appeared thoughtful, and asked only if the orthodontist's office was anywhere near the driving range.

The driving range? "It's about a mile that way. Why?"

"Can we go home that way?"

"Whatever for?"

Allison fidgeted in her seat. "Well, the truth is, Mom... I was really hoping you would take me to see Dora Klinger again."

Leigh steadied herself. *Of course.* The driving range was right across the highway from the assisted living facility. Allison might not be savvy with driving directions, per se, but she did have a near-photographic memory.

Leigh asked the obvious question. "Why do you want to see Mrs. Klinger?"

Allison fidgeted again. "Because... well, I want to ask her exactly where Theodore's grave is. We have to know for sure in order to read the map right. It's not like I'm going to the actual grave or anything. There's no danger involved. And you know she would love to see us again. She practically begged us to come back! Please, Mom?"

Leigh's jaw clenched. She had, in fact, been planning to return to Dora's just as soon as Ethan got home from school and she could safely stash both children at their Aunt Cara's. But she knew her daughter well enough to know that when it came to ferreting out information, frustration only bred more frighteningly bright ideas. If the orthodontist trip hadn't presented itself, the child would probably have spent the evening convincing her father she needed to work on her tee shot.

Twenty minutes later, Leigh and her daughter were once again settled into uncomfortable chairs, politely declining more hard candy. Their hostess, as promised, was delighted to see them. Yet even as she sat smiling pleasantly, all hunched over in a baby-pink cardigan sweater, it was clear she sensed the urgency behind their visit. "I've been thinking quite a bit about poor Mr. Pratt," she said sympathetically. "I hope you don't have bad news about him."

"Oh, no," Leigh said quickly. "We don't have any news, I'm afraid. But the police are working on finding him even as we speak."

Dora's crooked fingers fussed with the hem of her sweater. "I've got to say, of all the hauntings I've heard tell of, I can't remember a person ever just *disappearing*. Meeting their maker in mysterious ways, unfortunately, yes. Going missing for a spell, absolutely. But people go missing because they get frightened off. I'd think if that were the case with Mr. Pratt, he would have come home by now. Sweet, friendly man like that—he must know that people are worried about him. I don't understand it."

Given that no suggestion Leigh could offer was fit for her daughter's ears, she decided to change the subject. "We're trying to help the police however we can," she began, starting the speech she had constructed during the car ride over. If it hadn't occurred to Dora in the sixty some-odd years since she'd lived at the farm that she and her husband had been the victim of fortune-hunters rather than ghosts, it was probably best not to enlighten her now. It was also best, for any number of reasons, not to increase the number of interested individuals who actually laid eyes on Archie's map. "We think it was only a short time after Archie talked to you that he started making plans. He rented some equipment... as if he were going to make some changes to the farm. We just aren't sure what. I was hoping, if you thought back on your conversation with him, maybe you might have some idea? Was there something in particular about the farm that he seemed interested in? Kept asking you about in more detail?"

Dora's lips twisted in thought. She was silent for a long moment. "Well, he mainly wanted to know about the haunting, of course. We compared orbs—what paths they took, the seasonal patterns. He was particularly interested in the physical manifestations of the poltergeists."

I'll bet, Leigh thought to herself. *He wanted to know where everyone else had been looking.*

"Did he ask," she posed carefully, "about any 'manifestations' in the area of the tool shed?"

Dora's eyebrows rose. "Well, yes, actually. Now that you mention it. We talked quite a bit about that shed. It was my Bert that built it, you know."

Leigh remembered Lydie saying that the shed looked newer than the cellar underneath it; she had thought as much herself. "He built it on top of the root cellar?" she asked.

The wrinkles in Dora's brow deepened. "Oh no, that wasn't a root cellar. There used to be a root cellar dug into the hill over by the barn, but it had long since caved in when we got there. No, the cellar you're talking about was built for the old house. Bert and I tore that awful mess down ourselves, and he put up the shed in its place. Ew, Lordy!" Dora's face screwed up into a pucker. "Was that place ever foul!"

Leigh found herself perched on the edge of her seat. In her peripheral vision, she could see her daughter responding likewise. "The *old* house?" Leigh squeaked. "You mean there was more than one?"

Dora looked at her quizzically. "Mr. Pratt said the same thing. I don't see what's so shocking about it. The cabin was built way back—late 1800s, maybe earlier, I don't know. If Theodore and Tom Carr built the farmhouse you see now, where do you think they were living at the time? You can't build something like that overnight, especially not with a farm to run."

Leigh caught her breath. "Of course," she forced out, the wheels in her brain turning madly. "We never thought about that."

Dora shook her head. "Well, I don't know why not. Mr. Pratt was quite fascinated—wanted to hear all about how Bert built the shed. How he tore down the cabin. Whether we found anything unusual in it."

"And did you?"

Dora sniffed. "If you'd call it unusual for a crazy man in his eighties to live in a falling-down shack with rotten timbers and no plumbing, then yes—the whole thing was unusual."

Leigh swallowed. "Theodore lived there? I mean... *after* the new house was built?"

"I'll tell you what I told Mr. Pratt," Dora answered. "When we bought the land, the old cabin was a nasty, dirty wreck that reeked to high heaven. Reeked of what, I won't tell you, but I suppose you can guess. Mr. Trout—the nephew—he was very apologetic. Said as far as he could tell, his grandfather and his uncle hadn't gotten along too well at the end, and his grandfather had taken to spending time at the cabin. There had been a bed in there, and clothes and even some foodstuffs. His uncle never bothered to clean out the place after the old man died—just left it all to go to pot. For thirty years! Mess just sat there until Mr. Trout took over. He paid somebody to empty out the trash, but the cabin was too far gone to be of any use. So Bert and a couple of his buddies took mallets to the walls, and that was that. Foundation was solid enough, though, so Bert laid new floorboards and put up a nice, sturdy tool shed for himself. He'd be pleased to know it's still standing!"

"Mrs. Klinger," Allison said politely, "could I ask you a question?"

Dora smiled. "Of course, dear."

Allison rose, pulled a paper from her back pocket, and began to unfold it. Leigh opened her mouth to speak, but Allison, seeming to anticipate her concern, held the paper out for her mother to see. It was not *the* map, but a drawing of the area Allison had made herself, with the current landmarks in their appropriate places.

I'm not stupid, Mom! The girl's eyes said defensively.

Leigh cleared her throat.

Allison walked to the side of Dora's chair and held out the map. Dora reached for a pair of glasses on the table beside her and put them on. She studied the map a moment, then smiled. "Oh, yes. This looks familiar! That's my Bert's shed," she said proudly, pointing with a crooked finger. "Right there."

"I was hoping you could show me where Theodore Carr is buried," Allison continued. "We looked for the tombstone you mentioned, but it definitely isn't there anymore."

Dora nodded. "Mr. Pratt wasn't aware of the grave, either. I suppose the marker must have been gone a while now."

Leigh's ears perked. "Archie didn't know that Theodore was buried on the property? You're sure? You told him that when he visited?"

Dora looked up from the map, lowered her glasses, and studied Leigh. "He seemed surprised to me, yes. Though I still don't understand such a fuss over one old grave. Why, people used to be buried on their own land all the time. Not everyone was a churchgoer, you know."

Allison was becoming antsy. "Now, exactly where on here… could you point to it, please, Mrs. Klinger?"

Dora put her glasses back on and bowed her head. "Yes, well, it was a long time ago, you know, honey. But if the creek runs like this, down past the shed…" her finger trailed over the paper, trembling slightly as it went. "I'd say right here," she announced, tapping the paper with a fingernail. "The stone didn't stick up. It was flat."

"And what way did the writing face?" Allison pressed. "I mean, which way would you say the body is lying?"

Leigh cringed. Dora shot Allison a look of puzzlement. "Oh, my, child. I don't remember exactly. I suppose if you were walking toward the grave from the farmhouse, you'd read the stone head on." Her thin lips hitched up into a sideways smile. "Weren't planning on digging him up, were you?"

Allison's eyes flickered toward her mother. "Oh, no… I mean, I don't think so."

Saints preserve us.

Dora chuckled. "Oh, my. Such a delight, you are. Maybe Adith can bring you to one of our *phasma victus* parties sometime. You might find you have The Sight!"

"She doesn't," Leigh said quickly.

"Phasma victus?" Allison asked.

Dora laughed again. "We made it up. A couple of us here at the home. It's supposed to be Latin for 'living ghosts.' You know, like a seance, but with a festive touch. Your friend Adith seems very excited to join us."

No doubt, Leigh thought.

"But I told her the dog can't come," Dora added sternly.

Leigh rose. "Thank you so much for answering more of our questions." She gestured for Allison to join her. "But I'm afraid we have to be leaving now—my son will be getting home from school soon. But I'll tell Adith that any time she needs a ride over here, I'll be happy to bring her."

Dora smiled. "That would be lovely. Thank you. And bring your daughter, too!"

Over my dead body.

"Thank you for the invitation!" Leigh called, hustling Allison toward the door. After a few more exchanged pleasantries, they exited and made their way toward the van. Allison uttered not a word, but buckled her seatbelt, pulled the map she had showed Dora back out of her pocket, extracted a copy of Archie's map from a zippered compartment in her backpack, and commenced studying them side by side.

Her head was still buried in the task when Leigh pulled the van into their own garage. "Allison," she asked nervously, "what are you thinking?"

The girl's small, delicate chin lifted. She took off her glasses and gave her head a shake, tousling her dark brown hair like a mop. "Mom," she said with frustration. "I'm about to give up. No matter which way I look at it, this map makes *no* sense!"

Leigh worked hard to restrain a smile. Allison didn't need to know, but it was the best news she'd heard all day.

Leigh sat down in the chair next to Lester's bed and stared him straight in the eyes. "I just got back from a chat with Dora Klinger," she said evenly. "I know that Archie did the same and that afterwards he felt like he'd made a breakthrough. I know he rented the excavator to dig something up, and I know he thought it would be best all around if the two of you told absolutely no one what you were up to until you found whatever it is you're looking for. But someone else has been watching, Lester, and I know in my gut that that *someone* is responsible for Archie's being missing and most likely for knocking you out. Whatever you're looking for, it's not important enough to risk Archie's life or anyone else's. All this secrecy nonsense has to stop. *Now.*"

Lester looked back at her out of eyes that were bloodshot, puffy, red-rimmed, and miserable. After an excruciatingly long silence, he exhaled with a sigh. "I get what you're saying," he said hoarsely. "But I don't know how to help Arch, Leigh. I swear I don't."

"You can talk to the police."

Lester's head hung. "There's nothing I can tell them. I don't know for sure that anyone hit me. I didn't see anybody. Arch never saw anybody either; he didn't have a clue who was sniffing around. He knew people were trespassing... but he could never catch anybody. It always seemed to happen when he was away. After he disappeared, I thought maybe..."

"Maybe what?" Leigh pressed.

"I thought maybe there'd be a ransom note or something. You know, to trade Arch for—. Well, for what he was looking for. I tried to—" his voice broke up.

Leigh took in a sharp breath. *You tried to find it yourself, the night you got knocked out. And now you feel like a failure.*

Leigh had no desire to make him feel any worse. "But no ransom note ever came?"

Lester started to shake his head, then winced and answered instead. "No, nothing. I swear, Leigh, I don't know what happened to Arch! He didn't say a word to me. He wasn't afraid of anybody. I mean, he was always afraid that other people were trying to—. Well, trying to get what he wanted. But he never thought of what he was doing as dangerous! And now, just when he finally started to get close, suddenly he's... *gone*."

Leigh had never seen Lester look more pathetic. She was certain that he was sincere.

"I know what you're thinking," he said with sudden defensiveness. "You're thinking Arch found it and took off to cut me out. But that's not true."

"I didn't say—"

"I never wanted any part of it!" Lester interrupted earnestly. "It was his. All of it. I just wanted to help him out. And no matter what he thought of me, he would never have gone off and left his dog like that." Lester's eyes welled with moisture. His voice quavered.

"He loves that stupid mutt."

Leigh released a long, slow breath. In all the various scenarios she'd come up with, Lester's honestly, truly, not being able to help the police was a possibility she hadn't considered. "But if you can tell them exactly what Archie was looking for," she said with inspiration, "surely it would help. They could focus on suspects who would value the same thing!"

Lester's eyes swam with angst. Leigh could see the indecision. "Too many people already know," he said finally, intently. "If I tell more, it will only make things worse. Put more people in danger."

His eyes leveled a reluctant accusation. *He doesn't trust me, either,* Leigh thought. *Fine.*

"Look, Lester," she argued. "You don't have to tell me. I don't care. And I agree that the fewer people who know the nitty-gritty, the better. But the police need to know. They do this all the time—they keep certain facts about the case secret, so that when they run across people who know them, it's an instant red flag. They'll find out who else knows about it, who else wants it. And that's the way they'll *find Archie.*"

Lester's resolve began to waver. "You really think so?"

"I know so."

A knock and a clicking noise sounded behind her, and Leigh swung around. Knowing that Emma had gone back to the house for a few hours, she was hoping to see the detectives from General Investigations. She was not expecting to see Maura.

"Hello, Koslow. And Mr. Brown," the policewoman said formally, extending a hand. "I was hoping to have a word with you. Maura Polanski, Allegheny County PD, homicide division."

Leigh was confused. Maura might harass her fellow investigators behind the scenes, but she would never officially interview their witnesses. That would be overstepping in a major way. "Are the detectives coming?" Leigh asked.

"This is my case now, Koslow," Maura said evenly, her face revealing nothing. Her gaze shifted to Lester. "Your friend, Mr. Archie Pratt?"

Lester's lower lip quivered. "Yeah?"

"We found him."

Chapter 18

Lester's face went completely white. "Found him?"

"He's alive," Maura announced. "But he isn't well. For the past six days he's been in a community hospital in rural Ohio, slipping in and out of a coma."

"But he's… he's alive… he…" Lester stammered. "Is he going to be okay?"

"His condition is listed as fair," Maura answered. "That's all I can tell you on the medical side."

"What happened?" Leigh begged.

Maura cleared her throat. "He was found Tuesday night, lying in a field by the side of a two-lane road. Unconscious. The local police said he appeared to have been beaten up and dumped from a passing car. The owner of the property didn't recognize him and there were no witnesses as to how he might have gotten there, despite the story being on local news."

The small room fell silent. Leigh suspected that Lester, like her, didn't know whether to be overjoyed or horrified.

"Is he awake now?" Leigh asked finally. "Does he understand where he is, what's happening?"

Maura nodded. "As of yesterday, I think so. Apparently he can't speak because of a broken and rewired jaw, but he's following what they're saying. They've set him up with a tablet of some sort so that he can communicate, but so far he hasn't been able to control his hands well enough to do much except hit yes or no."

"Are they sure it's Arch?" Lester asked.

Maura nodded again. "The local police made a presumptive ID from the photos, but they're telling me the patient himself confirmed it. Picked out his name from a list."

"I want to see him," Lester blurted. "Will they let me?"

Maura's mouth twisted thoughtfully. "It's family only at the moment. His nearest relative has been notified. But I suspect that once he gets stable enough to communicate better, the hospital will let him decide for himself who he wants to see."

Lester's shoulders slumped. "He's not got any family he's close to anymore; they won't come. But he's hurt bad. He shouldn't be up there all alone."

Maura nodded sympathetically. "I'll be driving out to see him myself first thing tomorrow. I'll see what I can do."

Leigh's concerned gaze caught her friend's tired eyes. Maura was expecting the test results from her obstetrician within hours; she had sworn she would have "the talk" with her husband today. Yet here she was, working full speed and making plans for early tomorrow.

"Nothing personal, Koslow," Maura said stiffly. "But I need to talk to Mr. Brown alone now."

Leigh acquiesced. She bade farewell to Lester and walked to the door with the detective following. As soon as Leigh was outside, she turned around. "Maura, under the circumstances, couldn't you—"

"I'm fine," Maura returned gruffly. "I need to work."

Leigh decided to leave the issue alone. Maybe distraction was good medicine. "They do expect Archie to survive... don't they?" she asked quietly. "Why is the case yours now?"

Maura's voice sobered. "As far as we can tell, Koslow, a man was forcefully abducted from his home, taken across state lines, beaten till he was unconscious, and abandoned in a field. We have more than one charge for that, but the worst of them belongs in my department."

Leigh tensed.

"Attempted homicide."

Leigh parked her van in the Brown's driveway, but did not get out immediately. The sky had become overcast, just as the weatherman had promised, and the wind was picking up. Leigh thought uneasily of the mother dog and pups as she watched amorphous blobs of dark clouds scoot across the sky.

She wasn't even sure why she had come here. She felt a need to warn people—the whole neighborhood, if need be, that they could all be in danger. But figuring out what to say to keep them *out* of danger was less than obvious. As far as she knew, Harvey was the only one outside her own family who even realized Archie and

Lester had been on a treasure hunt. And since whoever had knocked Lester unconscious and tried to kill Archie was obviously hell-bent on protecting the prize, anyone else they so much as suspected might be on the trail could become the next target.

Including herself and her—

Nope. Not going there.

No one else was going to know. Period. And no one else was going to suspect that she—or her family—knew anything either.

She got out of the van. Just as she swung the door shut, her phone rang with an obnoxious cuckoo sound. She muttered under her breath and picked up. "Hey, Alice," she said with dread.

"Hey, Alice?" the voice of her longtime coworker, graphic designer, and cofounder of her ad agency barked. "Hey, Alice? Don't 'Hey Alice' me! Quote Leigh Koslow: 'I will get you the concept for the Rinnamon account by Monday morning at the latest. Really. I swear you'll have *plenty* of time to finish the mockup before you head off for that fantasy cruise you so richly deserve. And if I don't, I'll be happy to foot the entire bill for it myself—'"

"I never said *that!*" Leigh protested.

"Well you should have!" Alice growled. "I swear to God, Leigh, I'm heading for the airport first thing Thursday morning no matter—"

"I know, I know!" Leigh soothed. "You *will go.* I do swear it. But I don't have the concept yet. This weekend has been—"

"You hear the violin I'm playing? Don't tell me your problems, Leigh. You just get that snarky, totally undeserved, million-dollar imagination of yours in gear *now.* Go stare at a bunch of pottery crocks. Drink out of them. Sit on them. Spit chaw in them. Skeet shoot them. Line them up and roll bowling balls into them—*I do not care.* Just get me that concept!"

"Look, Alice—"

The line went dead.

Leigh muttered some more. *Pottery crocks!* How could she possibly think about something so mundane at a time when—

"Archie's dead, isn't he?"

Leigh spun around. Scotty O'Malley stood at the edge of his yard, his shorts dappled with a purplish liquid the color of beets, his hair sticking out in spikes as if he'd styled it with a tub of margarine. "Well?" he repeated, his tone as snotty as his expression.

"Isn't he?"

"No!" Leigh answered, a little more sharply than intended. "He isn't dead."

Scotty's eyes narrowed skeptically. "How do *you* know?"

Leigh's brain searched for the wisest way to answer. There was no point in trying to keep Archie's plight a secret; it had already been broadcast on local news in Ohio and might soon hit the Pittsburgh stations as well. She couldn't err by giving away his exact location because she didn't know it. But for everyone in the neighborhood to hear that something terrible had happened to Archie would surely increase their general wariness, and that was a good thing.

"The police have located Mr. Pratt in a hospital in Ohio," she informed. "He's been in a coma. But we're hoping he'll be all right."

Scotty's pupils widened and his jaw dropped. He let out a completely inappropriate expletive. "What happened to him? Did the ghosts maul him? Did he have, like, that green ecto-slime stuff all over him?"

Leigh prayed for patience. "The police think someone beat him up. But ghosts had nothing to do with it."

"You don't know that!" Scotty spit back. "I'm telling you, that place is *crawling* with ghosts!"

Leigh opened her mouth to issue her standard disclaimer about the supernatural, but something stopped her. "How recently have you seen ghosts out there?"

"I just saw the headless one again last night!" he crowed.

Last night? The same night that someone chiseled out most of the mortar from around the biggest stone in the cellar wall... after smashing her Aunt Bess's camera to bits. How had they known the camera was there? Had they seen it hidden in the dark? Or—the thought chilled her—had they watched Warren and Ethan set it up?

The camera had been placed in plain view, at least potentially, of everyone at the Brown's house. And if even one person had witnessed the event, the word was sure to travel. Anyone in the neighborhood could have heard about it.

Anyone *in the neighborhood.*

Leigh gave her shoulders a shake. She was getting paranoid. The camera had been hidden, yes, but only so well. The lens could have reflected in anyone's flashlight—the camera was probably easier to spot at night, in fact. And it did make the slightest of buzzing noises when it turned on.

"I see the headless one the most," Scotty continued. "It's the scariest, because it's got no head. The soldier ghost is more normal-like."

Leigh studied the boy's face. She believed that he saw what he said he saw. And why shouldn't she? Despite her attempt to believe otherwise, she had seen the headless "ghost" herself. Someone had been skulking around Archie's place both before and after he was abducted, and they were covering their tracks with a disguise designed to make sure any reported sightings were dismissed as nonsense.

And what of the "soldier" ghost? Leigh's mouth twisted with chagrin as she realized how easily Archie could have created that illusion himself. There were legends of hauntings at the farm already… who better than a Civil War reenactor to reach into his coat closet and play the part? If he dug at night, he most likely wouldn't be seen; but if he was, viewers were sure to doubt their own eyes. No harm, no foul.

Except now, they had both.

"What time did you see the headless ghost last night?" she demanded.

Scotty shrugged. "Don't know. Wasn't paying attention. Everybody was in bed already, but I remembered I left my phone by the crick. I ran down to get it and saw the ghost and ran straight back. It was, like, traumatizing!"

Leigh felt a little traumatized herself. "Where exactly did you see this ghost?"

Scotty pointed vaguely toward the creek between his house and the Brown's. "I don't know, somewhere around the woods on the other side. I didn't stick around. Ghosts can disembowel you if they stare you in the eyes, did you know that?"

"I did not," Leigh said charitably. "But thanks for the warning."

"Blood and guts everywhere!" he said with enthusiasm. Then his face turned wistful. "Wish I could see that."

Leigh turned away toward the Brown's house. "Be sure you stay in your own yard, Scotty," she warned. "Poking around Mr. Pratt's farm could be really dangerous right now."

He nodded his head sharply as he ran alongside her. "Oh, I

know. My mom won't let me out of the house!"

Leigh stopped and looked at him. "And yet… here you are."

The boy smirked. "Yeah. I'm *good.*"

Admonishing Scotty once again to go home and stay there, Leigh reached the Brown's front door and rang the bell. To her relief, the boy scarpered off just as the door swung open.

Leigh looked into the scowling face of Pauline. "So," the older woman said accusingly. "You going to make noise, too? Might as well. Can't hear my damned show anyway." With that, Pauline turned her back, tapped her bamboo cane on the floor, and shuffled off toward the sitting room.

Leigh followed. "Now, Adith," she heard Emma say with frustration. "You know what the doctor said. He said—"

Adith made a rude sound. "The *doctor!* That man couldn't pick me out of a lineup if I had my name tattooed across my face! He probably just prescribed whatever the last salesman in the door gave him a free beach towel to peddle! My old medicine was just fine. I don't like this new stuff, and I'm not taking it anymore. Period!"

"It's always best to follow your doctor's orders," Nora insisted, sounding like one of those welcome videos that hospitals loop endlessly on their in-house cable channels. "They have the training and they know what's best."

"And how exactly is falling asleep face down in my oatmeal *what's best?*" Adith railed. "I'm missing every halfway exciting thing that happens around here, and I'm sick of it. I'm allowed to make my own medical decisions, and I'm making this one. No more nod-off pills!"

Leigh poked her head into the sitting room just in time to see Adith cross her arms over her chest and stamp her foot.

"All right, all right, then," Emma soothed. "Of course it's your decision. But we'll have to call the office and tell them what you're doing. They may want you to try something else."

Adith's chin rose in triumph. "I got no problem with that."

"I can't hear my show!" Pauline roared.

"Excuse me," Leigh said tentatively. "I have some news for everyone."

Four faces turned toward her instantly. After a moment's pause, a fifth listener slipped through the partway open door to the screened porch and joined them. Derrick had a burp rag the size of a toga thrown over his shoulder, and despite the ambient noise, baby Cory was squirming contentedly within its folds.

"Is Harvey back yet?" Leigh asked, hearing no sound from the direction of his room.

Emma shook her head. "He's still at the library. I was just headed up to the hospital to see about Lester's discharge… what's happened?"

"The police have located Archie in a hospital in Ohio," Leigh announced. "He's been in a coma, but he's awake now."

Adith's eyes bugged with disbelief. Emma, Nora, and Derrick all looked horrified. Pauline seemed bored.

"A coma?" Emma repeated. "But *why?* How did he end up in Ohio?"

"That's all still being investigated," Leigh answered. "Archie can't talk because his jaw is broken, so he hasn't been able to communicate much yet. But apparently he was found in a field in a rural area. They think he was beaten up and left there."

The room went deathly quiet. Leigh hated being the bearer of such grim tidings, even if they did contain the good news that Archie was, at least, still alive.

"Well," Adith said hoarsely, breaking the silence. "Call me a buck-naked lizard. That poor, poor man. Who would have expected something like that?"

Pauline harrumphed. "I'd hate to see his hospital bill. Highway robbery!"

"But what—" Nora broke in with distress, "I don't understand. Why would he go to Ohio in the first place?"

"We don't know that he went voluntarily," Leigh responded.

"Kidnapped from his home!" Emma exclaimed, her apple cheeks suffused with red. "Lord have mercy!"

"Is that really what happened?" Nora implored, her own complexion ghostly white.

"We don't know," Leigh repeated.

"I've got to tell Lester," Emma cried.

"He's already heard," Leigh explained. "I was visiting with him when Detective Polanski told us both. She was still talking to him when I left."

"You mean your friend? Why is she talking to Lester?" Emma

asked with alarm.

Leigh took a breath. "It's a new investigation now. Attempted homicide."

Emma drew in a breath like a hiccup, her hand covering her mouth. Nora and Adith stood still as statues. Derrick, who looked every bit as pale as his wife, folded softly into the nearest chair. Pauline belched.

"They have to treat the case that way because of the seriousness of Archie's injuries," Leigh placated, hating to frighten them all. "They don't know what happened. It's just the routine." Then, remembering the role of a healthy fear in keeping them all safe, she amended. "Still, we all need to be careful, living so close, until it's resolved."

"Don't make no sense," Adith muttered. "Poor man wasn't bothering nobody. At least not nobody living."

"Derrick," Nora ordered, "You'd better take Cory on home, now that he's settled. I'll be there in an hour or so—as soon as Emma gets back with Lester."

Derrick rose obligingly, and Nora kissed her baby on the head and tucked the ends of the blanket around him. Derrick headed for the front door. "And don't forget his medicine!" she admonished, just before the door closed behind them.

Nora sighed. "He's going to forget the medicine."

Emma patted her absently on the shoulder. "Derrick's going to be a wonderful father, dear. Cory seems to feel quite safe with him—that's all that matters to a little one." Her gaze cast around for her keys or purse, or something. "I've got to get going now," she murmured, clearly flustered.

"Are you sure you're okay to drive?" Leigh asked.

"Oh, of course," Emma answered quickly. "I'll be fine, dear. I'd better be, because if I know Lester, I'll be driving him to Ohio first thing tomorrow morning." Her eyes misted. "Poor Archie. I just can't believe anyone would want to hurt that sweet man!"

"Don't make no sense!" Adith said again.

"Damn hippies don't care who you are," Pauline grunted. "Only a fool would trust a stranger!"

Leigh made no comment. She bid a sober farewell to the group and let herself out the front door. She wondered what Harvey had been doing at the library all this time. She wondered if Lester was finally confessing the whole truth to Maura. She wondered if the mother dog would get hungry before Leigh could get Maura—or someone else equally well equipped to scare off bad guys—to accompany her back to the tool shed to put out more food.

And she wondered, with every shaky step she took back to her van, whether Archie's assailants had been strangers at all.

Chapter 19

"Why don't you and the kids stay and eat with us?" Cara suggested as she dug into her refrigerator and began pulling out an assortment of organic vegetables. "Gil's got a business dinner, but Mom's staying. I can make that fabulous vegetarian casserole the men hate so much!"

With grateful assent, Leigh picked up a knife, washed a zucchini, and began to make her usual contribution to dinner at Cara's: chopping things. The women had a longtime understanding about the March's kitchen. Once any actual cooking commenced, Leigh got out of the way.

She was anxious. Cara, Lydie, and Warren all knew about Archie's being located; but none of them knew exactly how to feel about it. She had been looking forward to talking the situation through with her husband, but his meeting had run late and now he had a long drive back. The delay clearly perturbed him; he was anxious to get home, no doubt because he wanted to make *her* stay home. But of course he worried too much. She had sworn up and down that she would not go back to Archie's place to feed the dog with any escort short of an armed police officer, and she didn't *want* to go back, even then.

"Where is your mom?" Leigh asked, looking around. She had seen Lydie's car in the driveway, but the only voices she heard around the house were those of Mathias and Ethan hooting over a video game upstairs.

"She and the girls are in Lenna's room," Cara answered. "I'm pretty sure Allison is pumping Mom for more input on the map."

Leigh exhaled loudly. "I was hoping she'd given up on that."

Cara's eyebrows rose. "We are talking about your daughter, aren't we?"

"I know, I know," Leigh acknowledged. "She's a Morton woman."

Cara smiled. "In spades. Which reminds me..." she stepped to the doorway, cast a glance down the hall, then returned. "Something is definitely up with my mother. I'm telling you—she's seeing somebody."

Leigh remembered the "prior commitment" her aunt had claimed the afternoon before, yet refused to discuss. "You think so?"

"I know the signs," Cara insisted. "You can always tell when she's lying. Her mouth tightens and it stretches out her upper lip. She did that my entire childhood whenever I asked *anything* about my father. She did it when we were in college and she was seeing that dentist down the street in West View. She did it when Gil and I first started dating, and again right after Mathias was born—and I never even found out who it was those times. I've been suspicious on a few occasions since, but never anything definite, until now. And this time's different, because she's got this funny glow in her eyes. Whoever he is, I think this time she likes him back!"

"Wouldn't that be fabulous?" Leigh mused. "But why the secrecy?"

Cara shook her head with a sigh. "I think it's all wrapped up with her having spent so many years flaying herself for making a bad marriage. She's worried we'd all think less of her if she wasn't totally independent. Which is insane, but there's no talking to her about it. She will *not* discuss the subject. Period. Ever. It drives me bonkers."

Leigh's phone buzzed with a text. She pulled it out and looked at the number. The blood drained from her face.

"What is it?" Cara demanded.

"It's a text," Leigh said weakly. "From my mother."

"Your mother doesn't text!"

"Not when the gods were merciful," Leigh said morosely, sinking onto a stool. She turned her phone toward Cara. "Check it out."

This is your mother. I can text now!

"Oh, my," Cara exclaimed.

Leigh drew in a cleansing breath. Frances's well-meaning sisters had been trying for years to teach her the art of texting, but Frances had staunchly resisted all instruction. Leigh had secretly applauded her mother's refusal to join the millennium, but now, the worst had happened. Unsolicited household tips and cleaning advice would arrive with a ding, every two minutes, for the rest of her natural life.

Or until she got rid of her own phone.

Desperate situations...

"Act like you didn't get it," Cara suggested. "She'll think she didn't do it right or that it's not reliable, and she'll poo-poo the whole thing again."

Leigh smiled. "You are a brilliant and devious woman."

Cara grinned back. "I try."

Allison, Lenna, and Lydie appeared at the entrance to the kitchen. Allison's small face shone with excitement. "Mom!" she said proudly. "We figured it out. We know where 'The Guide' is!"

Leigh and Cara sat at the kitchen table. Allison stood between them, the map spread out before her.

"I couldn't stop thinking about Theodore's being buried on the farm," Allison explained ruefully. "That's what threw me off. That, and not understanding why the farmhouse was the only building at Frog Hill that the mapmaker drew in. But we should have figured that out the morning you found Lester, Mom."

"We should have?"

"Of course!" Allison argued. "Everyone else was focused on the cellar under the tool shed, weren't they? It seemed like maybe Archie had found 'The Guide' already and it was leading him there. But what Archie found out from Dora, right before all this started happening, was that Theodore had been living in a cabin above that cellar when he died!"

Leigh was not enlightened. "True, but didn't Tom Carr make the map?"

Allison frowned. "That was my fault. I *wanted* Theodore's grave to be marked on the map, so I found something that looked like a gravestone and made it fit. That's what screwed everything up so badly."

She smoothed the map with her hands. "Theodore's grave isn't marked anywhere on here, because Theodore wasn't dead yet! He's the one who drew it. And the building he drew as its focus wasn't the big farmhouse at all. It was the house he was living in at the time. The old cabin!"

Leigh and Cara both leaned in, their eyes focusing on the

scribbled square to which the arrow pointed. "The tool shed," Leigh said, pondering. "Of course. If you start the map there, every other building on the farm is in the cut-off area. No wonder there's only one square."

"I'm not certain," Lydie added quietly. "But my guess is that the man's idea was to hide his treasure somewhere on the farm, but leave a way for his heirs—someone besides his son, evidently—to find it someday. He must have assumed that the farm would continue to be handed down through the family. He made it a two-step process because he wanted somebody to work for it. He was intent on keeping it out of the wrong hands."

"That's where 'The Guide' comes in," Allison finished. "The spokes and Xs don't make sense without it. But if we had it, we would know which spoke is the right one, and which X is the right one. And that X will point out the exact spot where the real treasure is buried!"

"But there have been holes all over the neighborhood for years now," Cara said. "Even some in my yard! What were those people doing?"

Allison shrugged. "Probably trying to dig up every X on the map. But anybody who was trying to center the spokes on the farmhouse would be off by a mile."

"If the old cabin was leveled in the fifties," Lydie added, "it would be only natural for anyone seeing the farm after that to assume the map referred to the farmhouse."

"Including Archie," Leigh murmured, thinking of the ripped out drywall.

"What people forget," Lydie continued, "is the effect of time on the landscape. In Theodore's day the only woods left were on hillsides too steep to plow. But when the farming stopped, the forests began to expand again. The landscape looked different in the twenties, when he died, than it did in the fifties, when Dora saw it. And it looks very different now."

Allison nodded emphatically. "Aunt Lydie said that before, but we didn't understand how important it was to reading the map right. Look, Mom," she urged, pointing to the squiggle she had previously designated as Theodore's gravestone. "I thought this was just past the edge of the woods, because that's how Dora explained it. But *our* woods now go all the way down to here!" She swept her finger down the hill, past the squiggle and halfway to the creek. "If you think about it, all those trees are skinnier and younger than the ones higher up. They didn't even exist when this was drawn!"

Leigh's eyes pored over the sketch, imagining the woods as Allison described. A light dawned. "Of course," she said, looking at Cara. She pointed to the squiggle. "This is the rock you and I sat on the other day, when we were out looking for the puppies!"

Allison nodded so vigorously her whole body shook. "Exactly! Parts of the map still aren't perfect, like this farm—but I think that's because Theodore didn't come over here much. As long as you center the map right, the places he does know are drawn pretty well!"

"As soon as Grandma told us about the trees, I knew what the squiggle was," Lenna said proudly. "That rock's really cool. When we were little, Matt used to pretend it was his throne!"

"So what does all this mean?" Cara asked her cousin. "In terms of what's been happening in the neighborhood?"

Leigh's enthusiasm fizzled. "Nothing, really. Archie must have figured out that 'The Guide' was in the cellar. Although how he—" she broke off. "Of course. The hydraulic excavator. He and Lester probably took a half-hearted stab at chiseling out one of the stones, and then decided to heck with it. They would just dig the whole thing up and search through the rubble. I bet they still don't know *where* in the cellar it might be."

"I just hope Theodore didn't put it in the cabin walls or ceiling," Allison added bleakly. "If he did, it's already lost forever."

"I do think it's rather odd," Lydie mused, "that the mapmaker was so specific with the Xs, but left so little guidance about *where* in the cabin 'The Guide' might be."

Five heads lowered to stare at the map again. After a long moment, Allison squealed. "Mom! The stone that Mr. Pratt started to chisel—what did it look like?"

Leigh blinked. Had she told Allison about that?

Never mind. "There were smaller stones someone had worked on, too," she answered. "But the one that—" she hesitated a moment, then decided more secrecy was pointless. "The one that's received the most attention lately was in the middle of the wall opposite the stairs." She fell silent a moment, castigating herself. She had never stopped to think why that particular stone had been chosen. But it was certainly the focus of their 'headless ghost' as well. "It was close to rectangular, and it was the biggest stone in the wall. Maybe that made it the most likely candidate? Unless Archie knew something we don't know."

"Maybe he did!" Allison exclaimed. "Look at where it says 'The Guide.' Look close!"

Leigh looked close. All she saw were the same two words, circled by an irregular border with an arrow pointing to the house.

"The shape!" Cara exclaimed. "At first glance it looks like somebody's scribbled attempt at an oval. But what if those irregularities were intentional?"

"It's telling you what stone 'The Guide' is hidden behind!" Allison practically shouted. "It must be!"

Leigh stared at the shape. It did not seem to match her memory of the large stone, but that wasn't saying much. She had not paid close attention.

"I'm not sure," Lydie said, frowning. "I remember that stone as being pretty smooth on the edges. Besides, it wouldn't be easy for an elderly man working without power tools to pull out any of the larger ones by himself. Much less get one back in afterwards. And although you couldn't tell it now, putting in new mortar would have been a dead giveaway for quite some time afterwards."

Power tools. Lester said he had heard some kind of a motor running. A power chisel?

"But look at it!" Allison insisted. "I'm sure that's what it means!" She turned to her mother in earnest. "Couldn't we—"

"Absolutely not!" Leigh said firmly, anticipating the request. "No way, no how! *No one* is going back in that cellar until whoever hurt Mr. Pratt is behind bars. *Period.*"

"Your mother's right, Allison," Lydie said gently. "There will be plenty of time to finish the puzzle later, when it's safe."

Allison's head bowed. "I guess."

The crunch of tires sounded on the drive, and Cara rose and walked to the window. "It's Aunt Frances," she announced. She looked at her mother and Leigh in turn. "Were either of you expecting her?"

Both heads shook.

"Aunt Lydie," Leigh asked fearfully. "Please tell me you didn't already tell her what happened to Archie."

Lydie's face remained impassive. "Actually, no. I haven't."

"Oh well," Cara said with cheer, returning to her vegetables. "I'll have plenty of casserole. The more the merrier! Leigh, would you let her in?"

Leigh did a temporary disable on Cara's security system—which had been on "high alert" ever since Lester was assaulted—and opened the door. Frances strutted in with her usual air of authority, offering Leigh a stiff nod of welcome and then smiling indulgently at the girls. "Hello, darlings," she said sweetly. "Can you run along upstairs for a moment? I need a word with the other adults."

Allison displayed no reluctance, but quickly refolded the map, stuffed it in a back pocket, and retreated with Lenna in the direction of their brothers' still-raised voices.

Leigh wished she could escape as well. She especially wished she could do what Allison was doing now, lurking in the hallway outside listening to the conversation without having to be there.

"What's up, Mom?" Leigh asked.

Frances scowled. "You are living in an unsecured house in an unsafe neighborhood with no men present, and you ask me what's up? I've come to bring you and the children home with me for the evening. Your father won't be home till seven, but at least our house is in a nice area. Cara dear, you're welcome to bring your children, too. We'll have my meatloaf surprise. The children all adore it, you know."

Leigh froze. How did Frances know that Warren couldn't make it home? There was only one way.

Her loving husband was in serious, *serious* trouble.

Cara smiled, slowly and sweetly, without the slightest hint of insincerity. Leigh had always admired her cousin's acting chops. "Oh, Aunt Frances, that is so thoughtful of you! But really, there's no need. I've already got dinner started for everyone. The security system is on and Gil won't be too much longer. Won't you join us? Please?"

Damn, she's good.

Frances melted a bit. "Well, I—" she looked at her sister, who made no appreciable movement, but was probably twin-telepathing some form of encouragement. "All right, I suppose. Thank you." She looked at Leigh. "Did you get my message? I've learned to text!

Isn't that wonderful? I thought it was too complicated, but I was chatting with this delightful young man in line at the bank, and he offered to—"

Leigh's phone buzzed, and she swooped it up immediately. "Sorry, Mom," she lied. "I have to take this call."

She stepped aside and viewed the number with trepidation. It was the Browns' landline. She started toward the hall, but knew she would bump into Allison. Instead she turned, stepped out onto the sun porch, and closed the door behind her. "Hello? Emma?"

"It's Adith," a voice whispered. "Can you come over here?"

"What's going on?" Leigh asked, her heartbeat quickening.

"It's Harvey," Adith responded, distraught. "He's *gone!*"

Chapter 20

Leigh drove, rather than walked, to the Brown's house. She had no desire to be wandering alone around the neighborhood, but even if she did, the weather had turned ominous. It was not yet dusk and the sun had already given up, submitting to strangulation by an ever increasing mass of blue-black storm clouds. She could only hope that the mother dog had gotten her litter under cover somewhere, because the coming storm promised to be a doozy.

Leigh had told the other women only that Mrs. Rhodis wanted to see her about something, and that she would return before the casserole was done. It was a promise she intended to keep. She had barely shifted the van into park when Adith appeared at the front door of the house and shuffled out toward her as rapidly as her arthritic joints would allow. Leigh got out and met her in the middle of the yard, and Adith scanned the area warily before speaking. "Shhh!" she ordered, a finger to her lips. "You never know who's listening around here!" She led Leigh a few more paces away from the house, then let her story fly.

"Harvey's gone, he's missing, and Emma's totally frantic! We only just noticed a while ago, but there's no telling how long he's been gone. Lester doesn't know—his head was aching and Emma put him straight to bed and won't let him talk to anybody till he's better. She's such a fussbudget, you know. Why the last time I had the flu—"

"I thought Harvey was at the library?" Leigh interrupted.

"He was!" Adith insisted. "His friend brought him home hours ago and of course I met him at the door and told him about Archie straightaway. He seemed awfully upset but he didn't say much—just made a beeline for his bedroom and shut the door. When Emma got back with Lester, Harvey didn't come out to greet them, which I thought was strange. So a little bit later I went and knocked on his door. He didn't answer, so of course I had to open it. And he wasn't there!"

"Isn't there somewhere else he could be?" Leigh asked, desperate to come up with some nonviolent, non-Civil-War-related theory for his disappearance. "Maybe he went for a walk?"

Adith dropped her chin reprovingly. "Now when have you known that bag of bones to walk more than ten feet in any direction? Harvey doesn't go *anywhere*. He's always in his room, the sitting room, or the dining room. In nice weather, maybe the porch or deck, but even then he hates the sun. Emma and Lester are always offering to take him places, but he never wants to go. Only to the library. And not even that very often. Besides, will you look at this sky? No one in their right mind would be wandering around outside now!"

As if on cue, the clouds opened. Heavy raindrops at first fell sporadically, making scattered thumps on the grass and the women's heads. By the time they reached the cover of the porch, the rain was falling in sheets, and they hustled inside.

"I think you should call that detective friend of yours," Adith said, her voice dropping back to a whisper. "Whatever's happened to Harvey, I'm telling you..." Her usually mischievous eyes suffused with fear. "It's no coincidence!"

"I called her just now," Leigh admitted. "And I left a message. I'm sure she'll get back to me." Leigh *was* sure, although she would not lay odds on when. The call had gone straight to voice mail. Maura was technically off duty and almost certainly in the midst of a serious and personal conversation with her husband.

Leigh's phone buzzed, and she pulled it quickly from her pocket. Her shoulders slumped. It was another text from her mother.

Did you remember to vacuum behind the lint trap in your dryer?

Leigh stuffed the phone back in place. "That wasn't Maura," she explained dully. "Where is Emma, by the way?"

The question answered itself as rapid footsteps creaked on the stairs and Emma emerged from the hall door, her hair disheveled and face glowing with sweat. "Oh, Leigh! It's you," she said with obvious disappointment. "I heard the door slam and thought—. Well, never mind. Did Adith tell you? Do you have any idea where he could have gone?"

Leigh shook her head. "I'm sorry. No. I haven't spoken to him since yesterday afternoon."

Emma's countenance fell even further. "Well, I'm at my wit's end. I called his friend Amos and he was already back in West Mifflin—said he dropped Harvey off hours ago and hasn't seen or heard from him since. Adith and Nora and Pauline all saw him go into his room, but none of them saw him come out again. And I've searched everywhere! Upstairs, downstairs, every corner of the basement, the closets in the garage—I even called for him out in the yard. The man is just not here! He's never done anything like this before!"

"Under the circumstances," Leigh said as calmly as she could manage, "I think you should call the police."

Emma ran a hand through hair that was now half up in a bun, half down over her neck, attempted briefly to correct it, then gave up. "I think you're right," she agreed. "He's been acting so strange lately. Almost paranoid. I should have asked him about it, but with everything that's been going on with Lester—"

"Don't blame yourself," Leigh commanded as moisture welled up in Emma's eyes. "We'll find him. But we need the police. None of us can go out searching right now. It isn't safe."

"Amen to that!" Adith added.

Emma nodded. "I'll call 911 right now. Unless you want me to call your—"

"No," Leigh insisted. "You're right. Call 911 and get an officer out as soon as possible." *Any* officer, she thought to herself.

As Emma headed to the sitting room to pick up the phone, Adith grabbed Leigh's elbow and steered her—rather painfully—through Harvey's open doorway and into his room. "I looked on his desk already," Adith bragged, "and in his closet. His desk looks like he's cleaned it up. Almost like he was hiding something!"

Leigh cast a glance at the giant mahogany writing desk, which was indeed clear of folders, loose papers, and most anything else that would give evidence to what Harvey had been doing. Even the books he'd had out before were all back on their shelves.

"He doesn't even own a coat," Adith mentioned as she rummaged through the clothes in his closet. "Whenever he does go out, Emma makes him take one of Lester's. But he's not wearing it now. He wore it to the library—but he left it on the bed. See?"

Leigh did see. It certainly did not appear as though Harvey had prepared for a lengthy stroll on a stormy night. But it did appear as if he had prepared for something. "Have you ever seen his desk as clean as this?"

Adith shook her head emphatically. "Never! What do you make of it?"

Leigh's eyes roved the room, coming to rest on the small trash can by the side of Harvey's chair.

"Oh, I already went through that," Adith said dismissively. "It was full of scribbled notes yesterday, but it got emptied before... Well, all that's in it now is some tissues. That's what you usually find in Harvey's trash. Scribbled notes and tissues. Every once in a while a bandage wrapper or a toothpick. But those usually wind up in the bathroom."

How Adith knew these things, Leigh chose not to ask. But as she looked closer into the trash can, a flash of white just beyond it caught her eye. She reached down and picked up a small piece of notepaper, well crumpled, that had evidently missed its mark.

"Ooh!" Adith cooed. "I didn't see that! What does it say?"

Leigh unfolded the small square. It was covered with large, childlike printing, awkward and difficult to read. Three lines crossed the paper.

Have what you want

Will sell cheap

Meet me at dusk at Archie's

Leigh's breath caught in her throat. Behind her shoulder came a gasp.

"Ooh, Lordy!" Adith crooned. "I knew it! I knew something was up with that man! Who could it be from? How could he fall for something like that? Why would he go? Oh, mercy! They've lured him! Lured him just like Archie and Lester!"

Outside in the sitting room, Leigh could barely hear Emma's frantic call to the police over the omnipresent buzz of Pauline's television. "This isn't good," Leigh muttered unnecessarily. "Not good at all." A look out of Harvey's window confirmed the worst. The wind was howling, the rain was pelting, and dusk would almost certainly be setting in for real... *right about now.*

Leigh stared again at the note, trying to make sense of it. Where and how had Harvey received it? Had it been sent directly to him... or was it intended for somebody else?

Emma appeared in the doorway, her face drained. "The police are on their way," she announced. "I'm not sure they understood what I was saying about Archie and Lester and everything... but they're coming."

"Well, praise the Lord!" Adith said heavily, dropping into Harvey's chair.

A thought struck Leigh. "Where is Gimli?" she asked. "Has anybody seen him?"

Both women's eyes searched the room. "I'm sure he's here somewhere," Emma insisted. "Poor creature can barely stir himself to get to the litter box and back."

Adith's expression turned suddenly intent. "Fat old thing don't even get to the sitting room. He's always in here."

Leigh's phone buzzed with a text. She clenched her teeth and pulled it out. It could be Maura, after all. But it was not. It was Frances.

OH MY LORD! ALLISON HAS DISAPPEARED! SH

The text cut off. The phone buzzed immediately with another.

SHE'S RUN OFF TO THAT CELLAR!!!

Leigh's body flashed with heat. Her pulse pounded in her veins. She dialed her mother's number and Frances picked up immediately.

"She's gone!!!" Frances screeched. "They were talking about how to find that silly rock, and we had just put the casserole in and then the other children came down and she wasn't with them and they said they'd just seen her five minutes ago but now she's gone and I just *know* she sneaked out with that silly map to see if—"

Leigh didn't hear anymore. She stuffed the phone into her pocket and the crumpled note into Emma's hands. Then she ran out the front door into the storm.

Allison can't be in the cellar, Leigh told herself as she ran. *She just can't.* Leigh's orders had been too explicit. Allison was smart; she wouldn't go against them unless it was a matter of life and death...

What was the girl thinking?!

Leigh's eyes roved the generous slope of grass—now mud—that stretched between the Brown's back yard and Cara's place. If she hurried, maybe she could cut Allison off before she reached the cellar. Frances said she had been gone less than five minutes...

Sheets of rain pelted Leigh's face and eyes, making it difficult to see. She ran toward the creek bridge, stopping every few feet to scan the landscape for movement. Would Allison run across the open space, or would she make her way through the trees on the hill to be less visible? Leigh looked up into the woods, but visibility in that direction was even worse. The trees swayed and bowed in the wind; leaves not yet ready to fall were giving up and doing it anyway. A crack of thunder sounded.

Allison could *not* be out here. Had the child lost her mind?

Leigh reached the creek bridge. If Allison had come from Cara's house, she would not need to cross it to get to the cellar, because Snow Creek Farm, like Frog Hill, was on the far side of the creek from the road. But even if Allison had come through the trees, she could not get to the cellar itself without sprinting the last hundred feet in the open.

Leigh saw something. She started to cry out—then stopped. Whatever she had seen moving in the woods directly behind her, it wasn't Allison. It had been twice as tall.

She could have sworn it was a man. A man who, upon her notice of him, had ducked behind a tree.

Stay calm, she begged herself. *The police are already on their way.* She made no movement, but stood her ground. Her eyes were fixed on the tree, but the figure did not reappear. Had she imagined it?

She wished.

A vicious wave of chill bumps swept up her spine. Her clothes were soaked. Wet bangs drooped down over her eyes; her socks squished in her shoes. And clearly, she was not alone. But none of that mattered. All that mattered was stopping Allison from coming any closer.

She decided to go for broke. "Allison!" she called, cupping her hands and shouting against the wind. "Allison! Can you hear me?"

There was no response. The wind grew more forceful, whipping her wet shirt around her waist and flapping the hem of her capris at her calves.

It was no use. Allison could be fifty yards away and not hear her.

Leigh ran briefly in the direction of Cara's farm, scanning the creek bed as far as she could see. There was no one. Had she already missed Allison?

Her jaws clenched. She turned, ran back to the bridge, and crossed it. Beneath her feet, the creek was already swelling. Were she not already soaked to the bone, its fast-moving depths might have looked threatening, but the swirling brown eddies hardly registered in her mind. She ran on until the tool shed was in her sights, and she kept running until she had surveyed every possible angle of approach to it.

She did not see Allison anywhere. If Leigh had been too late to intercept her by the creek, or if Allison had slipped behind her mother through the woods, she could already be in the cellar by now.

Meet me at dusk at Archie's.

Leigh's eyes fixed on the cellar's wooden doors. They were closed. Her heart pounded.

She made another scan of the landscape around her. A flash of movement caught her eye, and her heart tipped into palpitation. *Another man.* Someone equally tall, ducking quickly behind the corner of the barn.

If she was not soaking wet, completely terrified, half-blind from rain and the other half from hysteria, she could have sworn she'd seen a Union soldier.

She drew in a breath, braced her spine, and clenched her teeth tight.

Whatever!

An entire forest of ghosts, real or imitation, could surround Frog Hill Farm and she wouldn't give a fig—all that mattered was getting her daughter the hell out of that cellar. The police should be arriving at the Brown's any moment now, and Adith and Emma would send them straight out. All she had to do was find Allison and keep the girl with her...

Leigh's eyes fixed on the cellar doors. Her lids narrowed and her hands balled into fists. Stupid hole was not going to defeat her. She was going back in the damned place one more time and that was it.

Throwing any thoughts of careful entry to the wind, Leigh threw open the cellar doors and rushed down the steps like a charging infantryman. "Allison Harmon!" she shouted, none too affectionately, "You get yourself back—"

Leigh stopped at the bottom of the stairs and blinked. The cellar was dark. But at least the rain had stopped pelting her. And she could see well enough to know that at least on the near side of the cellar, there was nothing to see.

"Allison?" she said again, this time in a whisper. "Are you here?"

She could not see into far corners where the dim light from the stairway failed to penetrate. And of course, she had no flashlight.

Oh, to hell with it!

Launching herself forward like a child playing airplane, Leigh extended her arms and ran a blind sweep around the far corner of the cellar. In three seconds, she was back where she started. She had seen nothing, felt nothing. Neither along the walls or under her feet.

Allison wasn't here.

Leigh thought no more. She put her feet into gear and charged up the stairs with the same speed she'd used coming down them. Just let somebody try to stop her now.

When in an instant she found herself safely above ground again, with the rain and the wind pelting her anew, she had to admit a certain surprise. She cast a glance at the still-open cellar doors and allowed herself a smirk.

You lose.

Once again, she scanned the landscape around her. It was growing darker, and fast. In a mere ten minutes there would be no light at all.

Knowing that Allison was not in the cellar was some relief. But it was hardly enough. If Allison hadn't gone into the cellar, where had she gone? What if she had reached it while Leigh was still looking downstream, and what if she had run into—

No. Leigh couldn't think that way. She just had to find her.

Lightning flashed. In the sudden burst of illumination Leigh could see a figure moving across the bridge. Not Allison... but someone. Someone who was walking straight toward her.

In a heartbeat, Leigh weighed her options. Then she moved slowly out from the corner of the shed and placed herself in a clearing that was within full view of both the approaching figure and—God willing—Adith Rhodis's trusty binoculars. To her surprise, the slightly bent figure kept coming toward her. Not hurriedly. Not aggressively. But as if, for all the world, he or she were merely out for a stroll.

When the figure got to within twenty feet of her, another convenient stroke of lightning showed his face.

"Derrick?" Leigh exclaimed with disbelief as they approached each other. He was wearing dress slacks, business loafers, and a cardigan sweater—all of which were thoroughly waterlogged. His hands appeared to be empty, but his limbs were taut, as if he were prepared for flight. "What are you doing out here?" she asked.

Derrick looked at her quizzically, twitching his nose as if he were about to sneeze. The resemblance to a rodent was comical. "What are *you* doing here?" he returned anxiously.

Leigh considered. It was a fair question. "I'm looking for my daughter," she answered. "She ran out of the house and I can't find her. Have you seen her?"

For all his obvious nervousness, the small man looked slightly relieved. "No, I haven't. Sorry. But it's hard to see much on a night like this. Why did she run out?"

Leigh's mind turned somersaults of confusion. Why Derrick was here, she didn't know, but he showed no signs of intending any harm. If anything, the man looked frightened of *her*. "I'm not sure why," she answered. "Have you seen Harvey?"

Derrick's eyebrows rose, then knit together again in puzzlement. "No, I… is he missing, too?"

"Maybe," Leigh answered, marveling at the absurdity of a conversation held by two people both equally determined to pretend that having a casual conversation in the middle of a driving rainstorm was an ordinary thing to do. "And why were you out here, again?" she queried.

Derrick's nose gave another twitch. "I just needed some air."

Leigh tried to think of an appropriate response to that. She failed.

"Well, I guess I'll be getting back now," he said awkwardly. "I hope you find your daughter. It's a nasty night."

Leigh nodded. "Yes, it is. Thank you."

Derrick returned her nod, gave a little wave, made an abrupt about-face, and headed back toward the bridge. Leigh watched him a moment, flummoxed. Then her fear set back in.

Where was Allison?!

She ran back over to the side of the tool shed, her nerves frayed to the breaking point. She felt as if she had fallen through the looking glass; nothing that was happening made any sense. It seemed as if she had been wandering around in the rain for an hour; in reality it had been only a few minutes. The thought of her daughter's being lost in the same nightmare brought sheer terror.

Stay calm, Leigh begged her beleaguered brain. *Don't be useless. Think!*

Her phone buzzed in her pocket. She whipped it out so fast she dropped it. With a cry she squatted down and began rummaging through the muddy grass with shaky fingers. After what seemed an eternity, she retrieved it, quickly curling her body around it to protect the screen from the endless rain. It was another text from her mother.

Never mind. She was in the bathroom.

Leigh's rear end collapsed onto the ground.

She remained sitting there, dazed, until she realized mud was seeping through her underwear.

Hang the fifth commandment, she resolved steadily. *Frances Koslow is a dead woman.*

"I think you'd better get up from there now," a deep voice ordered menacingly.

Leigh's head turned, with measured slowness, toward the source of the sound. Her predicament was so farcical, she could almost laugh. It did not surprise her, therefore—in fact, it seemed eminently fitting—that she would turn to find herself looking at the barrel of a shotgun.

"Hi, Joe," she greeted with the unnatural calm reserved for the hysterical. "What's up?"

Chapter 21

Joe O'Malley reached down a hand and pulled Leigh roughly to her feet. "What's up is that you're in the way," he growled. "What the hell are you doing out here?"

Unruffled, Leigh blinked back at him. "You have no idea how complicated it would be to answer that question."

He shook his head. "Forget it, I don't care. But you're not staying here. You'll have to come inside." He grabbed her by the arm and propelled her forward.

"Inside?" Leigh questioned, her tortured brain attempting to function again.

"In the house!" Joe spat out impatiently. Although Leigh was offering no resistance, the man seemed intent on half dragging her. "Before you screw up everything!"

Leigh's brow furrowed. They were headed for the backdoor of the farmhouse. "What do you mean—"

Joe clamped a beefy hand over her mouth. "Shh! Will you just shut up and hurry?" He removed the hand and commenced dragging her again. As they moved to Archie's back porch, Leigh caught sight of not one, but two other men doing a remarkably bad job of hiding behind trees. Realization dawned.

The reenactors. Why were they here?

"Go ahead," Joe ordered, pushing her up the back steps ahead of him. "He'll be in the living room."

He?

Another crack of thunder split the air, a flash of lightning hitting simultaneous with it.

Joe swore. "Gotta get this damn thing over with or we're gonna get ourselves electrocuted!"

Leigh put her hand on the doorknob. She was trying to be smart. Really, she was. But making informed decisions was challenging when one was floating upside down in rainbow pudding on the wrong side of the looking glass. Was Joe threatening her or not? He was hardly asking her to tea. But he wasn't pointing his gun at her, either.

She turned the knob and opened the door. If Joe was out to hurt her, trying to bolt now would only ensure that he did so—most likely immediately. And if he was not? Either way, she'd at least be out of the rain.

Leigh stepped into Archie's kitchen. The house had an unpleasant, stale smell to it. The mess that Wiley had left in his wake during the first days after Archie's disappearance had been cleaned up, presumably by Emma, and Wiley hadn't been free to roam in and out of his dog door since. Still, Archie's house seemed close and unkempt. All the ceiling lamps were off. The room was lit dimly by a small beam coming from the next room.

"Go on," Joe prodded, poking the butt of his gun into her back. "He knows you're coming."

Leigh took a deep breath and stepped forward. She walked through the doorway and out into the living room.

"For heaven's sake!" the familiar voice said with surprise, shining a small flashlight up and down her bedraggled form. "Mrs. Har— I mean, Leigh, what on earth are you doing out here?"

The question was a popular one. "I could ask you the same thing, Harvey," she retorted, her tone measured. "Everyone at the Browns' is worried sick about you."

His face puckered. "I'm sorry about that," he said sincerely. "But I had no choice. It was too dangerous for me to stay. I'm not ashamed to admit it—I was afraid."

Leigh was sure her head would spin 360 degrees at any moment. "Afraid of whom?" she pleaded. "Who sent you the note? Why on earth would you come? And why are all these men from the reenacting company hiding around in the trees?"

Joe let loose with an oath. "You *saw* them?" He groaned. "Amateurs!"

"Don't worry," Harvey told her, even as his own voice shook with that emotion. "It's all perfectly safe. Joe has everything figured out."

Leigh did not feel any better. "He has *what* worked out?" she demanded. "Harvey, talk to me!"

Leigh heard the buzz of a phone. Mercifully, it was not hers. Joe dropped a hand in his pocket and took a step away from them.

"Harvey," she said in a whisper, wondering suddenly if his presence was no more voluntary than her own. "If you were scared, why didn't you just call the police? Has Joe threatened you?"

Harvey's wiry eyebrows tented. "Has Joe... of course not! I'm the one who dragged him into this."

"But why?"

"Because I didn't know where else to go!" he said plaintively. "Once I figured out who the descendent was, I knew I couldn't stay in the house. But I thought I would have more time! I snuck over to Joe's to call the police, but he... Well, he talked me out of it. He said we didn't have enough evidence, and he was right. He convinced me we should go for a confession... with witnesses."

The pieces of the puzzle were at last assembling in Leigh's mind. But the process was painfully slow. "You wanted to catch whomever was offering to sell you the treasure," she reasoned, "so you asked Joe to help you? But why would anyone want to sell the treasure to you in the first place? Was the note even *for* you?"

Harvey cast her a sympathetic glance. "No, no, no. You don't understand at all!"

Joe gave them both a not-so-gentle push to the side. "Affirmative sighting at ten o'clock," he said excitedly. "It's time, Boss. Everyone to their stations!"

"Come with me!" Harvey whispered hurriedly to Leigh, guiding her in the direction of Archie's bedroom. "We'll have to hide you."

"From whom?" Leigh pleaded again. "Harvey, whatever you've got planned, there's no need to go through with it. The police are already on their way. They're coming out to look for *you!*"

Harvey stopped a moment and stared at her, wide-eyed. "Oh, but no! That will ruin everything!" He hustled her the rest of the way into the bedroom and opened Archie's closet door. "If they get here too soon, they'll tip her off, and then we'll never get a confession!" He spun Leigh around and attempted to push her gently backwards into the closet.

Tip *her* off?

"A confession from *whom?*" Leigh demanded, planting her feet.

"Places!" Joe whispered roughly.

Harvey groaned. "From the great-great-great granddaughter of Theodore Carr, that's who!" And with a strength that was surprising for a man of his size, let alone his age, he shoved her backward and shut the closet door in her face. "And *please* try to be quiet!" he added.

In the next two seconds, Leigh became aware of three things. One, that the closet smelled of cigarettes, even though Archie didn't smoke. Two, that some men's breathing can sound remarkably like Darth Vader when heard in an enclosed space. And three, that she was not alone.

"Um..." the man whispered sheepishly in her ear. "Hi there."

Leigh was proud of the fact that she didn't scream. She had never been a screamer, but if she were so inclined, this would seem a valid opportunity.

"Hi," she whispered back.

They heard the front door open. Leigh tried not to think about the fact that she was standing in a neighbor's bedroom closet in soaking wet clothes pressed up against a strange man about whom she knew exactly nothing except that he enjoyed marching in parades and running around historic battlefields shooting off blanks.

She had been in worse predicaments.

While her ears strained to hear what was happening in the next room, her brain worked feverishly to decipher Harvey's confounding comments. She had it all wrong, he had said. Had he meant that no one was trying to sell the treasure to him? That no one was selling the treasure at all? But the note said—

Of course. How stupid of her. No one had sent anything to Harvey, had they? It was Harvey who was in the driver's seat. Harvey who had reasoned out, without ever laying eyes on her map, that the best way to finger Archie's competition would be to find out who had their own copy. He had suspected from the beginning that a direct descendant of Theodore's would be the most likely candidate. He had spent all day at the library—and perhaps a courthouse or two?—finding out just who Theodore's living heirs might be. And evidently, he had found one.

One a little too close to home.

A chill swept up Leigh's bones, starting at the center of her soaking wet toes and traveling up to rattle her skull. Harvey hadn't received that note. Harvey had *written* it. Both the one she found—either practice or a reject—and the one he had actually sent. That incredibly cunning, gutsy old historian who never left his room had run out on a stormy night and enlisted the aid of the entire 102nd Pennsylvania Volunteer Regiment to bring the great-great-great granddaughter of Theodore Carr to justice before she flipped out altogether and hurt someone else.

And he had taken his cat with him.

"It's back here," Harvey was saying, his voice quavering. Leigh could hear him moving into the bedroom doorway, mere feet from where she stood. A woman's answering voice, low and indistinct, sounded from farther away.

"It's here, I swear!" Harvey pleaded, switching on the bedroom lights. "I… I overhead Lester and Archie talking and I knew what they were looking for. I stole a look at the map and figured out where to find it. They were off by a mile, but the location was obvious to me, and now I've confirmed it. It won't be hard to retrieve it—but that's your problem. That's stealing, and I don't want any trouble. I just want some money. Not much, considering what it's worth. All I want is enough to get out of the home and set myself up in my own place."

The voice that responded sounded much like a hiss. Leigh craned her neck uselessly, trying to identify the voice. But she could barely hear it.

"You can come on back, but I'm not showing you exactly where it is until I see some cash," Harvey insisted. Leigh could hear him backing up into the bedroom. He was trying to lure the woman deeper into the house, most likely so that as many hidden men as possible could hear her… and surround her.

"I want half before you leave here," Harvey continued, his voice advancing farther into the room. "If anything happens to me, the police will find a note explaining the whole sordid story. If you don't want that, I'd suggest you leave me to my business. When you've got it, you send me the other half. There's no risk for you. You own the land. All you have to do is bide your time, then find it "accidentally" while digging a fish pond or something. That was your plan from the beginning, wasn't it? If you couldn't buy the farm, land close by was good enough? Convince everyone it was found on your property, and it would *be* your property?"

You own the land.

Leigh held her breath as the second figure rustled through the bedroom doorway. Her eyes could see nothing, but her mind supplied the image with frightening clarity. A woman on the sidelines, unconcerned. A woman who could know everything, but whom no one gave credit for knowing anything. A woman who donned the cloak of a nurturer to mask the soul of a selfish, heartless witch.

"It *is* mine, you idiot!" the she-devil bellowed, her voice mere inches from Leigh's horrified ears. "It's *always* been mine! It belongs to my family, and it belongs to me! Archie was the one trying to steal it!"

"But you didn't have to hurt him!" Harvey chastised, raising his own voice to an impassioned wail. Leigh could hear the fear in his voice—understood it and felt it in her bones—but she also knew what he was doing. He needed a confession, and he needed it now.

"I didn't!" she screeched. "I didn't lay a finger on him!"

"But you hired somebody else to!" Harvey fired at her. "Hired them to 'get rid of him!' Didn't you? Well, *didn't you?!*"

"No!" she shouted, her temper rising easily to Harvey's well-dangled bait. "I only told them to scare him! To make him stop, to keep him away for a while! I can't help it if they're barbarians! But I can do the same to you all by myself if you don't show me where it is and get out of my way!"

In the distance, outside the windows and through the rain, came the distinct, high wail of a police siren. "Show me now!" she screamed. "Or I swear to God, I'll—"

"What?" Harvey pounced. "Bash my head in like you did Lester?"

"I'll do worse than that, you old goat, maybe even in your sleep! If you know everything there is to know about me you should know not to stand between me and what I want! Now, WHERE IS IT?!"

No sooner did the woman's voice move in the direction of Harvey's than a shrill mouth whistle sounded from the living room. The man behind Leigh immediately pushed the closet door open, shoved her aside, and leapt out into the room—handgun drawn. At his shoulder appeared Joe O'Malley, now sporting a blocky, mean-looking pistol that looked like something from a bad action movie. A third man had sprung up from the corner behind Archie's chest of drawers. A fourth leaned in the open window, his baseball cap dripping with rain.

"Oh..." the woman exclaimed, at first distressed, then incensed, as she backed away. "Oh, you think you're all so smart, don't you? Bringing your little toys? Well, look what I can play with!"

Leigh could no longer see the woman, but the sound of fabric rustling and buttons popping was followed by a collective gasp of horror from the men. Leigh hoped the gasp was not caused by what she thought it was. Her worst fear… yet, it couldn't be. Not unless everything else she had ever thought about the woman was a lie.

Leigh's limbs trembled as she moved to peer around her ex-closet mate's shoulder.

Nora Sullivan stood boldly, defiantly. Trapped between Archie's bed and the wall, her long wet raincoat unbuttoned to her waist. A handgun held between slim fingers.

Baby Cory nestled in a sling against her chest.

Chapter 22

"Unless one of you *soldiers* wants to go down in history as a baby killer," she sneered, "I suggest you step aside."

"Please, Nora," Harvey said weakly. "Don't do anything rash. Nobody wants to hurt either one of you."

"No, of course not!" she snapped. "You just want me hauled off to jail! You don't even know where it is, do you?!"

Harvey's face had gone white as a sheet. He licked his thin, dry lips thoughtfully. "No, I don't, actually. I've never even seen the map. So why don't we all put down our guns and—"

Nora spat out a laugh. The sirens in the distance had grown louder, then stopped altogether. The cruisers must have parked at the Browns'. The officers would be here any second. "You all can stay if you like," she said coldly. "Little Cory and I are getting out of here while we still can."

"Nora," Joe O'Malley said slowly, with what passed as his attempt at tact. "A half-dozen men here heard every word you said. I got a half-dozen more outside. You ain't going nowhere, police or no police. Now put the gun down."

Nora's chest swelled up; her eyes narrowed. "I am getting out of here. I'm going to walk right out that front door, and you and all your little friends who like to play dress-up are going to let me."

Joe's face flushed with ire. "Ain't nothing fake about the pieces we're holding, wench! And now we all know it was you who tried to kill our captain!"

"Is that so?" Nora put her free arm under Cory and lifted the baby to rest over her heart. "Well then, fire away. How good's your aim?"

The sound of a scuffle sounded from the living room. "Let me in! I can help, I tell you! Stop it! Let me go! *She's got the baby!"*

"Let him go!" Joe barked.

Derrick, wild-eyed, soaked, and bedraggled, stumbled into the bedroom.

Ignoring the men and the guns in the room as if they didn't exist, Derrick marched forward directly toward Nora, his chest heaving like he'd run a mile. "Give me the baby, Nora," he pleaded in a near whisper. "Just give him to me. Okay?"

Nora's brow furrowed with annoyance. "Go home," she said disdainfully. "I don't need you here. I shouldn't have sent you in the first place. Worthless coward."

The last of the fog before Leigh's eyes cleared away as she realized how much her impressions about Derrick had been formed not by her own experience, but by his wife's comments. Nora claimed that her husband was fascinated by the Civil War; but was he really, or had Nora coerced him into joining the reenactors just to keep tabs on Archie? Nora complained of his incompetence with the baby, but Leigh hadn't seen incompetence, had she? Only poor housekeeping. Everyone had assumed all along that it was Nora who stayed up nights tending to Cory, but now, seeing the woman in her trenchcoat, Leigh suspected that wasn't true either. Could it, all along, have been Derrick who stayed up nights changing diapers and giving two o'clock feedings—while Nora skulked about Frog Hill Farm with her coat pulled up above her head?

Leigh looked hard into the small man's frightened eyes, his tight-clenched fists, the determined set of his otherwise weak chin. Nora had claimed that her computer-loving geek of a husband wanted *chickens*, for crying out loud! The contradictions abounded, but Leigh hadn't seen them. She had believed the fiction—a fiction entirely of his wife's creation, designed to paint Nora herself as a devoted mother, nurse's aide, and neighborhood saint. And all to claim a treasure that could be worth a fortune.

Or nothing at all.

Dora Klinger had been right. Insanity did run in the family.

"The police are already here," Derrick said evenly. "I saw them starting down the hill. It's no use, Nora. Everyone knows you're looking for the treasure, now. But that's no crime, right? Everything's still going to be okay."

"The hell it is!" Joe interrupted gruffly. "You call having the captain beat to a bloody pulp not a crime?!"

Derrick's head swung back to his wife, his face drained of color. "Oh, sweetheart," he said softly, pathetically. "No. You didn't really... I know you talked to those two... But you didn't. You *wouldn't*. Please tell me you wouldn't go that far!"

Male voices raised in brisk conversation sounded outside. The police had met the reenactors. Nora was well and truly surrounded.

She glanced frantically around her, her eyes resting briefly, maliciously, on the silent figure of Leigh. For once, Leigh felt she could read Nora's mind. There was only one way out for a trapped gunman.

Taking a hostage.

Leigh took a surreptitious step back. But Nora didn't need her.

As the voices outside swelled to arguing tones, Nora raised her handgun slowly into the air, then pointed it straight down at little Cory's head.

"Move out of the way," she ordered coolly. "Put down your guns and let me walk out. And tell the police to do the same."

She's mad as a hatter, Leigh thought with horror, unable to imagine what twisted motivations—or violently unbalanced hormones—must be running through the young woman's body. Surely it was a bluff. It had to be. But how could any of them take that chance?

"Nora!" Derrick choked, his eyes welling with tears. "You can't do this. He's just a baby. He could get hurt. Please, please, *give him to me!"* He took a step forward.

Nora stiffened, her eyes wild, and screamed at him, "Get back, you idiot! I'll kill us both! I swear to God I will!"

A pall of quiet fell over the room. Even the voices outside had quieted. But within the void, Leigh heard something else. A low, rumbling sound that offered, even before her brain could place it, a thin ray of hope.

Quivering from head to foot, Derrick obediently stepped back. The men did the same, leaving a path for Nora to scoot out from behind the bed. But the man at the window was still too near for comfort, and as Nora sidled close along the mattress, Leigh's breath held with anticipation.

Oh, please, she begged silently, certain now that her hunch was right. *Go for it!*

Nora had not yet cleared the bed when she stumbled suddenly and uttered a sharp cry. The instant her attention was diverted, Derrick the nerd king launched himself toward her like a missile, knocking her gun hand up into the air and pushing her bodily back onto the mattress. The nearest men closed in, removed her gun, and secured her flailing limbs while Derrick swiftly extricated the baby from the sling.

Leigh watched as, without another look at his wife, Derrick cradled the baby to his chest and moved away. She had thought that the too-silent Cory might be sick—perhaps even drugged—but amazingly, the infant was wide awake and perfectly calm. As Derrick's face broke into a relieved smile, Leigh felt her own doing the same. What baby could stay content during so much turmoil? Ride the waves of so much excitement, noise, and tension with equanimity?

Perhaps one who really hated being bored.

Leigh stood still and stayed out of the way as the police entered and took charge of Nora, moving the ranting woman out into the larger room. Several more officers took Derrick and the reenactors aside for questioning. Leigh knew she would be interrogated as well, eventually. But this time, she didn't mind. This time, she really *was* just an innocent bystander.

Her family would be proud.

Not everyone in the room had been innocent, however. When the last of the men stepped out, leaving Leigh alone in the bedroom, she walked softly over to the far edge of the bed. No one else seemed to have noticed the thin trickle of blood that ran down Nora's bare ankle and into her shoe.

Leigh dropped to all fours and slowly, carefully, lifted the edge of Archie's bedspread and peered beneath it.

She couldn't help but grin.

"Way to go, Momma Dog," she praised.

"Please, Aunt Mo?" Lenna begged. "Now? Can we?"

Maura Polanski smiled at the Pack indulgently. Up to now, they had shown impressive restraint. If it had been up to Leigh, they wouldn't be here at all, but Allison had told Maura her entire theory of the map and the Guide over the phone already and Maura had asked Cara to bring all the children over to Archie's.

Objectively, Leigh realized it was safe. Nora had been arrested and removed an hour before, and Derrick had taken his still-happy, gurgling baby home. The reenactors had finished their high-fiving, coordinated a plan to stock Archie's refrigerator with his favorite beer in anticipation of his return, and left en masse to indulge in a round of their own in his honor. And to the amazement of all, Harvey Perkins had gone with them. The local officers had reported to Maura and departed. The storm had blown over and left only an occasional misting—and a lot of mud—in its wake.

Leigh herself had brought food and water for the mother dog and pups, all of which were present and accounted for, and which everyone had agreed to leave alone for a while. The rest of the time Leigh had been enjoying the telling smile on her best friend's beaming face.

"Yeah, okay, we can take a look," Maura answered. "But don't touch anything or try to dig anything up. Just *look*. Capiche?"

Lenna squealed with delight. The boys and Allison saluted. All four of them turned on their heels, pulled out their flashlights, and ran to the cellar doors. Cara followed dutifully after them.

"It disturbs me when they do that," Maura said with feigned annoyance, referring to the salutes. "Not teaching them how to snow me, are you, Koslow?"

Leigh grinned. "Who, me?" She looked from Maura's glowing face to that of her husband Gerry, who had come along on the call and hadn't moved six feet from his wife's side since.

For the first time all evening, the threesome was alone. "Can I assume that everything came back okay?" Leigh asked tentatively.

Maura Polanski, unbelievably, stole a look at her husband and *blushed*. "You can assume that," she answered with a grin. "In fact, you can assume that the obstetrician said my results were no different than the average thirty year old."

Leigh smiled broadly. "That's fantastic!"

"I think so," Gerry said smoothly, looking at his wife. On the job, Lieutenant Frank had one of the coolest poker faces in the business. But there was no mistaking his true feelings at the moment. The man's eyes sparkled like a kid at Christmas.

"Hey, wait up, you animals! This is my case!" Maura bellowed good-naturedly, breaking away to follow the Pack toward the shed. Within a few moments they were all in the cellar, although Leigh remained on the steps as a matter of principle.

"Look, Aunt Mo!" Allison said excitedly, standing near the center of the room, holding out the map for the detective to see. She moved her flashlight beam to the floor and tapped with a toe. "It wasn't in the wall at all! Aunt Lydie kept saying it would be really hard for a man Theodore's age to chisel out a big stone and put it back in, all without anybody noticing. The mortar would look different and unless whatever he hid was little bitty, the rock would stick out wrong. But he'd have no trouble digging up a rock in the dirt floor!"

Leigh gave in, stepped closer, and looked at the spot where several flashlights now shone. There were many rocks half buried in the ancient dirt floor, but only one had made Allison squeal as loudly as Lenna had. The rock in question was nearly flush with the ground, and the Pack had had to sweep a layer of dirt off it to see it properly. It was roughly an eight by ten inch oval, with two protuberances. Leigh had to admit, its two-dimensional outline was a near perfect match for the box drawn around the words "The Guide."

Maura studied the map and rock and gave a whistle. "I'd say you have a winner here, troops."

The children began to bounce. "Can we dig it up now?" Ethan begged. "I can look up in the shed for a shovel!"

Maura held out a steadying hand. "Unfortunately, no."

The bouncing ceased. "Why not?" Mathias questioned.

"Last time I checked," Maura said lightly, "None of you guys are landowners. This rock—and anything that might be buried underneath it—are the property of Archie Pratt. And only Mr. Pratt, or someone with his express permission, has the right to be digging here."

The children's faces deflated. But Allison was quick to buck up again. "Aunt Mo's right, guys," she announced, straightening her back and assuming her "mature" tone. "Mr. Pratt's been searching for this treasure for years. He got hurt really bad because of it. It's only fair to wait until he comes home and let him dig it up himself, don't you think?"

With only a little reluctance, the Pack agreed.

Leigh and Cara smiled proudly.

"We'll get this place sealed up, just to be on the safe side," Maura explained. "First thing tomorrow, I'm off to Ohio. I'll tell Mr. Pratt the whole story and we'll see what he wants to do."

The children began to buzz with talk among themselves, then

jogged up the steps and out of the cellar. Cara followed, with Leigh on her heels, but Maura and Gerry hung back. As Leigh reached the top of the steps and turned, she thought she saw—out of the corner of her eye—the dimmest silhouette of something she hadn't seen since the day she'd stood up as Maura Polanski's matron of honor.

The detectives were making out.

Chapter 23

A little over a week later, in the late afternoon of an unseasonably warm October day, an intergenerational crowd assembled at Archie Pratt's house and marched outside and across the lawn to the tool shed. Despite the fact that four of the attendees were over eighty, two of those were over ninety, and another of the group had just gotten out of the hospital, only Dora Klinger moved in a wheelchair. Everyone else, including Archie, was determined to make the march on their own, even if their progress was glacial.

"You're holding it wrong," Pauline barked, critiquing Archie's handling of his cane. "You got to pull it around a little more as you're moving. See?"

Archie imitated the older woman's movements, then broke out in a grin. "Well, what do you know?" he said slowly, his stiff jaw still muffling his words a bit. "That does help!"

Pauline sniffed in triumph.

"You should have let me rent that scooter," Lester insisted, sticking close to Archie's side in case he stumbled. Both Lester and Emma had been fussing over Archie like hens ever since his return, and Archie—never one to turn down either a free meal or friendly company—was letting them do it.

"You try to do too much on that leg too soon," Emma threatened, "and you can say goodbye to Pioneer Days at Perryopolis."

But Archie merely grinned again. He had been so happy to get out of the hospital and get home, he had been grinning almost constantly ever since, dismissing his healing jaw, fractured ribs, and deep bruises as a mere inconvenience. "Ain't *nobody* stopping me from marching at Perryopolis," he declared. "I may not finish the route till nightfall, but I'll be there with bells on. Or at least a canteen and a haversack."

He cast a wink at Allison, who smiled radiantly back at him. Scotty O'Malley, who had been dogging her heels the whole way, puffed up proudly. "I'm going to Perryopolis, too," he bragged. "As a drummer! And dad says if I get a D in pre-algebra, I can go to Fredericksburg!"

"You can do it, boy," Archie encouraged without sarcasm. "And so can I. By Fredericksburg," he proclaimed loudly, "I'll be good as new!"

Wiley, who had been running circles around the group as it moved, barked as if in agreement. His master grinned indulgently at him. It had surprised no one to learn that when Maura visited Archie in the hospital, the first words he had laboriously tapped out on his tablet were "dog needs fed."

When the crowd reached the cellar doors, only just unsealed by Maura and another woman from the local PD, the group split. Lawn chairs had been set out for those who needed them, and Pauline and Dora, along with Emma, settled in up top to await the good word. But everyone else insisted on crowding into the dank space below to witness the climactic moment.

"Now, you know we could all be making a big fuss over nothing, right?" Archie cautioned from the cellar's midst, his face illuminated by the glow of multiple flashlights. "Theodore Carr might not have had anything worth burying."

"He had the hat of that Southern general dude, didn't he?" Scotty asked excitedly, hopping from foot to foot like the floor was on fire. "The one who put his hat on his sword in the movie?"

Archie and Harvey exchanged a look of poorly concealed excitement. Despite their efforts at lowering the crowd's expectations, Leigh suspected the both of them would be hopping like Scotty if they could get away with it. "We don't know what he had," Harvey said. "It's all conjecture, because Theodore apparently kept the exact nature of his booty a secret, even from his family. The legend that passed down through his descendants was merely that Theodore had brought back a souvenir from Gettysburg that he was convinced was very valuable. At some point he hid it on the farm and wrote to his daughter that she was to come and get it when he died. He must not have trusted his son with it; though why, we don't know. Whatever happened between the two men, after Theodore died Thomas apparently told his sister that their father had nothing of value—that it was just an old man's fantasy. Theodore's daughter, whose married name was Leonora Trout, believed her brother. But she did keep the last letter her father ever wrote her, which included the map. She gave it to her son, David Trout, and told him the story. When David realized that his uncle wasn't mentally stable either, he must have started wondering: which man to believe?"

"It could be they were both loony," Archie conceded. "But I think that before David Trout sold the farm, he took a stab at finding that treasure himself. Not only that, but he must have shown the map to somebody else. Copy machines like we have didn't exist back then, but anybody could have taken a picture of it. And somebody must have, because according to Dora, there were strangers out here sniffing around even before Thomas died, when the place was still a rental. That points the finger to David as the leak."

"Where did you get your copy of the map, Mr. Pratt?" Allison asked.

Archie's eyes gave a twinkle. "Well, whose hands it started out in, I've got no clue. But it was given to me by a reenactor named Clive Haden, the man who recruited me. Fine old gentleman, passed away about ten years ago. Said he got it from another Civil War buff, along with the story that it marked the hiding place of..." he paused for proper effect, then gave a nod to Scotty. "The hat of Brigadier General Lewis Addison Armistead. Clive hadn't ever searched for it himself; he didn't even know where the farm might be, except that he heard it was someplace along the old Harmony Line. But once I saw the map, I was hooked. The very thought that it could be real, that a relic like that could be buried somewhere unclaimed, after all this time..." Archie's voice turned wistful, but with a sudden shake of his head, he sobered. "I got a little carried away, I'll admit. I figured out where the farm was, and then when I found out that it had once been owned by a Civil War veteran, well, I..." His gaze moved to the floor.

"You had every right to get carried away!" Lester broke in defensively. He looked around at the others. "Would you believe that at the very time Arch found this place, it just happened to be for sale? Now, how's that for a sign?" He looked at Archie again. "You didn't do a thing wrong. You had no idea if Theodore had any heirs, or if they even cared. Either way, they'd sold the place ages ago, and that includes anything buried on it!"

"But..." Allison asked hesitantly. "The story about it being

Armistead's hat. You said that didn't get passed down through Theodore's family. So how could anybody else know?"

Archie cast a shamefaced glance at Harvey.

"They couldn't," Harvey admitted, his own face turning equally sheepish. "That idea seems to have come from the Civil War buffs in the story. I suspect that they, like me, heard 'soldier at the Angle' and 'souvenir' and jumped to the most exciting possible conclusion."

"Yeah, we're optimistic like that," Archie answered with a sad smile. "I don't know why Theodore kept what he had a secret—maybe just part of his paranoia about somebody stealing it. But the story that came down through the family was bare-bones, like Harvey said. We heard it all from Derrick. He came to see me last night—wanted to apologize for Nora and try to explain. It turns out that when Nora's grandmother Sarah—she was David Trout's daughter—was on her deathbed, she gave Nora the original map and the letter and told her that one of her ancestors had fought in the Battle of Gettysburg and buried some treasure worth a fortune. But no one could ever find it and now the farm was sold. Nora was only twelve years old when she heard that story, and poor as dirt, and it caught her imagination and wouldn't let go. She's been determined to reclaim the treasure ever since." Archie cleared his throat uncomfortably. "I guess she considered it her birthright."

"Maybe so," Harvey said gravely. "But at some point, it turned into an obsession." He cast a glance around the group in the cellar, and Leigh suspected he was making sure not to be overheard by Emma, who felt horribly guilty for having hired Nora as an aide in the first place and was taking the entire affair very hard. "As it turns out," Harvey continued at a lower level, "Nora's been sniffing around the neighborhood for years, trying to buy the farm, or part of it, or something close to it. She would have bought your place" —he gave a nod to Leigh— "when it came up for sale five years ago, if she had the money at the time. But she couldn't afford to buy anything until after she married Derrick. Then she made a point of cozying up to Emma so that she could finagle a job, keep an ear to the ground in case any other neighbors wanted to sell, and—"

"And keep tabs on Archie," Lester finished bitterly. "She knew he was looking for the treasure. He and I would talk about it sometimes, secretly, of course, but somehow she—" He broke off, his face red.

"Well, I never trusted that woman for a minute!" Adith insisted. "I told you she was an eavesdropper. Ain't nothing lower than somebody who can't keep their schnoz out of other peoples' business!"

Adith crossed her arms and nodded her head sharply.

Harvey coughed.

Adith threw him a withering look.

"But Nora's rotting in jail now, right?" Scotty piped up, his face shining with glee.

"Her future is unclear," Maura answered gruffly, casting a look at Scotty that not only stilled his tongue, but made him slide a step behind Allison. The detective had heretofore made an effort to be unobtrusive, observing silently from the background. But Leigh knew that Nora's fate was a source of consternation for the prosecutors. Although there was no clear proof that she had assaulted Lester, there was ample evidence that she had hired two goons from her high school class to get Archie out of the way while she made one final, concerted effort at getting to the treasure before he did. But exactly what she had instructed the men to do was in debate, as was her mental state at the time. Her lawyers were pushing the theory of post-partum psychosis; the prosecution vehemently disagreed. Only one issue met with no debate from anyone: baby Cory belonged with his father. Fortunately, Derrick's mother—formerly banished from the home by Nora—was now helping Derrick with the housework, and by all accounts the baby seemed unaffected by his mother's sudden absence. Which was not so surprising given that, as Leigh suspected, it was Derrick who had been his son's primary caregiver all along.

Whether Nora had married Derrick because she loved him or because she wanted his income to purchase a house near the farm, Leigh could only guess. Derrick had told the police that he knew of his wife's desire to search for the family heirloom but had considered it a harmless quest, realizing only too late that her passion had morphed into pathology. The poor man seemed as amazed as anyone by the lengths his wife had gone to in the end. But despite the horror of the last weeks, he seemed to harbor no ill will towards the mother of his child. Amazingly enough, Derrick seemed optimistic that proper treatment could eventually bring

Nora back.

"So," Archie said loudly, infusing cheer into his voice again. "Who's going to do the digging?"

The Pack held up their tools. "We are!"

"Well then," Archie said with a grin. "Get busy!"

"Be careful!" Allison admonished as the foursome dug in with an assortment of small garden tools, and Scotty O'Malley, not to be left out, started pulling away the growing piles of dirt with his hands. "Don't break anything!" Allison ordered. "Remember what Aunt Lydie said!"

Leigh leaned toward her cousin. "Why isn't your mother here?" she whispered. "I thought she wanted to come."

Cara's lips twisted. "She did. But when I told her it was this afternoon she said she couldn't—she had to meet *an old friend.*"

Leigh grinned. "The mystery man again?"

"Without a doubt," Cara responded. "And where is your mother? Gotten any more texts lately?"

Leigh's answering smirk made her cousin laugh. Cara knew perfectly well that when Frances realized it was her own overzealous alert that had propelled her daughter straight into the jaws of potential death and dismemberment, she had banished the cell phone to the nether regions of her purse for all eternity. Never mind that it had been what Frances said, rather than what she texted, that had sent Leigh running out into the storm. If Frances wanted to blame the entire affair on the evils of text messaging, Leigh was only too happy to let her.

The Pack soon removed enough earth from around the stone's edges to make it wobble, and Archie leaned on his cane to loom above them. "Now, you kids have to realize," he lectured again, even as his own eyes blazed with anticipation, "the whole hat thing was just our own wishful thinking. Theodore Carr was a senile old man when he made this map—he could have been sleeping with a tin can under his pillow and calling it a cannon ball."

"The stone's coming up!" Ethan shouted.

"Let's pull it out!" Mathias ordered.

Five pairs of hands lifted the shallow rock from its resting place and set it to the side.

"In the middle there!" Archie shouted.

Ethan's fingers worked frantically to free the small, half-buried object near his side of the hole. "I've got it!" He stood up, brushed off its surface with a flourish, and held it out on his palm. It was a thin rectangular box, maybe three or four inches on its sides. "Here Mr. Pratt," he offered. "You open it!"

Archie, his eyes wide as saucers, took the item wordlessly in his hands.

"Well, I'll be!" Adith crowed from near the steps, looking through her binoculars. "It ain't no hat. It's a Prince Albert tobacco tin!"

"It's not the hat," Allison explained with awe. "It's *The Guide*."

"A rather clever way to hide an important paper," Harvey praised. "These tins were ubiquitous in the twenties."

"At least he was sharp enough to bury it in the center of the floor, where the ground stays drier," Cara commented, no doubt quoting some of her mother's archeological wisdom. "Otherwise it would have rusted through years ago."

"Open it!" Lenna said impatiently.

Archie put his hands around the tin and gently pried open the hinged top. The assembled crowd held their breath as Archie's pudgy fingers pulled out a yellowed, folded piece of paper.

Harvey stepped forward and took the empty tin. "Very carefully," he advised, as Archie's shaking fingers opened the paper. "Don't break the edges if it's brittle."

But the note, which was folded only once down its length, unfolded easily, and within seconds its surface was illuminated by the light of a half-dozen flashlights.

"Number three, number eight," Archie breathed hoarsely. "That's all it says."

"That's all it has to say!" Allison exclaimed. "That's the spoke and the X! Spoke number three and X number eight. See?" She held out her copy of the map for Archie, and as he took and studied it, he stepped back a pace from the crowd. Lester stepped back with him to keep a light on the map; the others gave them room.

The cellar went silent.

"Well?" Adith insisted at last. "Where is the danged thing? Let's go get it!"

Archie ran a hand over his sweating brow. "Can't do that," he said dully.

"And why not?" Adith persisted.

Archie looked up. "Hey, McClellan!" he said briskly, his voice all military.

Beside her, Leigh felt Warren start. He had been at her side the whole time, but up to now, hadn't said a word. Everyone else was looking at each other in confusion, but Archie was staring straight at her husband.

"Um… yes, sir?" Warren said uncertainly.

"You sure you're not related to Major General George B. McClellan?" Archie asked, a grin playing around his lips.

"Er, not that I know of," Warren answered.

"Well, that's a shame," Archie insisted. "Seeing as how you look just like him." His smile moved down to Allison. "And seeing as how whatever treasure Private Theodore Carr carried home from Gettysburg, he went and buried in *your* backyard."

Relocating the assembly a second time was no small task. The spot Allison and Archie agreed on as being marked by the X was technically on the Harmon's property, but it was on the far side of the creek from Leigh's house, partway up the hill into the woods, surrounded by spindly trees and just shy of another cluster of stones. The lawn chairs were set up again, this time at the nearest clearing on the flat part of the lawn, and stronger, sturdier tools were requisitioned from Leigh's garage.

When Mathias' metal detector went bonkers in the most obvious spot within the target zone, both Archie and Harvey gave up all pretense of hiding their enthusiasm. Unfortunately, neither of them was in any shape for hard digging, and Lester—who despite his relatively milder concussion, was still having headaches—was strictly forbidden any exertion whatsoever by his overprotective wife. Ethan and Mathias dug in with enthusiasm, and when they tired were replaced first by their sisters, and then by their mothers. But with eighty some-odd years' worth of root growth between Theodore's time and the present, the task went slowly, and only when Warren took a turn with an ax and shovel in tandem did the effort at last turn a corner.

Scotty, who had at first pretended to help by holding whichever tools weren't otherwise in use, had grown bored quickly. "You still have the puppies at your house Mr. Pratt?" he questioned.

Archie chuckled and threw an amused glance at Leigh. "Oh, I most certainly do. They're in charge of the house now, you know. I'm lucky I get to sleep on the couch!"

"She didn't stay in the box?" Leigh questioned. Randall Koslow had helped her fashion a whelping box to lure the mother dog to a more suitable location, and Leigh had succeeded in gradually coaxing her to move the litter out from under Archie's bed and into the area under the staircase. Although less than ideal, it was as good a spot as any for the dog to serve out her rabies observation sentence, and the one place in the house Leigh thought she might still feel safe after Archie returned home—provided he was willing to let the family stay. To Leigh's relief, Archie was more than willing... he cooed over the litter like a proud grandpapa.

"No, she didn't stay in the box," Archie reported cheerfully. "Her majesty prefers the fine shag carpeting under my bed. Her majesty also prefers I keep myself the heck out of there."

"Oh, no," Leigh said with chagrin. "Is she growling at you?"

Archie chuckled. "Not in so many words. Actually, she's a quite friendly little miss... ate some bacon right out of my hand this morning. I think she and I will get along fine. She can stay where she wants until the pups are older, though it'll be the devil to keep things clean. The couch is no matter. I'd be sleeping there anyway. It's easier to get up and down."

"That's very generous of you," Leigh praised.

Archie shrugged. "Can't very well turn her out, after such a selfless act of heroism on her part, can I? Besides, we have an understanding. I've talked to Wiley and he accepts his responsibilities." He put out a hand and patted the black hound's head. "I guess we'll take your dad up on that kindly offer of his."

Leigh smiled. Dr. Koslow had offered to vaccinate the pups and spay the mother dog when the time came—but only if Archie would also let him neuter Wiley.

"Hey look!" Mathias cried. "Uncle Warren's hit something!"

Everyone moved immediately to crowd around the edge of the hole.

"It's metal all right," Warren said, removing a glove to feel the flat stretch of surface he'd unearthed. "Maybe a tackle box. Or a foot locker."

"I can dig some more!" Ethan insisted, and Warren stepped back while the boys eagerly resumed the effort.

"So what do you see?" Adith shouted anxiously from the clearing twenty paces below.

"It's a metal box of some kind!" Leigh reported.

Harvey, who had been determined to make the uphill struggle, chuckled softly. "Haven't heard so much about hauntings lately, have we?"

Leigh grinned back. Despite Adith's newfound interest in Dora's *phasma victus* parties, neither woman had mentioned a word about ghosts, evil spirits, or orbs since Nora's arrest.

"I hope I didn't upset anybody with all that," Archie said apologetically. "I just thought it was all in fun, you know." He gave a surreptitious nod in the direction of Scotty, who was now scuffing his shoes anxiously at the edge of the hole, knocking some of the dirt back in. "The boy seemed to like it. And I didn't want him following me around out there when I was working, of course."

"You wore your blue army coat," Leigh accused. "You knew he'd think you were a ghost!"

Archie gave a mischievous smirk. "Well, yeah. That was the fun of it."

Harvey chuckled. "You don't have to give those men an excuse to wear those coats. Why, Jeb wore his to the farm the day of the sting! And when I asked him why, he shrugged and said that the wool was good in the rain!"

"What's taking so long?" Pauline carped from downhill. "I could dig faster with my danged dentures!"

"Look!" Lester cried, "You can see the corners of it! It's bigger than a tackle box… looks more like a trunk!"

At last the boys were able to grab the edges of the box and make it jiggle. After a few more minutes of concerted digging, Warren was able to lift it out.

"He's got it! He's got it!" Scotty screamed.

Warren stepped out of the hole and carried the metal box triumphantly down the hill to the waiting crowd.

"Oh, goody, goody, goody!" Adith exclaimed, clapping her hands as Warren set it on the ground in the middle of the group of chairs. Everyone stared at the object with reverence for a moment, despite its unimpressive appearance. The metal trunk was about a foot wide and a foot and a half long. It had a hinged top and a latch with a lock, but since most of the hinges were corroded, the lock appeared to be no obstacle. The surface of the trunk was rusted, but its integrity seemed otherwise intact.

"How on earth could an old man bury such a thing that deep all by himself?" Dora questioned.

"It wasn't that deep," Warren responded. "It just got covered over with tree roots."

"When Theodore buried it," Harvey explained, "those rocks would have been at the edge of the woods. He picked his spot well—safely above the flood plain, and with good drainage. Otherwise the metal would have rusted even more, after all this time."

"You think it's waterproof?" Dora questioned.

Harvey and Archie exchanged a troubled glance. "Not likely," Archie answered sadly. "Some water's bound to have leaked in over time. And it would only take a little..."

Harvey shook his head. "No way could a felt slouch hat survive over eighty years underground in a metal box. Theodore didn't plan for that, you know. He thought his daughter would come to pick it up soon."

No one said anything for a moment. After a while, everyone looked at Archie.

"Don't look at me!" he said with mock cheer. "It's not my property. Whatever it is and whatever's left of it, it belongs to the Harmons, fair and square."

Leigh and Warren looked at each other blankly.

"Well, *somebody* open the gol-durned thing!" Adith demanded.

With a mutual shrug, Leigh and Warren tugged at the metal lid until the hinges gave way and the top tipped off to the side. The crowd gave a collective gasp, but all anyone could see was the folds of a wool blanket, faded and partially deteriorated. Leigh reached in tentatively and lifted out the bundle.

"It's heavy," she commented. "There's something hard inside." Leigh's hands felt unsteady. Her eyes met Warren's for a moment, then both of them turned to Allison with a silent question. With an equally silent nod, the girl agreed. Leigh stepped over to Archie and gestured toward an empty chair. "If it's ours," she insisted. "We say *you* should open it. Now sit down and take this thing before I drop it."

With a grin, Archie complied. As everyone gathered close around him, he slowly unwrapped the folds of wool from the hard object within.

"Maybe it's a skull!" Scotty said brightly.

"Or some jewelry," Dora suggested.

"My money's on a gun," Adith added.

"Well, it ain't going to be an octopus!" Pauline griped.

"Nope," Archie replied as he pulled the last of the fabric away. "It's... a big jar."

"A jar?" Leigh said, unable to hide her disappointment. "What?"

Archie turned the vessel around in his hands with care, looking at all sides. It was ceramic, six or seven inches in diameter and just under a foot tall. It was sealed with a wire bail top. Archie's face turned sharply up toward Harvey. "Rubber gasket," he said breathlessly. "It's a long shot, but do you think... maybe?"

Harvey's cheeks flared red. "Open it!" he practically shouted.

Archie's own hands were trembling as he popped the metal wire off the lid, then slowly removed the lid from the jar and set it down in his lap. He looked into the wide mouth, inserted two fingers, and pulled out a yellowed piece of paper almost entirely covered with handwriting.

If this is a hint for some other place to look, Leigh thought with chagrin, *so help me...*

But before anyone could suggest it, Archie started to read out loud.

"My dearest Leonora," he read haltingly, his voice thick with emotion. "Thank you for coming. Your brother's mind is gone and my own is not as it used to be. You must take this, and you must keep it safe. I did not speak much of the war to you when you were a child. It wasn't worth speaking of. But now you have to know what you have and what you will hold. When I was a young man I served in the 71st Pennsylvania Infantry, and I was one of the few who left it whole. What I give you comes from what they call Cemetery Ridge at Gettysburg, where we lost nearly one hundred men. I will spare you much of that story, but what you must know is that I was lying on the ground, one dead man already on top of me, when I saw General—"

Archie's voice broke. He swallowed and started again. "General Armistead fall. He was still alive, but when he fell to the ground his hat and sword fell with him. I wanted the sword but couldn't reach it. The hat fell almost to my hand. I grabbed it and tucked it beneath me, and when I left that bloody field it left with me."

Archie stopped and took a ragged breath. Beside him, a flushed and unsteady Harvey leaned heavily on the arm of the chair.

"They gave the sword back." Archie continued. "Gave it back to the bastards who killed those hundred men—and so many others. This hat must never be returned to them. Never! Such fuss now over that rebel who did nothing but hold it high in the air! This hat is worth something, daughter. Sell it if you can, or keep it yourself, but you must promise me that you will sell it only to another Pennsylvanian, and that those damnable rebels will never worship at its altar again!"

Archie paused, then slowly lowered the letter. "Your loving father, Theodore Edward Carr. Dated May 27th, 1923."

"Two years before he died," Harvey said weakly. "And Leonora never came."

No one spoke. After a moment, Archie looked into the jar, then held it tentatively out toward Harvey. "You do it," he croaked.

Harvey stretched out a shaky hand and slid his fingers into the jar's mouth. With a slow, gentle movement, he extracted a misshapen lump of dull gray fabric.

"It's true," he said wondrously, his blue eyes dancing. "It's true, Archie. It's a hat! A felt slouch hat!"

"So it is," Archie agreed hoarsely. "It may never look like one again, but—what's that?"

"The hat pins!" Harvey cried out loud. "It still has his wife's hat pins in it!"

"So it's real?" Lester asked.

"Well, I'm no expert, but—" Archie began.

"It's real," Harvey said firmly. "It will have to be authenticated, of course, but… the style, the pins, what's left of the cords, the insignia… I'd stake my life on it!"

"Well, Lord love a duck," Adith murmured.

Everyone stood still. Held breaths were released. Eyes, both young and old, sparkled with excitement. Faces glowed.

"We shouldn't be touching it," Harvey said suddenly, letting the hat fall gently onto Archie's lap. "We could damage it. We should get it in some kind of protective case immediately." He looked up at

Leigh. "Do you have a cardboard box that would fit it, for now?"

"I'll get one!" Allison offered, and in a flash she was off the hill up toward the house, with Scotty and the rest of the Pack behind her.

Harvey looked beseechingly at Leigh. "We should call a museum... or something. What do you want to do?"

Leigh and Warren exchanged another silent communication. "If it's real, of course it belongs in a museum," Warren agreed.

"Who do you think we should call, Archie?" Leigh asked.

"The Gettysburg Foundation," he answered immediately. "They'll know what to do with it. They'll send somebody out right away. They'll want to see the box and everything, and take pictures..."

Leigh reached out and retrieved the jar and lid from Archie's lap, leaving him with the hat and the letter. A surge of unexpected delight coursed through her.

She stepped back out of the way, then looked around at the assembled onlookers as they began to file politely by, taking a closer peek at the precious relic which—despite the unlikeliest of circumstances—had managed to survive intact for over a hundred and fifty years, nearly ninety of them in her own backyard. Theodore Carr might have been paranoid and senile, or he might have been neither. No one might ever know what had transpired between him and his son at the end. But one thing was for sure. The man knew how to wrap a package.

Leigh slipped off, moved away from the sound of the crowd's assorted oohs and aahs and Pauline's "that looks like a damned dead vole," and pulled out her cell phone.

Her officemate Alice picked up the call immediately. "I'm not saying one word to you, Koslow," she began with venom, "unless you tell me—"

"Get your best photographer out to my house ASAP," Leigh interrupted. "I've got your concept."

There was a pause. "You mean it?"

"Would I lie to you?"

"Every other damned day! Is the SOB going to like this one? You know this is our last shot—and we need that account."

"No, he's not going to like it," Leigh answered, cradling the antique, salt-glazed stoneware carefully in her arms. She turned it over and looked again at the crock jar's bottom. With a finger, she rubbed away a smudge of decaying wool, revealing the remainder of the engraved maker's mark beneath.

Rinnamon & Co. Pittsburgh, Pennsylvania.

"He's going to love it," she said with a smirk.

Acknowledgements & Historical Disclaimer

Private Theodore Carr is a fictional character, and as far as I know, the ultimate fate of the hat of General Armistead remains an open question. I confess to completely making up the part about his late wives' hatpins, but otherwise, I have attempted to stay true to historical facts. There is no unit of reenactors associated with the 102nd Pennsylvania Infantry Regiment (at least not so far as I know), but I am in debt to the reenactors of the 38th and 40th Pennsylvania Volunteer Infantries for providing such informative websites. Many thanks also go out to those who willingly answered my historical, architectural, and police procedural questions, including Dr. John B. Vincent, Kate Gibson, and Maggie Price.

Author's Note

Edie Claire enjoys creating works of mystery, romantic suspense, women's fiction, YA romance, and stage comedy. She has worked as a veterinarian, a childbirth educator, and a medical/technical writer; when she is not writing novels, she may be found doing volunteer work, raising her three children, or cleaning up after an undisclosed number of pets.

To find out more about her books and plays, please visit her website (**www.edieclaire.com**) or Facebook page (**www.Facebook.com /EdieClaire**) If you'd like to be notified when new books are released, feel free to sign up for her "new book alert" on the website. Edie always enjoys hearing from readers via email (**edieclaire@juno.com**). Thanks so much for reading!

Books & Plays by Edie Claire

Leigh Koslow Mysteries

Never Buried
Never Sorry
Never Preach Past Noon
Never Kissed Goodnight
Never Tease a Siamese
Never Con a Corgi
Never Haunt a Historian

Classic Romantic Suspense

Long Time Coming
Meant To Be
Borrowed Time

Women's Fiction

The Mud Sisters

YA Romance

Hawaiian Shadows: Wraith

Comedic Stage Plays

Scary Drama I
See You in Bells

Made in the USA
Lexington, KY
06 March 2014